a love story

a love story

Denene Millner and Nick Chiles

DUTTON

DUTTON
Published by the Penguin Group (USA) Inc.
375 Hudson Street, New York, New York 10014, U.S.A.
Penguin Books Ltd, Registered Offices: 80 Strand, London WC2R 0RL, England
Penguin Books Australia Ltd, 250 Camberwell Road, Camberwell, Victoria 3124, Australia
Penguin Books Canada Ltd, 10 Alcorn Avenue, Toronto, Ontario, Canada M4V 3B2
Penguin Books (NZ), cnr Airborne and Rosedale Roads, Albany, Auckland 1310, New Zealand

Published by Dutton, a member of Penguin Group (USA) Inc.

First Printing, June 2004
1 3 5 7 9 10 8 6 4 2

 REGISTERED TRADEMARK—MARCA REGISTRADA

ISBN 0-525-94824-4
Printed in the United States of America

To Mari and Miles

*a love
story*

Nina and Aaron,
Part I

Only thirty-three minutes separated their emergence into the world, one thousand nine hundred and eighty seconds of elder wisdom that Nina would lord over Aaron for the next three decades. Already mocha brown with a thick thatch of jet-black hair, a brand new Aaron greeted his audience with an endearing whimper, eliciting a joyful noise from his exhausted mother, his exuberant father, and even the slightly indifferent resident who stepped in when it became apparent that Mom's obstetrician wasn't showing up for the big event. Eighteen miles away from Aaron's well-received entrance in Brooklyn, Nina was already swaddled tightly in the nursery in Queens, discovering the addictive taste of her own wrinkly knuckles. Nina's audience—even Mom—had been all too happy with her banishment to the nursery because the delivery room was still pulsing from the startling decibels reached by her maiden voice. The girl was loud, insistent, and, to all who observed, apparently angry about this new development. Nina, for years to come, would never live down the fuss she raised. Her mother would remind anyone who listened, whenever she had reason to note her daughter's aggressive volume, that "the girl been screaming ever since she got here."

Aaron was brought home to a small Brooklyn apartment whose rhythms hardly were altered by his arrival—though the space instantly was squeezed to a maximum, which wasn't a pleasant change in late July's summer swelter. His mother Josefina Simmons was still the same patient soul who could go months without ever raising her voice—even when challenged by the everyday outlandishness of her firstborn son, Carney, who seemed intent upon waking every morning to find a new way to ruffle all feathers in sight. Josefina's patience combined with her husband Ray's gentle humor to create a household that could easily rival the idyllic domestication of Josefina's favorite show, *The Brady Bunch*. Josefina was twenty-eight, born in postwar Harlem, so it didn't escape her notice that the world of Carol and Mike Brady was glaringly bereft of colored people. But she tried not to let tiring demands of racial consciousness intrude on her television viewing. After all, she thought, if you got worked up over things like that, you'd never have any peace. Peace was the goal in the Simmons residence, even in the early 1970s, when there wasn't much of it around them. Their goal was to achieve that airless, settled calm that one would normally associate with senior citizens—certainly not a home with two young kids. Pictureless walls, plastic sofa covers, dark-beige carpet worn thin not by footfalls but by excessive vacuuming. It was a place that could be lifted whole and deposited in the Smithsonian or the Museum of Natural History, in a wing entitled "Americana Living Quarters: 1970s." Aaron's father was a Manhattan doorman. His whole day was defined by adhering to decorum, overreacting—or not reacting, period—to nothing. Years later, after he left his parents' house, Aaron escorted a grieving friend to a funeral home and was startled by how comfortable he felt in the company of the dead—or at least in their sitting room.

Nina was carted home by a family that couldn't have been more different from the Simmonses. The home in Jamaica, Queens, was a cluttered mess, throbbing with so much intense energy and filled with so much stuff that the place always seemed about to explode in a shower of black militant outrage. The family's central theme, in fact, told much of the story: Nina's father Willy was a Black Panther who had spent the last two years in hiding. The NYPD believed, with good reason, that Willy Carruthers—also known as "Baby Ruth" by party loyalists— had played a key role in the botched robbery of a Department of Transportation parking meter collector. The idea, hatched a week after an unpopular fare and toll hike, was to take back the public's money and stage a very public redistribution—even giving some to white people—thus attracting attention and thousands of converts to their cause. But Baby Ruth and three accomplices wound up breaking the man's arm—for about $35 in quarters and a permanent APB with their names on it. Willy was just the driver—but unfortunately was using a car registered in his name. The public redistribution idea was shelved. Didn't take the police long to get to his momma's apartment in Harlem. Consequently, Nina's birth certificate read "Nina Andrews." It would take her twelve years to discover that the name really wasn't hers.

Willy Andrews—né Carruthers—spent most of his days poring over outdated, yellowing Panther literature, harassing his wife and claiming to look for work as a freelance auto mechanic. He wore a brooding scowl as his morning greeting and rarely found time—or inclination—to offer anyone a smile, including his wife Angelique. As a defense, she had long ago gone on the offense, berating him for his many faults whenever she got the chance. But still they clung to each other with a passionate desperation. And they seemed to find many opportunities to display that passion. It was a union that confounded all who knew them.

But as far as unions go, none was as surpassing as Nina's and Aaron's. From the first meeting, they became nearly the same person. It was no surprise to friends and family when eventually their powerful friendship turned into something more. Everyone just wondered what took them so long.

It took twenty-six years to build it up, fine little pieces of selfless-ness, layered on top of one another like the strongest brick mansion in the neighborhood. Twenty-six years of empathetic embraces, three-hour-long phone calls in the gloom of the night, bold and dramatic acts of courage with no thoughts of one's own well-being, jokes—oh, so many jokes—of such brutal wit that their bellyaching laughs would rumble into the next century; twenty-six years of plenty, of so much love and affection that they could smear jealousy over all who observed them like toddlers spreading a cold virus; two decades plus six years of a friendship for the ages.

And it was all over in exactly thirty-three seconds. Splintered by the same demons that had damned all of their individual attempts to forge meaningful love relationships with the opposite sex: the haunting presence of another woman, a creeping lack of trust, and the nasty drama of indictments and incriminations. Her name was Cocoa—and Nina just couldn't let her go.

"Why can't you just trust me, Nina?" Aaron asked his girlfriend, his voice cracking in exasperation. "Why, all of a sudden, are you trippin' over the dumbest little things? No wonder you couldn't ever keep a damn man!"

Nina removed herself from the kitchen and walked toward the living room, where her boyfriend was breathing heavy and wearing a scowl. There were veins visible on both sides of her neck. It looked like a long wiry creature was trying to escape by way of her throat. She clutched a pot in her hand so hard it trembled. It contained string beans. They were still frozen.

"Well, it turns out that every man I've ever known has been a lying, no-good snake," she said. Her voice was barely louder than a whisper, but she might as well have shouted from the rooftops.

They stared, almost as if they saw each other for the first time. Aaron shook his head sadly and headed for the door. He turned around just before exiting. When he looked at her face, he believed he saw unwavering rage and resentment. He did not see the tears in her eyes.

After the fight Aaron became a squatter on his best friend's couch, drifting through his days in a prolonged stupor, agonizing through nights at the club. He didn't even pick up a camera—there was too much of Nina attached to the camera. Nina became a worker bee, pressing herself into her job with the manic energy of a mental ward escapee. Her coworkers noticed her new single-minded passion for her job, but no one questioned her about it—after all, how do you query someone about suddenly becoming a good worker without subtly deriding their prior work ethic? Once she returned to her empty Lower East Side apartment, she'd collapse on her couch and stare at the images on the TV screen without seeing anything at all.

But then Nina started getting worried about her health. She

couldn't keep down any food; she didn't even have an appetite anymore; she found herself dizzy and winded after scaling just the first flight in her walk-up. She didn't know heartache could pack such a wallop. By the end of week two, her worry was building into a torrent of grief, remorse, and panic. She felt like her body wasn't her own, as if some bogeyman had invaded her bedroom while she slept and stolen the real Nina away. She stopped doing her hair; she even wore the same outfit two days in a row. Sensing that she was losing her way, that her control over the order and sense in her life was slipping, Nina summoned the courage to pick up the telephone. She had to overcome shame, to step over pride, to spin away from ego, in order to lift the receiver, which suddenly felt like a twenty-five-pound barbell.

"Aaron?" she said, her voice cracking from the effort. It was past midnight. Aaron was still in the club, but preparing to leave. He pressed the cell phone closer to his ear, thinking that the voice must be an aural mirage, his mind tricking him.

"Nina?" he said.

"Aaron, I need you to come over here. It's important," she said, still shaky.

Aaron could hear the trembling. He felt a pain in his chest, a footprint of fear. He couldn't even hazard a guess what went wrong. A dozen questions crowded his mind at once. Was she sick? Was she hurt? Was she dying? Was she in danger? It was almost an involuntary reflex on his part to rush to Nina's aid—he'd done it so many times that his body could act without deliberation.

"Nina, what's wrong?" he said, already rushing toward the club exit. But he heard nothing. "Nina? Nina!" His cell phone was dead. He ran.

him

I think I made a mistake. As a matter of fact, I know I made a mistake. And it wasn't the insignificant kind that you forget about a day later—like forgetting to put the gas cap back on after you fill up, or walking away and leaving the ATM card in the machine. Those aren't the kinds of mistakes that can tear your heart out of your chest and leave it hopping around on your living room floor like a doomed fish. That's how this drama with Nina has me feeling. Why did we have to leap off this cliff anyway? From the moment I first opened my eyes the morning after the consummation, I had been grappling with this dread smacking me in the back of the head. Why couldn't we just leave it alone? Wasn't a friendship crafted by the angels enough for us? What was it about the human condition that made wanting more so inescapable?

Nina was the kind of friend that most men never even dare to dream of—smart, funny as hell, tough, competitive, and as loyal as a Labrador. She had been in nearly a half dozen fights over three decades in some way defending my ass. Most of us don't think we'll be lucky enough to get half of those qualities in a friend—I've had them smart and funny and I've had them competitive and tough. I've even had them loyal—but so dumb that you'd be tempted to pick the

Labrador in a battle of wits. But in her I got it all—and the fact that it was wrapped in a beautiful package added something to the mix, but in retrospect I'm not sure it was something good. Her beauty just confused me. Well, if I'm being honest here, *confused* probably isn't exactly right. The confusion came in after that other thing—I believe it's called lust.

What do you do after you sleep with your best friend, a woman you have loved for more than twenty years as if she were a part of you—the way you love the strength of your hands or the curve of your calves—who has been your life's most dependable part? In our case, we began what had to be the craziest, most intense love affair the world has ever seen. Or at least our friends and family had ever seen. A love affair for which I'd regularly sleep in the hall outside her apartment door, awaiting her return. (Nina despised cell phones.) A love affair in which she once lay in the bed for three days straight, holding me tight as my feverish body shook from the ravages of what turned out to be pneumonia. A love affair during which her irrational suspicions and hefty baggage pushed her to track my every move, like some kind of curvaceous TV detective on CBS.

And what happened to our friendship, you might ask, this precious thing that seemed to breathe a purer form of oxygen and radiate in its own self-sustaining photosynthesis? In fact, that's a damn good question—I'm still searching for the answer. Before our troubles, Nina might have told you the friendship was still going strong, enhanced now by the drug of sexual exploration and physical intimacy. And I would have to agree that the sex was, indeed, earth-shattering, like some New Age tantric gymnastics that could only be achieved after years of emotional dependency and physical familiarity. But if this thing doesn't make it, if the jagged edges we keep tripping over manage to induce permanent bleeding and injury, will we emerge as best friends still? Somehow I don't think so. Something tells me that my lover will bring the same passion to discarding me that she now brings to loving me—that she brings to every single thing that she does.

I want to tell you about my lover; I need to. But first I have to un-
burden myself about the power of friendship. If you've never had a
true friend, this might sound foreign to you, unbelievable even. But if
you've been as lucky as I, you'll likely find yourself nodding in hearty
agreement.

Probably the first necessary ingredient in forging one of these
Hall of Fame friendships is that it start as early as possible, preferably
in childhood. Only the youngest souls are free of the instinct for self-
protection and the latent jealousies that eventually doom most human
relationships. After we've been around for a while and seen the pain
that humans easily inflict on one another, how can we fail to put up
every barrier and wall in our reach to fight off a stranger's probing interest? To put it simply, people are fucked-up. They do incredibly
foul things to each other, often in the service of some objective as trite
as excitement or as ugly as ambition. In a world where stressed-out
mothers drown their children and bored teenagers torch homeless
men, where hungry ghetto thugs murder Chinese food deliverymen
for an order of pork fried rice and absentee fathers pretend their children don't exist, how consoling it is to know that your flank is always
covered—you shall never be alone. That's what a true friend brings.
Companionship, a kindred soul. In fact, the word *friend* doesn't even
feel adequate enough to get the point across. I prefer something more
dramatic, like *limb*.

Of course, friendship is easy when we're young, when the special
interests and likes that can be so idiosyncratic later on are more likely
to coincide. If it's enough that you have a new football or the latest
hot video game to lure a new buddy, something extra must occur to
elevate the ones that last. I think it's a psychic connection, some kind
of linking of fates and experiences at a level so deep that we never
even see it, like the synchronization between two PDAs as they exchange information. And I think I actually remember when Nina and
I achieved that synchronization, when we clearly were more than just
friends—we had become *limbs*.

Nina likes to tell people about the day I moved onto her block, how she knew I was the man for her when I offered her a piece of candy like a precious little gentleman. Though my recollection is a bit different—I only offered her the candy after she brazenly asked me what that was in my mouth that I was suckin' on like I was *"scared it's gonna run away"*—that's not even the karmic moment I'm talking about. My moment came several years later, after both of our libidos had started revving like NASCAR engines. Nina, in effect, became a *pimp* for my benefit.

We had become obsessed with the kiss. Everything about it— what did it feel like, what separated good kisses from bad kisses, was it nasty to take someone else's spit into your mouth? As I recall, Nina was of the opinion that anything having to do with spit was nasty. I was a bit more ambivalent, considering the spit part of the cost of getting involved in the kiss business. Our mutual obsession—which probably was shared by every twelve-year-old on the planet—could be traced to a movie my mom took us to see one memorable weekend called *Flashdance*. A lot of the action probably flew right over our heads, but we did in our own way pick up on the sexual tension that flowed from the screen in waves. I don't think my mom was prepared for all the sexual innuendo. I'm judging this by the frown she wore on her face throughout much of the movie. When the female star, Jennifer Beals, took out a piece of lobster and let it linger suggestively between her lips, my mother audibly sighed in frustration—signaling to the two twelve-year-olds in her presence that something nasty was happening, though exactly what we weren't certain. But then at the end Jennifer and Michael Nouri get engaged in a furious lip-lock that produced a strange reaction in my lower extremities. It was one of the first times I remember getting an erection that was linked to a sexual image, rather than the arbitrary gust of wind or shifting in my seat. We fled the theater that day giddy from the sights we had seen and desperately wanting to escape my mother so we could analyze it together.

"Have you ever kissed somebody like that, with your mouth all open and stuff?" Nina asked me later, as we leaned lazily against the rusty old swing-set in her backyard. Many years had passed since those swings were deemed safe enough to hold the actual behind of a child, but they were far enough away from the open kitchen window of Nina's house that no one could hear our conversation. The swings had become a favorite spot for us to start exploring the complexities of the boy-girl interactions that swirled around us at our middle school and created loads of confusion for everyone involved. Adolescence might be an exciting time, but we already sensed that it was confusing and scary as hell.

"Uh, well, yeah, kinda . . . I don't know," I stammered. Only recently had Nina and I started discussing these quasi-sexual matters and I still wasn't sure what kind of posture to take with her. The cool, experienced pro, which I instantly became around any male friends, or the truth?

"I think I know the answer, Aaron," Nina said with a little giggle. The giggle intensified my natural embarrassment—I felt a hotness on the back of my neck. "You've never done that before. Well, that's okay. I haven't either."

There was a silence. I couldn't look her in the eye. We had stumbled onto unfamiliar terrain for us. I had thought we could talk about anything.

"Would you like to?" she asked, hesitating just a little. Now I turned my head toward her. She was trying, unsuccessfully, to look blasé. I nodded and then ducked my head. Looking down at the ground, I opened my mouth and forced out my own question. It sounded like a cross between a mumble and a throat clearing.

"Would you?"

I looked up just long enough to see Nina also nod her head. But the difference was that she was looking at me as she did it, her already large eyes widened. Was she telling me that she wanted *me* to do it, to kiss her? I was so startled that I felt an intense need to flee. I looked down at my wrist, even though I wasn't wearing a watch.

"Uh, well, I gotta go," I said, clearly lying. "See ya." And with that I disappeared around the side of her house faster than a frightened cat. The shame flowed through my body like hot lava, making me want to melt into the cracks in the sidewalk as I scurried back to the safety of my house and my room.

That was the background to explain why, less than a week later, I was crammed underneath the band shell in a nearby park with my lips and tongue nervously engaged in a wrestling match with Tonya Billings, a fast little seventh-grade classmate that Nina had convinced to accompany me to the park. The circumstances weren't really explained to me until afterward—and neither was I told that Nina was spying us from behind a tree about thirty feet away. Tonya knew everything; I knew nothing.

About the kiss? It was fantastic, magical, earth-shattering, and utterly terrifying. Tonya did most of the work: she approached me just before the final bell and asked if I wanted to come to the park with her "to hang out for a little while." I knew Tonya's reputation—well, what I knew was that one boy in the eighth grade had told a few of his homies that he had "made out" with Tonya and she had let him feel on her titties. I guess that constitutes a reputation. Tonya had never paid me more than a passing interest. She wasn't mean or indifferent to me by a long shot, but she had never indicated that I'd soon be on the receiving end of an invitation to accompany her to the park. One of my friends, Paul something (I can't remember his last name all these years later), had heard Tonya's request and I glanced over and saw that he had already reported it to two other boys. So now Tonya and I had an audience as we exited the school building together and walked toward the nearby park. Though we were only about a foot apart as we walked, we weren't really acknowledging each other's presence. I was paralyzed with fear, indecision, and cluelessness. I didn't know what to say so I just shut up and walked.

"Can I ask you something, Aaron?" Tonya said softly. I stole a quick glance at her and nodded my assent. What could it be?

"Do you like Nina?" she asked. I looked at her a little more closely this time. We were less than a half block from the park now. Curiously, I don't remember other students streaming past us, though school had just let out and it was a bright spring day—I do remember that much. It was almost like the streets had been cleared for our big scene.

"You mean, do I *like* her like her? Like a girlfriend?" I asked.

Tonya nodded. I looked at her again. She had a round, pleasant face—not as pretty as Nina but certainly not ugly either. Somewhere in the middle. Her brown eyes seemed to sparkle when she smiled, which made you want to see her do that as much as possible.

I still didn't know that Nina was the mastermind behind this whole production—though the questioning was Tonya acting alone.

I shook my head vigorously. It had certainly begun to cross my mind what it might be like to have Nina as a girlfriend, but I knew enough about these matters of the heart to understand that in this situation, while heading toward the park with a different girl, it was best to deny *any* interest in somebody else.

"We're just friends," I said. And it was the truth.

My answer was followed by more silence—enough so that I could hear my heartbeat pounding in my head. When we got into the park, Tonya appeared to know where she was going—straight toward the octagon-shaped band shell that sat in the middle. It was a grand little brick-and-steel structure that had been erected in another era when families came to this Queens park to be entertained, before television would come along to splinter and isolate them. We made our way to a staircase that led to an area below the band shell. At the bottom of the stairs, we probably would be invisible to most passersby, unless they were specifically looking for us. Tonya had a certainty about her step that told me she had been down here before. I saw her give a lingering glance up and behind us—at the time I thought she was checking to ensure we had our privacy, but I soon found out she was making sure Nina was in position. I was expecting an odor as we descended—this was the kind of location where a boy could do some serious pissing if he couldn't get to a bathroom—but I was happy to smell nothing except faintly the grass and trees and cement and rubber, the odor of urban outdoors.

Tonya looked at me with sudden passion, or as close as a twelve-year-old girl could come to it. It looked more like the facial expression of a girl who had to go to the bathroom. She stepped forward and pressed her lips against mine before I had a chance to prepare, to object, to scream, to get scared. She smelled like strawberry Bubblicious; I opened up my lips enough to taste the lab-created strawberry glucose that lingered on her lips. I pressed my eyes shut and marveled at the thickening sensation I was feeling in my crotch. I was getting a woody! Tonya moved her body closer to mine, almost as if she knew what was transpiring down there. My first instinct was to thrust my butt out to keep my loins away from her, but I didn't do that. Instead I let her flatten herself against me until the unmistakable bulge pressed into her groin area. Her lips pulled away slowly, causing my stomach to do a quick flip. I opened my eyes long enough to see her staring at me. I was tempted to apologize for the bulge, but I didn't. Turned out I didn't need to—Tonya smiled. But she remained silent and shut her eyes as her lips came at me again. This time she opened her mouth. I followed her lead and opened mine too, tasting the strong flavor of the chewing gum.

"Wait," Tonya said, pulling her mouth away again. She reached up and removed the pink wad of gum. I laughed and she smiled as she tossed the gum behind me.

How do you describe the thoughts that race through your head during your first kiss? The EKG printout would undoubtedly resemble a person in the midst of a heart attack. I tried to focus my energies on my tongue, imagining that it might scare her if I let it get too wild but also being aware that this wasn't supposed to be boring. But there didn't seem to be much danger of scaring Tonya with an out-of-control tongue. Not when *her* tongue was probing every crack and crevice of my teeth and gums, like an adolescent dentist conducting a cleaning. And what about my hands? Where should they be, what should they be doing? Was I supposed to be grabbing stuff, squeezing and stroking? How long did you have to wait before you could get a feel?

I decided that I had nothing to lose at that point, that I might as well go for it. Slowly my right hand snaked its way up her side, stopping for a moment several inches below her left breast, as if it was resting up for the big expedition breastward. I plunged my tongue deeper into her mouth, thinking that it would serve as a distraction. My hand settled lightly on top of her breast, waiting for a reaction. I got one. She didn't move her mouth away, but the sharp intake of breath scared me. I considered moving my hand, but I knew once the hand was gone it wasn't going back. So I hung in there. Started searching with my forefinger for nipple. Not so easy with the various lumps and bumps on the surface of her bra. Tonya had actual breasts, proud grapefruit-sized globes that had brought her significant attention for the past ten months or so from grown men, many of whom were technically old enough to be her father. Having located a swelling in mid-breast about the size of a thimble, I moved the forefinger around and over it, back and forth, wondering whether my ministrations were being received by Tonya with less discomfort than I was feeling. I heard a sound almost like a rumble that started deep down in her gut and rolled its way from her mouth to mine—actually I felt it more than I heard it. If I wasn't losing my mind, it was an actual moan. And then she did it again, clearly intending the sound effects to deliver a message. If I could chart the three decades of my sexual life on a long, hilly graph, with the early hiccups representing perhaps the accidental penis encounters of my young hand and then moving to the penis–hand encounters that were quite intentional and usually initiated under the covers in my bed before sleep, the moan that Tonya emitted that afternoon under the bandstand would be depicted by a mountainous rise not matched until my junior year of high school four years later. I couldn't have planned a better induction into sexual exploration, this early encounter with the joy of giving women pleasure. The chill that raced down my back and the hardening bulge in my pants sealed my future unselfishness as a lover—much thanks to Miss Tonya Billings, wherever she now may be.

Alas, my hand was allowed to venture no further than the left breast, but that was okay. My indoctrination had been complete. After Tonya and I finally pried our bruised and swollen lips away from each other, we shared very little conversation. We had "made out," yes, but we still had no intention of talking about it. What was I supposed to do, thank her? With little more than a glance in her direction—and her in mine—I scurried up the stairs and out of the park. I did turn around after several minutes to watch her retreating form—and was shocked to see her huddled next to a tree, in deep conversation with Nina Andrews. Huh?

It only took about another twenty-five minutes for Nina to call me on the phone, demanding that I meet her outside at the swings.

"Okay," she said in a loud whisper as soon as I rounded the corner of the house, "you just *have* to tell me everything!"

her

In order for you to understand my feelings for Aaron—indeed, my feelings as I sit here at this very moment—you need to know about all the knuckleheads who've staggered through my life over the past seven years. It has not been pretty. My friends tell me the reason why I've collected such a stable of losers is because of my ridiculously high standards—though I'd prefer to think of my rules as absolute necessities for an intelligent, pretty, got-it-together girl who deserves nothing more than what? The best. Topping my Man Must-Have List? It's simple, really. Rule Number 1: He's got to be tall, chocolate, and fine—but that's a given. Rule Number 2: He's got to be at least four years older than me (you know, to make up for that maturity curve we women have over these dumb little boys). Rules Number 3 and 4 and 5: He must be at least four inches taller than me (when I put on my most prized possessions, my Manolos, Ferragamos, and Choos—not necessarily in that order—I want to still be able to look up at my man, not down), have at least the same level of education as I (I've got a BA in business from Emory, and a year completed toward an MBA from Columbia University—Mama didn't raise no fool), and a serious desire to keep bettering himself educationally, financially, mentally, and emotionally. Number 6? He has to be able to know how to dress (I've been known to dismiss a potential suitor if his pants hung too low off his waist, the tag in his jacket didn't match at least one advertiser in *GQ* magazine, he owned more than two pairs of sneakers—means he spends a little bit too much time playing, not enough time making money or figuring out ways to make more money—or the worst of offenses, his shoes are busted.) Numbers 7 through 18: He has to be well-traveled. A sense of humor is a huge plus. So is sensitivity. And strength. And a healthy respect for culture. He's got to know Jesus. He can't be a liar, a cheater, distrustful, dishonest, or disrespectful. And he's got to appreciate the fact that I'm not perfect, and be ready to accept me as is—faults and all.

That's for starters.

Now, I've been known to deviate from The List. I've recently concluded that the reason why my relationships with all these boys didn't work out is because of said deviations. Too many concessions. Like Stephen. I met him on a rainy Tuesday afternoon at the deli near my office. I went there with a jones for chicken soup—I wasn't feeling well and wanted something hot for my throat, which had begun a slow throb that, along with my stuffed nose and sleepy eyes, was a sure sign that a cold was coming. Stephen saw the glaze in my eyes and, without prompting, handed me the soup he'd ordered for himself, along with his business card. "I'd be happy to bring some Alka-Seltzer and orange juice to your house later on if you're still not feeling well," he said with a smile. He strolled away as cool as you please without saying another word. Suit? Donna Karan. Slides? Cole Haan. Title? Esquire, Pierson, Lehman and Fitzgibbon. By Saturday evening, we were clutched in a furious tongue-wrestle in Central Park (my cold conveniently forgotten by us both), where we went for our second date (Rule Number 22, no passionate kissing until at least the fourth date to ensure the man truly respects you). By Monday, I was calling in sick to work so that I could lie up in his bed while he burned the eggs—a clear violation of Rule Number 23, no giving it up until at least three months of dating have occurred. Six Mondays after our passionate love affair began, Stephen wasn't bringing soup, wasn't offering to stroll with me through anybody's park, sure wasn't serving a sistah anything in bed except his own special brand of (mediocre) hot beef, and was supposedly so busy at work that he could only dial my digits late night, during which he'd kick off his feeble conversation by asking me what I was doing "right now" (Rule Number 24—never, never ever never, become the booty call.)

Then there was Wallace the Millionaire. He was a trader who made a killing renting out the Sag Harbor mini-mansion his parents left him to use for summer vacationing (I loved that he was so industrious). He opened doors (Number 46), always made sure I arrived home safely (Number 47), was a stimulating conversationalist (Number 19), and claimed to be quite smitten with the idea of commitment. "I can't wait to be able to call someone my wife, and to hear my child call me 'Daddy,'" he said to me over breakfast during one of our short weekend getaways to the Hamptons.

Damn if I wasn't hanging in for that title.

Alas, it wasn't to be. Come Thanksgiving, we both realized that we'd made plans to go to the Washington, D.C., area—he to visit his family, me to visit my best friend, Kenya—and eagerly laid out plans to hook up. But for some reason, that Negro, who drove one of his three rides wherever he went—never got around to offering me a lift, even though he knew I was headed down on the ruthlessly nasty Amtrak. Rude. I kept waiting for my phone call invite, but it just never came. In fact, in the few days before it was time for both of us to leave, I couldn't get him on the phone, and he only returned my phone calls when he knew I wasn't going to be around—at home in the afternoon, at work in the wee hours of the early morning, all of which just got me more steamed. Finally, he fessed up in an e-mail that he was stopping in Delaware to visit "friends"—whoever the heck they were— and that he wouldn't be able to see me until *after* Thanksgiving. "Maybe we can meet up for a movie or something," he said. A movie? Was his mama going to go to the movies, too? Would his beloved aunties and cousins be there? How, exactly, does one offer to "hook up" with his girlfriend in his hometown, and not once offer to bring her over to meet family?

Uh-huh, I thought he was dead wrong, too.

So I holed up at Kenya's and didn't bother calling him—not that weekend, and not anymore after that. In an e-mail a few weeks later, he said that he needed to "take a break" from our relationship so that he could "sort out some things." I heard through a few of my friends that he was sorting out some blonde named Lanya.

Then there was Dana, the perpetual liar.

Jason, the mama's boy.

Tysaan, the thug who just stayed in the gutter and seemingly liked it there.

I even tried a few white boys—Liam, Mark, and Michael—but I was fooling myself; they were just as doggish and immature as any black man, just not as blatant. Besides, my girl Kenya wasn't with the interracial dating, and I was tired of listening to her racist tirades about how white men can't "measure up" to "beautiful, strong black men." She sounded like my damn daddy, but more on that later.

The question was, if not white boys, then who? "Well, where are all those beautiful, strong black men? Because I keep coming up short with all these perfect guys you keep fantasizing about," I said to her one day as I hurriedly stuffed a few of my bathing suits into my over-sized overnight bag. We were headed to the Hamptons for a short midweek getaway with Aaron, who, during his bartending travails, got invited by some guy to use his beach house for a few days (he was an old, rich white guy who liked the way Aaron conjugated his verbs and mixed rusty nails)—free of charge. Aaron, of course, invited me and Kenya to hang.

"What do you think, there's some open field somewhere, where they're all waiting on line to meet you?" Kenya said, slightly annoyed. She always got a little snippy whenever we found ourselves having conversations about boys, which was often. "You have to put yourself out there, be willing to talk to guys even if they're not wearing Prada, even if he's not making a million bucks, even if . . ."

Blah, blah, blah. That's what she always ended up sounding like to me—like the teacher in *Peanuts*—you know, *wonk wonk wonk wonk wonk*. She wasn't telling me anything that I hadn't already considered, or done. Frankly, I'd grown quite bored with her boy proclamations— they were clichéd, tired, stale . . . until she said "it."

"I mean, I just don't get why you two don't just go on ahead and do it—it's not like you're not perfect for one another," I heard her say just as I tuned her back in. She'd gotten my attention now.

"What did you just say?"

"You heard me," she snapped. "I said *Aaron*, heifer. That's your man right there. I can't figure out why you all keep playing around and acting like you're not perfect for one another. Anyone with eyes can see it."

"Aaron?" I said, incredulous. "He's my best friend. That'd be like, like . . ." I was searching for the words to describe how preposterous it would be for me to get with the man who'd been my boy, my ace, my road dog, for practically as long as we'd both been on this earth. He's been the man in my life from age five, when his family moved into Ol' Mrs. Johnson's house. She was the old lady who always sat out on the stoop in a pink-flowered housecoat that smelled like that nasty medicine my mom used to force down my throat when I couldn't move my bowels. Ol' Mrs. Johnson never wanted anyone to walk in front of her house, particularly kids, which I always thought was bizarre, considering if you were walking on that side of the street, you had to walk past her house to get where you were going. I guess that never occurred to her, though, because she'd get to shooing folks—kids in particular—the moment their big toe hit the first block of sidewalk in front of her house. "Y'all git, now—git on from in front of my house!" she'd yell, all loud, crinkling her nose to the side of her face and waving her hand like she was pushing away flies. She was scary, but for some reason, she was always trying to kiss on me. "Lord, if that ain't the cutest little baby I ever did see," she'd always say to my dad as he held tight to my hand while we walked to the corner store for the morning paper. "Mornin' Mrs. Johnson," my dad would call back, and then mumble under his breath as he tugged on my hand. I don't really remember what he'd be saying—I was only three at the time—but I knew enough that what he was saying wasn't nice. He didn't seem to like Mrs. Johnson. Or anybody, for that matter. Daddy was one of the most bitter men I've ever known; the most incidental of things would set him off into a tangent of tirades—against "the system," "the man," "pig-headed women," "the racist governmental structure," "backwards-ass Negroes." Hardly anyone was spared his wrath, which came loud and often, depending on whatever misstep—real or imagined—a person might have made against him, his family, or black people in general. See, Daddy was what he called "a Black Panther sympathizer," someone who was down with the movement, but didn't really participate. He was more like the fan on the sideline, who draped himself in the team's colors, painted the quarterback's number on his face, furiously waved signs for the cameras, and yelled at the referees whenever they made a call against his team. Though he preferred to describe himself as a race man who cared deeply for his people, most of the people who came in contact with him just thought he was a little loopy.

Anyway, Daddy would straight clown Ol' Mrs. Johnson—would talk about her silver wig and her loud mouth and how she was "setting back the movement" by wasting her time sitting on the stoop "instead of helping the people." And then, one day, Ol' Mrs. Johnson was gone, and Mommy and Daddy started whispering about what would happen to her house. I was too young to know that Ol' Mrs. Johnson was gone forever; she'd just stopped chasing people off her front walk. But I was more than happy to look out our front door one day to see a little boy standing next to this great big old truck in Ol' Mrs. Johnson's driveway, with a fistful of Now and Laters, this new candy I'd seen on the counter next to the cash register at the newspaper store. Daddy wouldn't let me eat candy—"a black woman has to be in the best of health to help her people, and candy's not good for you," I remember him saying whenever I'd ask for a piece—and I didn't really know how to get my hands on any, seeing as I couldn't reach it, and I didn't have any money to buy it, anyway. But there was Aaron, sucking on a Now and Later like his life depended on it. I was going to get me a piece, too.

"What's that you suckin' on like it's gonna run away?" I said, walking up to him. I'd caught him by surprise—or at least that's the way it seemed, because he didn't say much of anything. His eyes just got wide as saucers. But he kept right on sucking that candy. And then he lifted his right hand toward me and said, "Grape. Want one?" A total gentleman, I tell you. Just as I'd popped that magnificent burst of sugar into my mouth, his mom made the most spectacular entrance I'd ever seen anyone's mom make: "Hello, dear," she said, cupping my face. Her hands were soft, her fingernails were creamy, her hair perfectly coiffed—like one of those white moms on TV who never got mad, even when their kids did something that, in my house, would have meant a quick ass-whooping followed by a really long lecture. "Aren't you lovely? What's your name?"

"Nina," I said, trying to push the candy deeper into my cheek to keep it from falling out while I talked.

"Nina," she practically sang. "What a pretty name for a pretty girl. I take it you've met my son, Aaron. How nice it is to have someone on the block to look out for him."

My cheeks were hot—from excitement, embarrassment, too. I was searching my brain for something to say when my mom threw water on the new neighbor parade: "Nina! Get your butt back across this street. You know better than that!"

"I gotta go," I said quickly, turning around to look both ways before I crossed the street, something I wasn't supposed to do without permission and a grown-up watching. "It was nice meeting you Aaron and Aaron's mommy!" Aaron never did say anything—he just waved his Now and Laters at me as I scurried back into my house.

It was the beginning of the most sincere friendship I've ever had. We went through our first (terrifying) day of kindergarten together, slept over each other's houses, talked to one another into the wee hours of the morning about everything from what our favorite chocolate was to who we'd let touch us down there, to what college would best match our ambitions. He cut all my hair off when we were six—my mom forgot to put away the scissors and I thought it would be cool to see what my ponytail would look like on my favorite dolly; I insisted he take ballet with me so that we could practice our dance moves together—and he did (much to his dad's chagrin). When I got my first period, I told him before I even told my own mom and sister. I dressed him; he dressed me. I approved his girlfriends. He had final say on who I was dating, and if he didn't like him—out the door the guy went, no questions. Nothing was off-limits for us, and anyone who knows us knows that we're tighter than some married couples.

But actually *getting* with him? Like, in a man-woman kinda way? That wasn't really something we ever considered. Well, at least not out loud. Come on, now—we went through puberty together, slept in the same bed with one another, saw each other naked. To go through our entire twenty-six-year friendship without at least wondering what it would be like to get with the other person would have been nothing short of abnormal. I'll admit to cuddling next to his solid, chiseled back in search of warmth and my body shivering from sexual energy—not necessarily the chill in the room. I'd found myself wondering what it would be like if he loved me the way a man should—usually when he was telling me about some freak he'd posted up after a hot party or whatever. I'd even gotten jealous of some of the girls I deemed unworthy of such a jewel, particularly when even I, his hot best friend, hadn't sported him. There were nights when climbing in bed with him was damn near unbearable (usually when I'd gone without sex so long, my thongs had cobwebs), his gentle (friendly) touch so incredibly sensual that only the most passionate of lovers would have known what to do with it.

Alas, we never went there. "Sleeping with Aaron would be like sleeping with you," I told Kenya incredulously. "I might as well be a lick-sister!"

"Um, I hardly think sleeping with fine-ass Aaron would be like sleeping with a girl," Kenya shot right back. "He is all man, honey."

"Uh-huh—just not my man," I said. "Let's drop it, please."

I hadn't thought about what she said again until later on that night. I still don't know if Kenya was sick for real or if she was just faking cramps when she said she couldn't go to the "rhythm and blues fest" at the local nightspot near where we were staying, but Aaron and I left her sucking down Aleve and nursing a cup of hot tea.

"Go ahead, have a good time without me," she said pitifully. "Don't you worry—the kid's going to make a comeback. I'm going to be bigger, better, stronger—just not until tomorrow morning."

"We'll get in a dance for you," Aaron tossed back as he grabbed my hand and headed for the door. "Later girl," I said, waving. She was winking at me, with a really mischievous look in her eye. Wasn't nothin' wrong with that fool; she was just trying to get Aaron and I to hook up.

It worked.

The so-called "rhythm and blues" concert was a white-people version of R&B—all Elvis and Jerry Lee Lewis and other white musicians who'd co-opted black artists' styles, watered them down for the masses and, with a twist of their hips, got folks to call it soul. You couldn't tell the good white people of Sag Harbor that they weren't listening to some real music—they were just clapping their hands and doing their awkward, stiff-legged, jerky-hip dances and singing off-key. Not even three shots of tequila, two berry martinis, and a lime-flavored Corona between us could get Aaron and I low enough to sit through that madness; we hung in there for about an hour and then blew the joint in search of somewhere quiet, where we could enjoy our buzz and a break from the locals. We ended up on a bench in front of a short stretch of a public beach frequented by families during the day, but, as we soon discovered, lovers by night. Couples, mostly teenagers, were fogging up their parents' oversized SUVs and expensive—but practical—rides, coming up for air only when it was time to steal away back to the places where they wouldn't have dreamed of doing what they'd just done in their daddy's backseat. The night was starry and still—its beauty, and the chill in the air and our liquor-induced buzz tempting us to draw closer. The air was electric. I rested my head in the crook of his neck. He smelled incredible. The liquor made me say that out loud. Really loud. He busted out laughing.

"Why you yellin'?" he said, just as loud.

"Who's yellin'?" I said back, trying my best to stifle my giggles.

"Why you got your nose buried in my neck?" he said, shouting again.

"I'm cold."

"Well so am I, but you don't see me with my nose all up in your neck," he yelled.

"You want me to move?" I asked, raising up. "Fine—I'm going to go over here to this side of the bench. Doesn't smell as good, but if it makes you more comfortable. . . ."

Aaron followed me over to the other side, sliding dramatically to make his point: "Nah, nah, baby—come on. Let's be warm together."

"Warm together, huh?" I said, nuzzling back into his neck. This time, though, it was my lips, not my nose, that was doing the nuzzling. Without thinking, I dotted my sentence with a series of sweet, soft kisses. He tilted his head just slightly, giving me more access—an access I happily took. I was certainly getting warmer.

"Yeah," he said, turning his head toward mine. "Warm."

We were silent for a moment—the pause pregnant with possibilities. For years, we'd played with one another, teased and threatened, lingered, suggested. But we'd never followed through—never gone there, because, at the end of the day, it was the friendship, the loyalty, the respect, that kept us coming back for each other. Still, I'd felt this incredible urge to break all of our unwritten rules, to face head-on the years of sexual tension that buried itself beneath our friendship, our trust, our years together. This very night, he was all I'd ever dreamed of having in a man—stable, familiar, capable. I wanted him. But I didn't say that. I buried my desire to touch him beneath my insecurity—refused to follow my instinct into the unfamiliar. So I burst out laughing—the spit from its force sprayed his face. "What the fuck was that—'Yeah, warm,' " I said, in a deep and mocking voice. "What are you, Barry White now?"

"Oooh, you dissed me," he said, raising up off the bench enough to make me tumble backward. He used his pointer finger to nudge my forehead, then started heading for the car.

"Aw baby," I said, mockingly. "Come on now baby, don't be mad."

We were quiet heading back to the house, the silence thick with questions. What had just happened? Was I really trying to put the moves on my best friend? Was he willing to accept my advances? Would we have . . . nah. We were drunk. Wasn't much else to it.

That's what I thought, at least, until I got back to the house and climbed into the bed with Kenya. "I think I almost kissed Aaron." She didn't say anything. I was silent, too. Then I said: "I think I wanted to kiss Aaron."

"Of course you do. You want to marry Aaron, have his babies, and live happily ever fucking after. I don't get what took so long for you to get this. Duh. Now what you gonna do about it?"

A few weeks later, I did something about it, all right. A few weeks later, I had sex with my best friend. And it was incredible. And he was incredible. And we were incredible. Two people, with a shared history, mutual admiration and love for one another, perfect for each other in every way, together. Finally. Perfect match, right? One would think. Everyone says it's important to be friends before you're lovers if a relationship is to last. The reasons are obvious: Only with full disclosure can you truly decide whether someone is worthy of sharing your pillow for the rest of your life. Is he honest? Do you trust him? Do you really love him? Does he love you back? Are you still down to call him your friend, despite that you know what his nastiest habits are? Does he treat you different from all the other tricks he's run up in without giving a second's thought to how they'd be affected once they realized they were just another piece of ass, and not The One? In Aaron's case, all of my answers were a resounding, "Yes." After more than two decades of unconditionally loving each other beyond limit, it was only natural that we progress—together. The only thing anyone who was remotely privy to our long-standing friendship wanted to know was, "What took you so long?"

Well, we broke down and did it. And now our friendship is broken down, too. All the things that seemed special, endearing, about my best friend are now making me question whether he's really the man for me—or if he's going to end up on the heap of failed relationships that made me reach out to Aaron for companionship in the first place.

Nina and Aaron,
Part II

After his cell phone went dead, Aaron's knees sagged momentarily. What was wrong with Nina? He stepped outside and felt dread washing over him. But it gave him energy. He burst onto Broadway, already waving his arms in search of a cab. Past midnight, black man alone, looking a bit unstable—who was he kidding? He spied a white woman stepping from a cab across the street. He darted in front of a speeding car, praying that the cabbie wouldn't see his rush into oncoming traffic. With a final sprint, he caught the door before the fortyish blonde woman could close it. He forced a smile onto his face, that comforting gesture he had been trained to offer white women on the Upper West Side. Uneasily, she smiled back.

He saw the concern furrow the driver's brow as he stared into Aaron's visage in his rearview mirror.

"Lower East Side. First Avenue and Third Street," Aaron said. He leaned forward. "And you can relax, man." The cab driver, of unclear Mideastern origin, did not relax at all. But Aaron didn't have time for racial sensitivity training. As he watched the brightly-lit streets of Manhattan fly by the window, his mind went to Nina. So many shared moments, so much history filling up the backseat of the cab with him. As usual, Nina's presence was overwhelming—even when she wasn't present.

Nina, her hand still clutching the phone, sat motionless in the corner of the couch. She hoped that if she didn't move, if she slowed her breathing to a shallow ripple, she would be able to hold back the tears that were welling just behind her corneas, floodwaters at a dam. Like Aaron, she sifted through their past. With considerable trepidation, she asked herself: Could they handle this?

him

I think this would be an ideal time to tell you about our first time. Actually, I'm sure there would be better places in the story to describe the thunder of our first intimate moments, but this is a memory that can still bring tears to my eyes—so please indulge me for a few minutes.

All I can say is I will be eternally grateful to Mr. Jack Daniels and his unparalleled powers of persuasion. Try to imagine the tension that had developed between us, twenty-five years of prolonged stares and double meanings and jealous fits, twenty-five years of physical contact and stolen glimpses and intoxicating scents. We were like two superpowers, watching each other for decades so closely that we could predict each other's movements, so similar that over the years we had morphed into mirror images—both waiting with escalating anxiety for a massive culminating engagement. It finally came on a fateful spring night—forever will I believe the poetic declarations of spring's lustful power. Come with me for a moment and picture the excitement, the anxiety, that filled her Manhattan bedroom.

I had called her up at the last minute to invite her to see her boy Maxwell, her absolute most beloved singer—at least at that time. The story behind the tickets was a little cumbersome—a regular big-spending customer at the club where I tended bar presented them to me quite unexpectedly. He was a well-compensated attorney in midtown whose client list included a firm that promoted a large percentage of the country's music concerts, so he always had a stack of gratis tickets to hand out like business cards. He was also a white man with an unhealthy obsession: black girls. Or to be more specific, black strippers. For a white man such as he with an obsession such as his, the strip club was an invention that made his life a lot easier. He had begun to use me as a middleman, passing messages to the club's performers— and thus contributing to the ease with which he could feed his obsession. You shouldn't distract yourself with the fact that I was employed at such a club. It was just a side hustle while I worked on starting up my photography career. At times it becomes necessary to put aside moralistic judgments in order to make a few dimes. And anyway, the place wasn't sleazy—it was an establishment where men could have some good clean fun and attractive ladies could make a few extra dollars for tuition, since they all claimed to be paying their way through school.

"Wait, are these some tickets from that dude you were telling me about—the one you're pimping for?" Nina asked me over the phone, chuckling at the "pimping" line because she knew it would piss me off.

I sucked my teeth but didn't go for the bait. "Do you want to see Maxwell or not?" I said, my annoyance clear.

"Shoot, you know the answer to that. He's my secret Love God," Nina said.

I laughed. "Does that mean you kneel down and pray to him every night in your bedroom? Or maybe you invoke his name when you pull out your vibrator."

"I told you, I will not have you trying to mock my little friend!" she said. "A girl can get lonely on those cold New York nights. But anyway, I don't give a fuck if these are pimping tickets—I'm going to see my boy. What time you picking me up?"

When Nina emerged from her building, a somewhat ratty Lower

East Side walk-up, I nearly choked on my breath mint. It had been only a couple of weeks since I had last seen her; she seemed to grow more stunning every time we came together. In my experience, a woman at age thirty was like a high-performance engine at its peak, all the cylinders firing, the horsepower ramped up to its zenith, the strength and majesty of the carriage drawing appreciative stares and comments at every turn. Nina appeared to float down the stairs toward me, her heart-shaped face lit up by a broad grin and her outrageous curves caressed by a clingy, short black dress. I shook my head as she approached.

"What you shaking your head at, sexy boy?" she said with an impish gleam in her eye.

I shook my head again. "You lucky I'm your best friend," I said.

"And why is that?" she asked, her arm slipping inside mine as we started down the street. With her on my arm, I thought, I might even be able to get a cab.

"Because if I wasn't, I'd be all over that sexy ass of yours," I said, assuming my usual teasing posture with her. But her response was not *her* usual. Instead of throwing something sassy back at me, Nina grew silent. I thought her silence was a bit odd at the time, but I didn't dwell on it for more than a second or two. Now that I look back more than a year later, it's clear that she had something planned already, a bold move that would change everything forever.

Maxwell onstage proved to be the world's most effective aphrodisiac. By the time we had drifted out of the relatively small club where he sang, danced, crooned, and moaned for more than two hours and we had sucked down a few shots of Jack Daniels and enough apple martinis to fill a couple of carafes, we were both virtually throbbing with sexual arousal. The air around us was different than usual—thick with the danger of altered states. Sometime during the cab ride back to Nina's building, some unspoken messages were passed back and forth between us. With her back leaning heavily against my shoulder, Nina gently slid her left hand up the inside of my right thigh. It was a grand dramatic gesture—and it worked as forcefully as a scream in my ear. Nina had probably touched me a thousand times over the previous twenty-five years, on virtually every inch of my body—the casual tickling, poking, prodding of best friends of the opposite sex who didn't exactly mind a little physical contact. But immediately I knew the cab caress was different, as if she could pass her intentions through her fingertips. She let her hand come to rest, about four or five inches from my straining erection, which had slipped out of my boxers and was now banging against the inside of my trousers. I was no longer breathing—couldn't risk the disruption of movement. I waited for her hand to continue its ascent up my thigh—but it had stalled. Was she scared? Had she changed her mind? Maybe she had made the mistake of considering the long-term consequences. If her hand moved a few more inches, our lives could very well be permanently changed. That thought would have been sobering to anyone—anyone except for me. I decided to take the initiative, to plunge ahead. Slowly I draped my arm over her shoulder, reaching around and around, searching for her right thigh. My hand made contact with the soft silky fabric of her dress and quickly I felt the smoothness of her bare leg just below the hem, which had ridden up nearly to the crotch. It was like my fingertips had never before made contact with her flesh. I felt a jolt in Nina's bones, like my fingers carried an electric current.

"Aaron?" she whispered my name softly, hesitantly, asking a thousand different questions at once. She was giving us one last chance to pull back, to give this a second thought. She was telling me that she was aware of how much things would change—she wanted to know if I was equally aware. I heard all this in her voice, but I was too far gone to really give the matter the deliberation it deserved. My mind was clouded by the fog of a lust so many years in the making that it had grown massive and feral and clumsy. Once aroused, it lumbered to its feet like an awkward Goliath and took ground-shaking strides toward its prey. This advancing beast could not be stopped—not by the plaintive whispers in the back of a smelly New York City cab, certainly not by abstract sentiments of a possible friendship lost. Pushed by the beast, I forged ahead, stroking her bare thigh, trying with all the might of my inebriated will to move her hand up to my crotch. Nina followed her whispered question with a moan of pleasure that was as distinctive and clear as an alarm clock. I saw that the cab had by now turned onto her street—we would be faced with the pivotal question before we had a chance to answer it with our actions. The cab slowed in front of her building; I reluctantly reeled in my right hand.

"This you, right?" asked the cabbie, a middle-aged black man with a thick Brooklyn accent.

I wasn't sure if I was sorry we had reached her place—though I would be sure if she told me I should just stay in the cab and go home. Nina sensed my hesitation—if it were possible to spend so much time with another person that you could read their thoughts, Nina and I would be there.

"Why don't you just stay over here?" she said sweetly, confidently. I needed no further prompting. Of course I had slept over at her place on several occasions over the years, but clearly this was different.

"That sounds like a great idea," I said, as I handed the cabbie a $10 bill for a $7.90 ride. "Keep the change."

As we were scooting out of the taxi, I caught the leer on his face—and I didn't like it. I leaned in close to the fiberglass partition.

"Yo, man, you need to keep your eyes on the damn road. Your business is not back here."

The half smile on the cabbie's face quickly disappeared, replaced by a smirk.

I don't even remember the walk upstairs to her third-floor apartment, nor do I remember her pulling out keys and opening the door. Like a child whose life begins at age four because he can't remember anything prior, my memory bank with Nina begins in her bedroom, on her bed. That's when our new lives began. I was deathly afraid that there would be an awkwardness and a shyness between us. Hell, we had both done enough trash-talking about our skills in the bedroom that it's a wonder I was even able to sustain my erection once it became clear that I'd actually be using it, putting all those years of idle words to the test. But all my fears turned out to be far, far off-base. From the first passionate kiss in the middle of her bedroom floor, me wearing my pants around my ankles and my just-freed penis bobbing up and down in the stale air, her with the black dress tugged above her ass cheeks—thanks to my eager cupping of her fleshy derriere—we moved together like a well-practiced duo. The intense familiarity paid off handsomely. That's not to say that we both didn't get our share of surprises. Her breasts were larger and her skin softer than I had imagined. She later would tell me I was more muscular than she would have guessed. She said my dick was almost exactly the length and girth that she'd conjured in her mind's eye. I wasn't sure if I was proud or embarrassed by that fact.

As my tongue explored the inside of her mouth, the taste of her peppermint breath mint still lingering, I was still partly disbelieving that Nina and I were about to have sex. It was something that I had given many hours of thought over the years, but a few years back when Nina was immersed in a relationship that I assumed eventually would lead to marriage I had decided to dismiss the idea of us altogether. It was almost a necessary mental exercise for a man to undertake when you had a best friend as fine as Nina—you had to excise all erotic thoughts about her if you were going to be able to function in her presence and carry out all the best-friend duties, such as listening to her describe sexual experiences with other men. I could feel—or maybe I could sense—Nina's left hand slowly dropping down toward my crotch. I got so distracted from the anticipation of her making contact that I almost forgot that I had been attempting to unzipper her dress in the back with one hand.

We drifted onto her bed somehow, our bodies intertwined and our hands furiously groping, squeezing, stroking. I had an urge to pull back to take in Nina's lovely form—I was gaining confidence now, knowing that surely there was no turning back. It was time to relax a bit, let each of my senses in on the action. I pulled away from her and gazed down at her naked body, awestruck at its perfection. My God, there wasn't a blemish or scar in sight. After all those years of falls and scrapes, somehow perfection had emerged. Her breasts were large enough that even on her side they kept their spherical form—but still perky enough that they didn't sway to the side. I reached down and ran my hand along her back, thrilling in the way it sloped dramatically inward and then jutted out precipitously as it grew into her large rounded ass, like a dome on a glorious European cathedral. She turned over onto her back and looked up at me with widened eyes, no doubt wondering what was racing through my head. I hoped my big grin was enough to let her in on my thoughts. I leaned over and pressed my nose into the hollow of her neck, inhaling the fruity sweetness of her scent, a springtime bouquet of lilacs and roses. She reached out and slowly ran her fingers over the hills and crevices of my chest and the taut muscles of my stomach. My well-defined abdomen was a source of pride for me—I worked hard with a regular nightly regimen of crunches and twists to maintain it as my body's primary showpiece. I was grateful for the work now as I watched the giddy expression on Nina's face while she toyed with my "six-pack." I leaned down and pressed my lips against hers.

"You are so beautiful, Nina," I said in between kisses.

A smile spread across her face but she didn't say anything in response. She cupped my face in her hands and blanketed it with little affectionate pecks. I grew eager to sample the rest of her. I moved my mouth down to her neck, my lips and tongue leaving a trail along the way. I paused at her breasts, circling around with the tip of my tongue until I closed in on her enlarged nipple. A deep moan started in her belly and passed all the way up to her throat. I went back and forth, left to right, sucking in the nipples like pulling on a straw. Her squirms told me she enjoyed this. But I was eager to move on. I slid down her torso, stopping at her cute little navel to give it a few licks; moving down. I paused for a few seconds of contemplation as I stared at the dark triangle of bushy hair—Nina clearly was not a frequent trimmer. Many women may be taken aback a little by this, but I knew the next thirty seconds were perhaps the most important half minute we would encounter in determining whether there would be a relationship that had real meaning. Nina had to pass the smell and taste test. Perhaps that sounds a bit crude, but let me tell you, my last relationship had failed to take off because I could not will myself past my lady's (okay, her name was Sophie) rather unpleasant taste. And we're not talking necessarily about hygiene here—Sophie was fastidious about cleanliness in all parts of her life. This is more elementary than that, bodily juices whose wells and springs were not influenced by soap and water. These are factors almost completely beyond a woman's control, I know, but if I'm going to spend considerable time in her nether regions, I need not feel my stomach turning at the thought. The lands were likely littered with women who had been cast off for failing the taste test—women who would never really know why their boyfriends had fled or their fiancés lost their will. This hadn't been my only problem with Sophie, but it was a major deal breaker.

Maybe Nina could read my thoughts—she kept her legs clamped firmly shut. I was a bit confused. I looked up at her with my eyebrows raised. She looked back at me; she appeared a bit frightened.

"I don't like that," she said in a tiny hesitant whisper.

I was stunned. A thirty-year-old woman who had been sexually active for the past thirteen years, had been living in Manhattan for seven of them, had had numerous boyfriends and even more sexual encounters—and she didn't like oral sex? All this time, you think you know someone and you make a discovery of this magnitude. Some clueless loser had gone down there and so thoroughly botched the job that she was now exercising an opt-out? I found that unforgivably sad.

"Really?" I answered, my shock evident.

She nodded her head without looking at me. Clearly she was embarrassed.

"Just let me do you," she said, staring at the ceiling.

No, I could not have that. The karma would be all wrong, imbalanced, off-kilter. I took a deep breath.

"Let me give it a try, Nina. You can stop me if you want."

My plea sat there for several long painful seconds. I became more aware of my surroundings—the faint glow cast through the window by the street lamp, the bedroom clutter in every corner, the subtle pleasant aroma of female sweat. I stared at her nostrils, which I could see slowly expanding every time she took a labored breath of her own. I saw movement below and looked down to watch her legs slowly opening. I was giddy with excitement and apprehension, a man who had been granted entry to the vault but still had one more combination to solve before the bounty would be his.

Before I could be paralyzed by the implication, I plunged ahead. Almost immediately, I knew that this was a place I never wanted to leave. Faintly sweet, tangy but not overpowering, like a carefully seasoned dessert treat.

I settled in to go to work, so relieved and pleased that I wanted to shout out. But first I had a crucial rescue mission to complete—Nina's introduction to a vital sensual delicacy. How could you even call yourself a sexual being without having made its acquaintance?

Rather quickly, several minutes into the job, my work paid major dividends. It started with her legs slowly tensing—I could feel her thigh muscles growing taut around my jaws. Then her head thrashed back and forth on the pillow and she began to groan. Encouraged, I increased the pressure and tempo of my ministrations. I slid my hands under her ass cheeks to gain more control, pulling her in even tighter. She responded enthusiastically and loudly to my taking control. I had one more trick for her, a tongue movement that had never failed me. Again it worked fantastically—Nina thrust her pelvis against my face with force, lifting her hips (and my face) off the bed. She moved her hands down and pushed on the back of my head. I could no longer breathe, but it was a small sacrifice. The scream must have started down at her toes, which tensed and pointed downward like a ballerina's. It began as a rumble, a release of emotion, pleasure, frustration, and tension that stirred together into a guttural cocktail of noise. By the time she opened her mouth, she was screaming so loud that there must have been 911 thoughts all up and down the building and the street. I moved away and watched the scene unfold, her trip back to my world, her body slowly deflating. When finally she opened her eyes, she granted me a wide smile.

"Aaron, my God!" she said through her exhaustion. I saw the twinkle in her eye. "Can you do that again?"

her

Now that Aaron and I are drifting in this netherworld of angst, both of us waiting to see whether the bough will break, I am trying to figure out why I seem unable to do this, to make one of these work. I know what a psychologist would say—that I'm incapable of having a stable relationship because I've never seen one up close. That would be fair. I grew up, after all, in the jumbled stew of anger, instability, and indifference that was the marriage of Willy and Angelique Andrews. My mother? She was perpetually unhappy. My dad? A complete jackass who never did deliver on the promise he made to Mommy the day he sweet-talked her onto the 6 train headed for City Hall: "Of course, I'll take care of you, Angie. I'm a man—and that's what a black man does," he'd said, as he pushed the pen into her hand and nudged it toward the marriage license. "We takes care of ours." Young and desperate to get out of her mama's house and two months pregnant with a child she wasn't sure she really wanted, much less could feed, Angelique signed on the dotted line, said, "I do," and walked down the aisle toward her mediocre life with a man who talked big but delivered real, real small.

Of course, Angelique had seen just how black men "took care" of their women. Her father, Simon, was what the old-timers referred to as a rolling stone—an O.G. playa who'd made babies in two different states with three different women, refused to marry any of them, and made minimal effort to even so much as learn his children's names, except when he came around to get some money or some time in their beds or both. Angelique's mother, Violet, recognized Simon's pattern pretty early on, and, unlike the others, decided to let someone else keep her bed warm at night. But men of that generation—or at least the ones who bothered to pay Violet any kind of attention—didn't believe in taking care of anyone else's bastard child, no matter how swell her Sunday dinners were. Violet insisted loud and often that she wasn't bitter—"I loves my baby, even if her daddy and these other no-count men won't"—but the lectures she tortured her daughter with made it clear her heart had grown cold after years of inattention, promises not kept, ache. "Get yourself a good man, Angie. Not no no-count niggah who don't want to do what a man 'posed to do. Ain't no man a man if he ain't working hard to keep his family together." She'd said that so many times that Angelique could sense when the speech was coming, and damn near mime the words right along with her mama. The words stuck, though, so Violet accomplished what she'd set out to do: keep her daughter out of similar familial predicaments.

Alas, they were just words. Angelique looked up one day to realize she had two daughters of her own and a husband who did the right thing by marrying her, but did everything else ass-backward. So consumed was Willy Andrews by what he was being denied, that he never really made the time to take care of his family the right way. He couldn't hold a job? It was the Man's fault. The fight he had with the brother in the bar landed him in jail? It was the Man's fault. His children were eating chicken broth and soup for dinner again? The white man was keeping his black family from eating right. But while he was complaining about what they didn't have, Angelique was scrambling to hold her little family together. Sometimes, even, to Willy's disdain.

"Well how else are these babies going to eat?" she'd once said to him, punctuating her sentence with a roll of her neck before she snatched on her jacket. It was snowing outside, and it was cold inside, too. Willy swore by saving heating costs by making us bundle up in as many sweaters/socks/long johns as possible to avoid turning the thermometer up—saved him a bundle in heating costs, he always bragged, even when our teeth were clattering. I remember looking at my mom, mouth agape—but I can't remember if I was more surprised that she'd snapped at my father, or that she actually thought she'd be warm enough in the thin, raggedy coat she was pulling over her shoulders.

"We got plenty to eat here, Angie—don't give me that!" Daddy yelled at her. "Ain't no woman of mine gonna go to nobody's welfare office to beg The Man to feed *my* children."

"Where, Willy? Show me where the food is and I'll take this coat off right now and go in that kitchen and cook us a meal." Her hand was on her hip now. My father's nostrils were flaring.

He flew into the kitchen and whipped open the cabinets; my mother was right on his heels. Wham! He slammed down "Flour! You can make homemade biscuits if your cooking was half a damn." Wham! "Beans! You can feed a family of ten with a pot of these." Wham! "Tuna fish. Mix some mayonnaise in this here and we got sandwiches for everybody. We got food, Angelique. Don't tempt me up in here."

"Tempt you? Tempt you! If I feed these children one more bean, they're going to fart clear to the moon, Willy! These babies need meat, and cheese and milk and healthy things so they can think straight. Hell, I'm a grown-ass woman and I can't think straight from being hungry. And I know not eating is affecting you because clearly you done lost your damn mind up in here slamming my damn food around this kitchen."

And then, a grunt—and a smack. I heard my mother's body hit the counter, and though I wasn't in the room—so paralyzed with fear were me and my sister that we didn't dare move—I pictured my mother holding her face and reeling back from him. She was crying—I could hear from the shakiness in her voice. But she wasn't scared—

no, sir. "Put your hand on me one more time, Willy Andrews, and I declare before God I will call the police and tell them to come get your silly ass from out of my house," she said through clenched teeth. "See if I don't do it, hear?"

"Do it and it'll be the last time you dial a number, the last time you talk to a human being, the last time you take a breath—you hear me, woman?"

But he left her alone. He walked slowly out the kitchen and back toward their bedroom. I heard him gently close the door. My mother? She wrapped her scarf around her neck real tight, put on her gloves, and headed out the door. It wasn't the first time my father had hit my mom. And it certainly wasn't the last. Still, we ate real good that night.

Daddy wouldn't touch his food. Just drank water and stared at the wall. Finally, he pushed his chair back from the table—loud and abruptly—and stomped up the stairs. My mother hadn't looked up from her plate until just then. "I'm thinking about divorcing your father," she said flatly. And then, with more conviction, she added: "So if we split, what's it gonna be? You gonna go with him, or me?" When I lifted my head, my eyes met hers. They were cold, distant. Tired.

Truth of the matter was, I didn't want to go anywhere with either one of their asses. They were both crazy as bedbugs, and I was fast becoming just like them. I wanted out. No, what I wanted was for Aaron's family to adopt me. His mother always said she wished she had a daughter. Here was her shot.

"Man, your leftovers are better than what I get for dinner on a good night," I told Aaron as I eyed his lunch. He'd spread his cloth napkin across the table, and was carefully placing his smoked ham sandwich (carved from the Sunday ham his mother baked on Tuesday), sliced carrots, applesauce, and Twinkie on it when I walked up, free lunch of mystery meat, stale bread, warm milk, and brown apple in hand.

"Ah, but I gotcha covered though," he said, without looking up.

He grabbed a napkin out of my hand, and pulled out a second sand-wich—this one fatter than the first. "My mom knows how much you like her ham, so she made me bring you one, too."

I had to stop myself from drooling right there on the table. "Thanks," I said, trying hard not to snatch it out of his hands. "Hmm hmm. Just the way I like it, too—lots of mustard, slice of cheese, extra ham," I said, as I pulled out a few pieces of meat to sample before biting into the bread. "I know you're going to share your Twinkie with me."

"You can have some carrots, too."

"Uh, no thanks," I said. But inside, I was smiling—smiling at the fact that Aaron's mom thought so much about her son's health that she actually hand-peeled carrots, chopped them into slices, and packed them in her boy's lunch box. My mom never did *that*. "Lunch is one of the most important meals of the day, dear," she once told Aaron on one of the many occasions I just *happened* to be over their house during dinnertime. We were gathered around the table—Mrs. Simmons, Aaron, his brother Carney and me (Mr. Simmons was working late—again), and Aaron was trying to make the case for why he should get $1.20 per day to buy the school lunch, instead of hav-ing to "lug that big ol' lunch box to school every day." I looked at him like he was a natural-born lunatic, but that didn't stop me from eat-ing my meat lasagna. I was determined to go home full enough not to even need to eat oatmeal for breakfast the next morning. "The lunches aren't so bad. Right, Nina?"

No, this Negro wasn't trying to get me to cosign this foolishness. Here his mom was, cooking him nice, hearty dinners, and then stack-ing his lunch box with goodies for the next day, and this bonehead was trying to say he wanted to eat trays full of mystery meat? See, that's what happens when people don't appreciate shit. At least that's what I thought at the time. Mrs. Simmons didn't work outside the home, but she held down her job inside it. She was a regular June Cleaver in blackface—never complained, always had her household in order, al-ways looked impeccable, always made sure her kids and her man were clean, well fed, happy. She signed Aaron and his brother up for Little League every year, then stood on the sidelines and cheered them on; signed them up for swimming lessons, then sat on a perfectly ironed and lint-free towel hung with love and sun-dried on the line just for the occasion, with a rapt eye on her sons while they romped in the water at the local pool. She never missed a PTA meeting. Baked cookies for all the functions. Held Tupperware parties at the house, with the ladies-who-lunch crew showing up in their pretty dresses and dainty talk, praising her for being such a model mother and wife. Never missed a Sunday at Mt. Calvary Baptist Church, or a Saturday of volunteering at the church's weekend food pantry. I'd find reasons to be around her—she with me. "Nina, why don't you come on over and help me and Aaron make brownies this Saturday. I sure could use your help," she'd said to me more times than I could count. One time, she even invited me on vacation to Atlanta with them—like clockwork, they visited Georgia every spring to see Mrs. Simmons's family, and Chicago every fall to check out Mr. Simmons's people—but my father wouldn't allow it (though I suspect that's because he couldn't afford to send his child anywhere, and he refused to let someone else do it). She settled for my spending the night a few times (when we were younger, of course; there was none of that once we hit, like, ten). Those were the most glorious; we'd play board games and she'd tell really corny jokes ("Will you always remember me?" she asked once, quite earnestly. "Of course, Mrs. Simmons," I'd say quickly. "How could I ever forget you?" "Okay, knock-knock," she'd say back. "Who's there?" I'd answer. "See? You forgot me already!" I remember collapsing into giggles on more than one occasion to that one, mostly to spare hurting her feelings—it was really a bad joke, even for my equally corny nine-year-old self). She'd even beg me to bring over my comb and brush so that she could braid my hair ("I always dreamed of having a little girl with beautiful hair like yours. Instead, I got two knotty-haired boys!" she'd say as she loosened out my Afro puffs and gently comb through my cottony-soft corkscrew curls). Her husband would come in and kiss her cheeks and hug her and disappear into the den, a cup of coffee in hand. She'd smile. Always smile.

If there was anyone to thank for her son's tenderness, it was this tender woman. Make no mistake about it; Aaron was by no means a punk; I suspected he could throw down with the rest of the boys in our class. But he was raised right, and fighting was always the last option for him. His mama had taught him the subtle art of negotiation—how to use his mind, instead of his fists, and get along with even the biggest of enemies. It was a trait that served him—and me—well, and I loved him for that. For being my protector, without having to be a brute, for never hesitating to tell me what's on his mind, but always being gentle with my feelings. They're traits only a son raised by a woman with some sense would actually adopt. And those traits often served me well—like the time when I got together in ninth grade with Boobie, the basketball star, who decided he was going to have his way with me, even if I disagreed. Aaron got him real good. But I don't even know if I can tell you about that right now—the memory still pains me. You might have to ask Aaron about that story. However, I can tell you about Dana "the wifey beater" Jeeter, whose acquaintance I made in the tenth grade. I'd heard the tales—one girlfriend showed up to school with a black eye, talking about how she fell down the stairs; another with bruises all over her back, supposedly from a fight she'd gotten into with her little brother. But we all knew the deal: Anyone who went out with Dana eventually got their asses kicked by him for whatever minor infraction—real or imagined. It would always start out good—who didn't want to be the jewel on the handsome football player's arm? But the glory of being Dana's girl never really made up for the abuse—at least not for some of us. If you sassed him, you got cussed the hell out with a quickness. If he felt like you disrespected him, well that was worth a quick slap. If he caught you looking at some boy the wrong way, or heard you were looking at some boy the wrong way, or imagined that you looked at some boy the wrong way, well, that was grounds for a beating. And rumor had it that he meted them out often. That didn't stop the girls from dating him, though, including my dumb ass. "But Nina, you know you can't control your mouth," Aaron pleaded with me when I told him Dana had sent word through one of his boys that he was interested. "He'll go upside your head in no time. Why you wanna put yourself in danger?"

"Who says I'd be in danger?" I asked, my neck rolling. "It's not like I can't handle mine. Shoot, I can keep you in check."

"Come on Nina, I'm serious. You're just asking for trouble here," Aaron said, defensiveness ringing his words.

"And so am I," I pleaded back. "Look Aaron, you know me. I wouldn't put myself into any situations I couldn't handle. Plus, Karen and Laurie were two really weak bitches who spread rumors about him because he didn't want to go out with their sorry asses anymore. I mean, how do you know he was the one who blacked Karen's eye? And Laurie's a nasty heffa anyway—those bruises everybody thought they saw on her back when she was changing in the locker room were probably dirt marks anyway. Plus, Dana's fine. And I'm not weak like them. So don't worry."

Aaron just looked at me and shook his head. I walked away, searching for my girl Tonya to send a message back to Dana. I was interested. Dana bit. And before you knew it, we were an item.

It was a good look for me—for a few weeks at least. My popularity stock rose eightfold—because I was dating the football star, or because everyone wanted to see if Dana would put his hands on me (depending on who you talked to). He was nothing but a gentleman— blew kisses to me up in the bleachers when he was on the field waiting to go back on offense, drove me home after school before he'd have to rush back to the locker room to suit up for practice, took me to the movies on the weekends (well, the afternoon shows, at least— my father wouldn't let me go to any movie theaters later than 4:00 P.M. He was such a freak that way).

And then one Saturday after a game our school lost to our archrival, Jamaica High, he snapped. "Nina!" he called out to me, all loud. I was talking with my girlfriends, making plans to spend the night at

Tonya's house so that I could go to a sweet-sixteen party I would have never gotten to go to if I were home and waiting for my dad's permission. I looked at Dana, then turned back toward my friends to tell them I had to go and that we would make plans later. But I guess I didn't move fast enough, because Dana lurched forward and put his face right into mine and started yelling. Loud. "Yo, whassup with that. Didn't you hear me calling you?" I looked at him like he was out his natural-born mind. "Yes, Dana, I heard you loud and clear. But I was in mid-conversation. Can I finish, please?"

He grabbed my arm and, through clenched teeth, said, "Come here."

"I don't have to go anywhere with you," I said, snatching my arm away. "I think you need to calm down." My girls were quiet now, as was I. I could see the fire in his eyes, feel his hot breath on my neck. And I was scared. I imagined that he was silently deliberating when, exactly, he would knock my two teeth down my throat, and then how much that would hurt, and if I would have to walk around toothless for the rest of my life because my parents couldn't afford to send me to the dentist for a cleaning, much less to get two false teeth.

"You know what? Walk home."

"Fine," I said, and turned my back on him.

It was a brave act, but I wasn't fine. In an instant, I knew he was going to come for me, and that our meeting wouldn't be pretty. "See, I told you your mouth was going to write a check your behind couldn't cash," Aaron said to me later, when I told him what happened. We were sitting on his porch sipping hot chocolate his mom had poured fresh from the pot. He shook his head and took another sip.

"Well, I need to do something to him before he comes for me," I said.

"Like what?" Aaron asked.

"Like get someone to beat his ass, so he won't come near me," I said quickly. "Maybe I could sick my dad on him." I thought about that prospect. My father would kill that boy. I didn't want him to die. I just wanted someone to hurt him really good. "Nah. How about your brother? He's kinda little, but he's tough. The two of you could take him."

I was just kidding—kinda. But Aaron took me seriously.

"Oh, like I took Boobie—and almost got myself killed? Nina, I am not going to go get my brother to beat up no Dana Jeeter. He could take both of us over tea. I'm afraid you're gonna have to take your ass-whoopin' like a man" he said, half-laughing. I didn't see the humor. He saw that and dropped the giggles. "Look, you can't stop violence with violence; in the end, everyone's going to get hurt, whether it's from you getting your butt handed to you on a platter, or someone finds out and tells the principal, or worse, your moms. The true strength of a person comes when she's brave enough to speak up without using her hands."

"Well, tell that shit to Dana—he's the one who's gonna beat my ass when he sees me."

Aaron was silent for a minute. He knew that much was true. "Look, don't worry," he said softly. "I'll take care of it."

"You will?" I asked, suspicious. "What are you going to do?"

"Don't you worry about that. I'll take care of it."

Well, his taking care of it came in a conversation with the damn principal, whom Aaron met with early Monday morning to tell him all about Dana and his penchant for beating on people who weren't his own size. The principal, while sympathetic in their early morning meeting, didn't do anything, though. Dana was, after all, one of his prized football stars, and who was going to punish the guy who made the school look good? Both Aaron and I had heard through the grapevine that the principal had the coach say something to Dana— no punishment, just a "warning" to handle his ladies a bit more "discreetly" or he'd be suspended indefinitely from the starting lineup—but that both of them dimed Aaron and me as the two who told the principal about his hand problem. Aaron was successful in one area: Dana didn't bother me anymore. But coach never said he couldn't kick Aaron's ass.

Though Dana threatened Aaron something fierce, he never did

lay a hand on him. But I knew once again that Aaron was willing to take a beating for me—and it made him even more of a hero in my eyes. What man would stand up for a woman who wasn't even his girl like that? Not many, I'll tell you that. Josefina Simmons taught her son well, and I appreciated her—and him—for skipping the "how to be a thug" lessons mothers those days were teaching their men children. After all, I'd seen men who could crack heads—Dana, my dad. But at the end of the day, where did that get them besides being bitter men who beat up on their women? Josefina Simmons, in my book, was the woman.

Until I got into a relationship with her son.

Nina and Aaron,
Part III

B y the time Aaron knocked on Nina's door, his mind had convinced him that some disaster had already struck. When she pulled it open, her eyes wide, dark bags sagging underneath them, his pulse quickened several beats. His first thought was that she had some type of debilitating illness, like leukemia or late-stage breast cancer. She gestured for him to follow her. He saw that she was carrying something, a colorfully packaged rectangular box. She glanced at him and followed his eyes downward. She held the box up toward his face. He nearly choked.

"I needed you to be here," she said without looking at him. Her voice was surprisingly barren of emotion. She walked toward the bathroom. "Just wait here."

He watched the door close and stood motionless for several moments, as if his legs were rooted to the spot. As he made his way toward the couch, his mind grappled with a jumbled mass of images, of crazy thoughts. He sat down and tried to think logically, to put events in some kind of order. What would he do?

On the other side of the bathroom door, Nina covered her face with a towel so that Aaron couldn't hear her sobs. She was so consumed by terror that she had to think about each of her movements, to force the messages down the brain stem to her fingers and hands. She removed her robe and sat down on the toilet seat. How the hell had she landed here? Her mind tried to wrap itself around the last year, but even that wasn't far enough. She had to go much further back to make sense of this.

him

My mother always told me if you want to know what a girl will be like when she becomes a woman, check out her mom and her surroundings while she's growing up. Those two clauses probably best summarize why I am scared stupid right now. I saw Nina's mom and her surroundings from *waaay* too close while growing up. While it's perfectly fine and even entertaining having a best friend from a crazy family—I spent many an evening profoundly engrossed by the drama her parents and her sister Nikki could create over every tiny issue that made its way into the house, and in fact, they often went looking for them—it's not advisable for a lover. Just imagining an iota of that spectacle up in my house was enough to break me out in hives. I need peace and lots of it. Household drama makes my dick shrivel up.

Maybe at one time Willy Andrews had been a strong, productive, hardworking man, but by the time Nina and I were old enough to keep an eye on him, he had become almost a caricature of the angry, bitter black man who can't catch a break—and ain't really investing much time in looking for one either. If you got up the nerve to ask him and weren't frightened away by his sour exterior, he'd probably tell you he was fighting for "the liberation of African peoples." He

55

told me and Nina this on more than one occasion when we were young. In fact, as we ran around their backyard once playing tag, he even verbally attacked us for not dedicating enough of our lives to "the liberation." Try to imagine how such a comment would be received by two eight-year-olds. We had enough consciousness to know that we both were, indeed, African peoples—though even that at times seemed a bit abstract to me since I knew Africa was thousands of miles away, I had never been there, nor had my parents and my grandparents, and the people had peculiar but wonderfully melodic accents that in no way resembled the way me and my folks talked. So the "African peoples" part was faintly comprehensible; he meant black people. But what about this "liberation" stuff? We were two carefree children racing at will through the streets of Jamaica, Queens, with hardly a care between the two of us and certainly no sense that our lives were at all limited by our blackness. We giggled when we'd peek out from Nina's room and watch her father bop his head—one of the few times we ever saw anything like joy in his soul—as he played his James Brown records and gustily accompanied James in yelling out "I'm black and I'm proud!" We had just discovered the Sugarhill Gang and Kurtis Blow—James had nothing to say to us.

Mr. Andrews, as I respectfully called him, was a mechanic. But he didn't work at a garage. He was a freelancer. During the gas crises of the late 1970s, when people were driving their cars as seldom as possible, this wasn't exactly a job with huge growth potential. Mostly Mr. Andrews sat in the house and brooded. He always appeared to be waiting for someone, looking out the window a lot, but usually while he stood behind a curtain. Now that I look back, the image reminds me of the pictures I've seen of Malcolm X peering out a window while hiding behind the curtain and carting an enormous semiautomatic rifle. By any means necessary. Turns out this image wasn't too far off.

I should add that I don't think Mr. Andrews was a very good mechanic. He always had somebody yelling at him through the door about how he had ripped them off because their car still didn't run right. One time he even got into a fight. He was underneath an old beat-up Cadillac that was sitting on blocks next to the house. The car had been there for weeks, prompting several loud shouting matches with his wife concerning her displeasure with "this ghetto shit." Nina and I weren't sure who owned the car or if it even had an owner. We had grown so used to its presence that it was now a handy hiding spot for the neighborhood games of hide-and-go-seek.

One afternoon in the middle of a steamy summer, a large, glowering bald man drew our attention as he stalked past us as we scrawled our names all over the black asphalt with the multicolored chalk Nina had gotten for her birthday a few weeks back. He wore the familiar olive green shirt and pants that was our neighborhood's blue-collar uniform and he looked intent on inflicting major damage. I can remember the brief chill that raced down my back as I watched his stiff-legged stride move in the direction of Nina's dad. I had no desire to see him hurt; I was excited about the drama that was sure to liven up the lazy day.

"Where's that man going?" Nina whispered to me. From the alarm in her voice, I knew she probably already had her answer.

We both followed the angry bald man, careful not to draw too close. The man didn't hesitate a second before walking right up to Willy, rearing back his right foot and delivering a vicious kick to Willy's left leg, landing it in the vicinity of the calf. Despite the summer heat the man was wearing heavy black Brogans. I heard something close to a pained grunt come from Nina, as if she was the one who had received the blow. Both of us were frozen in mid-step, afraid of what would happen next—but knowing there was nowhere else in the world that we'd rather be at that moment. Yes, the slightly deranged Willy Andrews kept things lively on our block, but we had never seen an actual altercation with another grown-ass man. Usually the brunt of his wrath was saved for his woman and children.

"What the fuck?!" Willy bellowed from beneath the Caddy. He moved quickly from beneath the car, sliding on the nasty old towel that had been blackened and slickened from its usual home under his back under a car. Willy scrambled to his feet, his fists already clenched. He glared at the taller man, but Willy didn't make any moves. His face wore an evil mask. The other man's mask was even more evil.

"Foster, what the hell is wrong with you?" Willy hissed.

The man called Foster thrust a long, straight finger in Willy's face.

"You know what's wrong with me, muthafucka!" Foster said loudly, his voice verging on a shout. "Where my damn money? You done had two fuckin' weeks!"

I had forgotten to breathe. I desperately wanted to see if anybody else was witnessing this theater, if I had an exclusive front-row seat, but I couldn't turn to look because I might miss something. But more than my excitement I felt Nina's fear, her young body so tense that her shoulders would later ache and she wouldn't understand why. I had an urge to reach out and pull her close to me—and I felt a quick shame that I had toyed with a brief glee at the specter of her father getting his ass kicked. At that moment, expecting this to get drastically uglier, I was blown away by what happened next—Willy Andrews somehow called on reserves of a previously hidden charm. His fists unclenched and a smile spread across his face, opening a crease in the scraggly growth of beard. Willy Andrews was not an unattractive man—when he smiled, at least. For one shining moment, he was damn near handsome. I could see the man that Angelique Andrews had become so attached to. He reached out with his left hand and playfully squeezed Foster's biceps.

"Look at you, Foster, all bulked up and ready to hurt somebody," he said with a chuckle. "You know we ain't got no business fighting each other, as much as we been through together. We should be ashamed. We need to redirect all this hostility. Shit, would Huey and Bobby have let some dumb shit come between them like this?" Mr. Andrews looked away for a split second—perhaps realizing that the last line might have been a bit too corny.

Maybe Foster was as stunned by the transformation as we were— or maybe it was Willy's summoning of the Panthers' twin deity,

Bobby and Huey. As if someone had let the air from a tire, Foster's body deflated and relaxed. A smile also crossed his face and he instantly became a different person—warm, approachable, even nice. Nina took a few steps closer to them and I followed her lead.

"Is he your friend, Daddy?" Nina asked.

A quick shadow passed over Mr. Andrews's face. I braced myself for the coming storm. Nina had committed several breaches of child etiquette, especially in Willy Andrews's manual, the foremost being that she was now minding grown folks' business. But to my surprise, Willy reached a hand toward her and addressed Foster.

"Foster, you remember my daughter, Nina? She's the older girl." He placed his hands on Nina's shoulders and turned her toward the big man, who appeared to be at least four inches taller than Willy, who was well over six feet himself. Nina looked up at Foster with widened eyes. He looked down at her and smiled. He wasn't nearly as scary. Foster offered her his right hand, waiting for her to shake it. But Nina wasn't quite ready for that. This man had just kicked her father like he was a mangy dog.

"Why did you try to hurt my daddy?" she said.

Foster looked perplexed; clearly he had no idea what to say. Willy Andrews chuckled.

"Sorry, Foster. The girl is not shy."

Mr. Andrews cast an eye in my direction. I took a step forward, waiting for my introduction—I was planning to show Nina up by giving Foster a bone-crushing handshake. But there would be no introduction. Mr. Andrews's gaze paused on me for just a split second—he appeared to be making a calculation. Whatever he turned over in his head, I came out at the end with a big-ass zero. He looked back at Foster, patted Nina on the head in an attempt to show affection, and led Foster into the house, neither of them bothering to give us another glance.

We could hear Angelique Andrews cry out a loud hearty greeting for Foster. Angelique Andrews did nothing quietly, nor was she capable of holding back any emotions that might be coursing through her ample yet shapely limbs at any particular moment. Through the front window I could see her giving Foster a hug. My disappointment at the brutal dismissal I had just received was quickly crowded out by the sight of Mrs. Andrews in action. I had gotten to the point where I couldn't even hear her voice on the phone without getting a flashback of a recent image that was still rattling around in my head like a pinball.

A few months earlier, Nina and I had stumbled across her parents in the throes of some serious sexing. I think they probably forgot that she and I were in Nina's room, engaged in a marathon two-person checkers tournament. (For some reason I can still remember that I held a twenty games to fifteen edge at the time.) It was a Saturday night, approaching 9:00 P.M., and I knew I better leave soon before I got the summoning phone call. This was at least a year before *Flashdance* and the kiss under the band shell, but we were old enough to be more mesmerized than repulsed by anything having to do with sex. How can a ten-year-old boy see the big round ass of his best friend's mother, bouncing up and down on top of her naked husband's body with such vigor that it made a loud slapping noise each time she connected with his thighs, and not turn to jelly for the rest of his life every time she looked in his direction?

There's nothing quite so mind-altering to a prepubescent child than to stumble upon a sex scene in the house. I wasn't in my own house, but the vision still left me shaken to my toes. In fact, the salaciousness factor was substantially elevated because I wasn't related to the participants. In other words, it's a lot easier to get excited from seeing two people screwing if they're not your parents. Of course, as I said, the sight of Angelique Andrews would send me into hyperventilation for the next year as I had to fight back the flashbacks that would come flooding in of her big brown ass. But I didn't suffer irreparable damage. I can't, however, say the same thing for my friend Nina.

Our first reaction was paralysis. There was fear, mixed with fascination. We couldn't move because we were afraid of getting caught and because we couldn't tear away our eyes. I was prepared to bolt at the slightest provocation—I looked to Nina for the cue. But Nina's mind was a thousand miles away; her face wore an expression I couldn't read. Was she embarrassed, angry, disturbed, ashamed? I hadn't a clue. And we wouldn't talk about it either—at least not for another fifteen years or so.

After that night, I paid a little more attention to the Andrews marriage. Their relationship was so different than what I saw in my own house on a daily basis. At a glance, the husband and the wife seemed to despise each other—they never let pass an opportunity to attack each other's weaknesses and highlight the failures. Even in front of a neighbor's child. And so for years I wondered in the back of mind why they still stayed married to each other. I even asked my own mother about it once, but she didn't really have much of an answer for me. She just looked at me with a frown and went back to stirring the beans in the pot. So in my mind's shorthand, I probably stored something that looked like this: Andrews marriage—fighting—bad.

But after the sex, I started noticing other little things of interest—how Angelique would stroke Willy's head or pat his butt everytime she walked by him, or how he would sometimes cup her booty with his hand or stick his nose in the well of her neck and sniff, coming away with a big grin on his face. This stuff didn't happen all the time. Didn't even happen a lot. But it certainly happened more than it did at my house, where my parents barely seemed to acknowledge each other's existence, never mind openly exhibit signs of affection. It was clear that the Andrewses had strong feelings about each other. On some days those feelings manifested themselves in nasty, painful arguments. On other days, those feelings came out as nasty, bed-rattling sex. Even back then, I wondered whether you could have a passionate marriage without all the fighting. Or a peaceful marriage that didn't look all but dead. Could peace and passion exist in the same household? I was determined to one day answer that question in the affirmative, with my own household as exhibit A. How could I know that I'd be trying to create a peaceful household with the Andrewses' spawn?

her

"I'm just saying, I like Mr. Ho Ming Chow and all, but damn—do we have to eat fried chicken wings and pork fried rice every other night?"

There Aaron was, complaining again. There I was, thinking that our moving in together wasn't the brightest idea in the world. There we were, about to get into yet another random argument about, well, nothing.

"Don't eat it, then," I said, settling down in the couch, plate in one hand, remote in the other. "More for me." I just didn't feel like getting into it with him that day, particularly after having had my boss give me a hard time all day. Did you send out the invitations? Did you put Nickolai Taylor on the VIP list? Did you lock in the dj at the price I wanted? Will they be serving fresh sushi at the bar and passing the crab cakes by hand? Trust me, all I'd ever wanted to do in life was to be in the marketing and promotions business, but working for the New York division of Golin Estates wine company was making me re-think my career decisions. My boss rode my ass all day, every day—half because he didn't think I knew what I was doing, half because he damn for sure didn't know what he was doing. And on this day? He'd strapped the harness on for a *long* ride, bareback. We were planning a book party for a young hip-hop author with a huge New York City following. The concept was simple: We'd get together the guest list, invite the people, rent a space, let the author sign his books, and provide Golin cocktails for the attendees. You would have thought I was planning Charles and Diana's wedding, that's how much my boss was micromanaging the project. After the eighth time he yelled at me for something incredibly stupid, I stopped counting and made a point of being really numb. It was the only thing that was going to get me through the day without stabbing his ass.

So the last thing I wanted to do was to come home to a nagging-ass man.

"I didn't say I wasn't hungry. I just said I'm tired of Chinese food."

"Well, I'm sorry you're tired of Chinese food, dear. Would you like me to cook you an eight-course meal? Would that make you happy?" I said sarcastically.

"Actually, yes I would, now that you ask. It would be nice if you cooked every once in a while."

No . . . he . . . did . . . not.

Now, I knew this man did not say to me, after sitting his ass up in this house all day, with absolutely nothing to do but get ready for his little bartending gig down at the stripper-ho club, that I should have come home from a hard day's work, where I make real *legitimate* money, and cook. Tell me he didn't just say that.

"You know what?" I said, snatching up my plate. "I'm going to remove myself from this room while you think about what you just said."

"I know what I just said," he shot back.

"Well, you know, I figured that since you didn't have a problem cooking yourself breakfast and lunch that you would have considered whipping up a little dinner while you were at it. It's not like you were using your extra time around the house to clean up after yourself," I said, with a whole lot of bass in my voice.

When it comes down to it, I'm not so sure I appreciate the man Josefina Simmons molded with her own two hands. I mean, when he had his own place, I didn't much mind that he was a slob. Or that he expected his girlfriends to do things—cook, clean, and coddle—that no self-respecting black woman with a mother who taught her better would do. Or that he didn't make a whole heck of a lot of money. Or that most of his cash came from his job down at the strip club. I'd even tried to put out of my mind the fact that he spent a majority of his evenings ogling a bunch of half-naked, stanky, sweaty, writhing women while he poured drinks for a bunch of dirty old men.

But this? This had to stop. I was quickly finding out that all the things I found endearing and quirky about my best friend were annoying as hell now that he'd brought his bad habits to my house. Let's be clear: I'm not a neat freak, but I do like order in my home, and I think I work hard enough to deserve a little peace and quiet—sans nagging—after a hard day's work. I'd long craved that, particularly after having a little sister who thought that just because we were kinda, sorta the same size, that she had the right to squeeze her fat butt into my jeans, and her flat feet into my stilettos and her little fingers into my most prized possessions—my diaries, my keepsake boxes, my jewelry chest. She was always in my stuff, and, when she wasn't borrowing my things, she was busy taking over our room like it was her own personal fiefdom. I'd walk in after a tough class and want to just lay down on my bed and chill, and there would be my little sister, splayed in the middle of the floor, her clothes and shoes and books and stuff spread out all over her bed, my bed, the dressers. And no amount of yelling, begging, pleading, or cleaning could convince her that she was disrespecting my space, and me, by acting like she was the only one living in our tiny room. She and her nasty ways were the reason why I got all A's in my freshman year—I was determined to use my good grades to get a scholarship to a real school, real far away. Sophomore year, I was at Emory University, on a full academic scholarship—far away from home and in my own neat, sparkly dorm room. And no one had the key but me. I so enjoyed that freedom— the freedom to have my own space, unencumbered by other peoples' drama, mess. So enamored was I by the idea of living alone that when it came time to come back home for summer vacation, I found reason to stay in Atlanta—to work, to intern, to scrub kitchen floors. I didn't care, so long as I didn't have to go back to that house and those parents and that tiny room with the old New Edition posters on the walls and the curtain of beads running down the middle of the room to separate my side from my sister's. I craved alone time, solitude, space, and made sure to have it when I moved out on my own.

I hadn't considered these things when I agreed to let Aaron move into my apartment. Our coming together just seemed, well, natural: We'd loved each other a lifetime without conditions, and spent so many days together that it was weird when we were apart. So why wouldn't we, as lovers, take the next logical step and move in together? He actually had tears in his eyes when I handed him the key to my place; I'd made him a special dinner, laid out my good china and some candles, and set a gift-wrapped box with my key in it right in the middle of his dinner plate. "I'd be happy," he said, "to stay with you all day, every day, for the rest of your life." And then I got misty, too. Our lovemaking was passionate that night, and for many nights after that. But with every wet towel left on my bathroom floor, with every bed that went unmade, with every dish that piled up in my kitchen sink, with every toilet seat left carelessly wet with pee, I'd begun to despise what I'd once found endearing about my man. I'd grown bored quickly of cleaning up behind him, doing his laundry, even cooking his dinner, which I thought I'd never tire from, considering I actually liked doing it. Nothing soothed me more than being in the kitchen, watching the steam rise from my pots as I prepared delicate, flavorful meals for me and my man. I'd often start my day poring through my cookbooks, picking out a new, scrumptious meal to cook for dinner. After work, I'd head straight for the market—the one in our neighborhood was scuzzy, so I'd take another two trains to get over to the white side of town, where the ingredients, while considerably more expensive, were quite fresh and worth the trouble—and collect what I needed to put whatever recipe I'd found that day onto my man's plate.

I stopped that, though, when I realized that the old saying, "Why buy the cow when the milk is free?" was starting to come to fruition. Clearly, I was the Bessie of the situation. Aaron hadn't a problem enjoying my home-cooked meals, or walking into a clean bathroom and kitchen, or being able to reach into his dresser drawers for clean socks and underwear whenever he needed them. But he never really bothered to say, "Thank you." What's worse is that he quickly started expecting me to do all the heavy lifting around the house—like I was his maid or some shit. It'd always be, "Babe—did you get a chance to do any whites?" or "Babe, what's for dinner?" or "Babe, we're out of toothpaste—can you pick up some when you go shopping?" It never really occurred to him that if he didn't have drawers he should drag his behind down the street to the washing machines, or that he should stop in the Duane Reade down the street from the stripper-ho club to pick up some Colgate if he saw we were running out. Right before my very eyes, Aaron was becoming an aggregate of my exes—all of them needy, none of them willing to give, but always quick to take. Without gratitude.

I know I'd be a long-suffering fool waiting for a man to bow down and kiss my feet for fixing him a meal, but is it wrong to expect an occasional "Thanks, babe!" or "Since you cooked, let me wash the dishes"? I don't think that's so much to ask. It's kind of like when you politely hold the door open for someone when you know you could have just kept on walking and let them open the door their damn selves, and then watching them walk through and away without so much as giving a nod of thanks for your politeness. I never took well to rude people. Or ungrateful ones. Which is why my address book is littered with the numbers of ex-boyfriends whose mothers apparently failed to teach them a thing or five about gratitude.

But I never expected this from Aaron, especially since he'd always seemed appreciative of my efforts to hook his sorry butt up. I'd often found myself bent over his stove, making straight miracles from whatever scraps he had in his cupboards and refrigerator, which, had it not been for my scrubbing and discarding of old, moldy takeout, could have probably walked the hell away from his junky apartment on its own green, hairy legs. I even knew to buy extras when I did my big every-other-week grocery shopping to pick up a few extras for him, because if I didn't, the boy wouldn't have so much as condiments in the refrigerator, let alone real food. Aaron my friend always thanked me kindly and repaid the favor by doing something sweet for me, like spotting my movie ticket, or taking me on his little adventurous get-away hookups.

But the new Aaron? All he did was eat, sleep, and mess up my place. When I'd grown tired of his dependence, I started staging miniature work stoppages—I'd leave the bathroom a little funkier than it should have been, or leave the dishes in the sink a little longer than they should have been in there, ignore the laundry until it just couldn't hold any more. It never seemed to bother him, though; in fact, once, when he ran out of underwear, that fool used money he could hardly afford to waste to buy a new pack of drawers—because I told him I didn't have time to do the laundry. What is that? Not once did it occur to him to take a stack of quarters and walk his sorry butt on down to the Laundromat and hook up a load.

But mess with a Negro's stomach, and he'll complain every time. We were eating Chinese food almost every night because I wasn't in the mood to cook an elaborate feast, only to have him gulp it down like he would a Happy Meal, and then remove himself from the kitchen like what he had wasn't special-prepared by the hands of his lovely, hardworking girlfriend after a long day at the office. So pork fried rice and chicken wings it was. Again.

"I'm just saying, you were hooking up dinner before—what happened?"

"What do you mean what happened, Aaron?"

"You used to like cooking. What happened?"

"You know what, Aaron? Sometimes, women get tired. Did you know that?"

"Huh?"

"Well, which word didn't you understand? Tired! I work hard all day, and the last thing I'm really thinking about is cooking a meal for someone who clearly doesn't appreciate it." Then, I went in for the kill. It was like that—I never really knew when to just shut the hell up. "Despite what you saw our moms doing growing up, not every woman enjoys being a doormat while she cooks and cleans for a man who barely acknowledges the fact that he's getting hooked up out of love, not obligation."

His eyes grew dark, distant. He was glowering at me. "I know you're not talking about my mother, not after all the nights you had your feet planted under the dinner table, grubbing and begging to spend the night so you could eat a good breakfast, too. You certainly ate better at my house than you did at your own, that's for sure."

"So what you saying—that I didn't have food at my house? My mother didn't take care of me? Fuck you, Aaron! Not everybody grows up with two silver spoons in their mouth and leftovers to spare. Don't you dare talk about what was happening in my home—we lived a hard-ass life, and my mother did everything in her power to make sure her girls didn't go to sleep hungry. It wasn't easy, but I will not have you sitting here making light of that!"

Aaron was silent. The glare had left his eyes; nervousness had settled in them. I could tell he knew he'd crossed the line, and he was trying to find the right words to recover from it.

But I wasn't interested in giving him an out.

I took my plate of chicken wings and rice, stomped past him and into the kitchen, and dumped everything—my good, ceramic plate included—into the garbage. I heard the plate shatter to pieces, but I was too busy making a beeline for our bedroom to care. I slammed the door behind me.

Clearly, the honeymoon was officially over.

him

How ironic that Nina and I should now be confronted with the relationship equivalent of a third world war. I say this because she was so instrumental in molding the man I became—if she got problems with the way I turned out, maybe she should blame herself for missing a few steps along the way! I'm only half-kidding—in any boy's life, there is usually a small cast of men and women who play pivotal roles in making sure enough of our destructive male instincts are tamed that we can grow into productive citizens. If that cast is missing a key player or two, or one of the players is lunching, that boy will be inadequately tamed—often with disastrous results. In the African-American community, the jail cells, drug treatment centers, street corners, and neighborhood basketball courts are filled with the by-products of failure—men who were missing something important, whether it be compassion or kindness or basic common sense.

Among other things, Nina taught me how to be tough. How many men can say *that* about their ladies? It pains me to make this admission, but in my early years I was a bit of a punk. Maybe it had something to do with the excessive coddling of my mother—but on second thought I don't even want to engage in the typical blame-the-mother speculation. That's too easy. Too common. What I do know is that my skinny fourth-grade ass was scared to death of the chubby Puerto Rican kid down the street. Raul Orosco was two years older than me, but we were somehow in the same grade—something about losing a grade in his move from PR and then having considerable trouble escaping from bilingual classes. There were quite a few Latino kids in our Queens neighborhood—enough so that I learned how to insult someone's mama in Spanish before I did in English. My observations in my early years had led me to conclude that the kids in bilingual classes were kinder than your average, everyday Latino. Maybe it had something to do with their general insecurity about their place in this new world that swirled around them. Or maybe not—hell, I'm no sociologist. But anyway, Raul wasn't like the others. He was perpetually pissed, as if he were overcompensating for the kindness of his bilingual class members. Like the Hulk, my favorite comic book character when I was a boy, Raul soaked in the hidden rage that churned around him and used it to grow into a massive, frightening monster. Uh, okay, maybe I'm exaggerating a bit. He was more fat than muscle and I'm not sure he ever picked on anyone his own size, which would have been the sixth graders. Raul decided a few weeks into my first marking period in fourth grade that he couldn't stand me. I have no recollection of whether I did anything to incite his scorn, but I do remember regularly fleeing the classroom every day before the chime of the last bell had even subsided. I had several different escape routes that I used to avoid running into fat boy. And because he lived just one block over, I had to be just as careful about my forays outside during after-school and weekend hours.

My embarrassing weakness drove Nina crazy. She didn't care about my quickly eroding manhood or reputation—she was just pissed that her best friend had been taken away. And she didn't hesitate to let me know about it.

"Aaron. You can't run away from Raul all the time!" she said harshly as we crossed the park after school. "We don't even play no more."

I looked up in surprise. It was a month into my Raul fright and I had been so focused on my daily survival that I hadn't thought much about how it was impacting Nina. I knew she had been upset a few times when she came to my house after school and I created one excuse after another for why I couldn't come outside. But I didn't expect this desperate plea for my time.

"You think I should fight him?" I said, trying hard—and unsuccessfully—to keep my voice from shaking. Boys learn fairly early that fists are supposed to solve most of our problems. At about the same time boys learn that they rarely do.

Nina crinkled her nose and gave me a smirk. I wasn't sure if that were an answer. I leaned in closer to her.

"What?" I said. "What does *that* mean?"

She shrugged her shoulders. "I'm not saying you should fight him. He's way older than you." She turned to me. "Maybe *I* should talk to him."

"Huh? You? What could *you* say?" I didn't mean it to sound so much like a put-down.

She shrugged her shoulders again. "I don't know. I'd tell him to leave you alone because you're my friend."

I was about to object, to tell her how unlikely that was to succeed—but then I stopped myself. I thought about the times I had seen Raul neutralized, or at least less enraged than usual. Usually there was a female involved. That's certainly not to suggest that this big doughboy was any less goofy or boneheaded around girls than the rest of us fourth-grade losers. In fact, he probably was even more awkward than most of us. But Raul, perhaps because he was closer to the razor's edge of adolescence, seemed to care more than the rest of us. And it was that vulnerability, that chink in his armor, that might give Nina some weapons. Eventually we would all be so vulnerable—those of us that started caring, that is. But how would it look from my fourth-grade perch if I let a girl step to Raul in my defense? It would look bad. Especially in the eyes of the male portion of the fourth-grade population. That could prove more humiliating than just letting Raul kick my ass and continue to terrorize me.

"Nina, just let me handle this," I said.

"How are you handling it—by hiding in your house?"

I pivoted quickly, to see if that was supposed to sound as nasty as it did. Nina's facial expression changed from frustrated to a bit sheepish. But she didn't retract the comment. She just stared back at me, blinking.

"I got an idea," Nina said brightly. "How about we do it together?"

"Huh?"

"We could go together and have a talk with big bad Raul," she said. "What's he gonna do, beat both of us up?"

"Uh, yeah," I answered, nodding furiously. I had to come up with something quick to squelch this plan. I knew Nina well—once she got an idea in her mind, there was no reversing that charging locomotive.

"Nina, why don't we just leave him alone? He'll get bored soon and forget about me."

She looked at me like I had an extra nose. "Aaron! There are eight more months until the end of the school year. When you think he might get bored of scaring you—'bout March, maybe April?"

I didn't care that she was making fun of me. I tried something else.

"Maybe we could tell somebody," I said tentatively. "Like maybe I should tell my dad."

Nina shook her head. "He's not gonna like you running away. Dads don't like to hear about that."

I thought about her father, his apparent lack of attention to Nina and her sister Nikki. I wondered when he could have given Nina an idea of how he might react to such an admission.

"What about your brother?" Nina offered. "You could get Carney to beat up Raul."

Carney wasn't exactly my idea of a bodyguard. He was nearly the same weight as I was as a seventh grader and we didn't really get along very well. If Carney knew somebody was preparing to beat my ass, he'd be more likely to sell tickets than try and stop it.

"Nah," I said, shaking my head. "He wouldn't help me."

Nina shrugged again. "Okay, well I guess it's the two of us then. We'll do it tomorrow."

We were nearly in front of her house now. I realized the discussion was over—it was a done deal. I was already shaking. How was I going to last another twenty-four hours with this impending disaster hanging over my head? I walked through the front door of my house and immediately fled to my room. I had an idea—I was going to try to sleep for the next twenty-four hours.

So there we were, two frightened and witless fourth graders, waiting outside of PS 202 to ambush Raul Orosco. We didn't really have a plan, so to speak. Nina just told me that I should let her do the talking. I suspected that I would be able to retain a little bit of dignity—assuming I actually had some—if this encounter just came down to Nina and Raul engaging in a pleasant discussion about our relationship.

"Hey, fat boy, why don't you leave Aaron alone?!" Nina yelled out as soon as we saw our pudgy nemesis step out of the side entrance of the school. There were at least a dozen other kids within earshot and each one of them contributed to the chorus of laughter that rained down on Raul's head. He wore the aghast look on his face of a little boy who just peed in his pants at the front of the classroom. I couldn't have imagined, in my worst nightmare, a more horrible way for us to start this conversation.

"Nina! What are you doing?" I whispered in her ear. But the girl was ignoring me.

Raul started toward us, first glancing around to see exactly how many witnesses we had. Certainly he had to resort to some serious violence to find the appropriate response. But I saw the slump of his shoulders and there was a fear—or maybe it was an embarrassment—in his eyes that I had never seen before. I began to feel a glimmer of hope—but I was still shaking.

Raul walked straight up to Nina, trying to intimidate her with the full extent of his five feet nine inches or so. But Nina wouldn't back up or even blink as she stared up at him. The other kids had gathered around in the familiar elementary school fight circle, with the three of us in the middle.

"Hey, what you call me?" Raul asked in his heavily accented English. But everybody within fifty feet of us knew exactly what she had called him.

"You heard it," Nina said softly but firmly. I was amazed by how calm she sounded, like she was having a normal conversation with a friend. I think Raul was startled, too. Nina had quickly put him in an impossible situation—he couldn't really fight her and save face, but if he didn't do anything he certainly would be stripped of his dignity. And his veneer of invulnerability would be destroyed.

I saw Raul glance at me and immediately I knew what he was going to do—he needed to bring the focus back on me and away from this bold girl in his face.

"Whas da matter, you little sissy boy? You gotta get a chica to fight for you?"

About a thousand responses raced through my head but none of them seemed quite right. So instead I said nothing. Just stared back at him, trying to look hard, tough.

"You need at least two fourth graders to equal one Raul," Nina said. The crowd greeted that line with more guffaws and snorts of appreciation. Raul looked even more panicked now, his eyes flashing like a spooked horse. He clearly had absolutely no idea what to do. I got a settled feeling inside; I knew instantly that my days of terror were ending. Raul was going to run away.

"You better watch your mouth, little girl," Raul said, sounding a little unsure of his message. Nina picked up on it right away. Girl didn't miss a beat.

"Or what? You gonna beat up all of us?"

I wasn't quite sure what she meant by "us"—until I turned around. The sight made me giddy. At least a half dozen of my classmates, all girls, had materialized alongside us, all glaring at Raul as if they were trying to bore a hole through him. For the first time in my life, I understood what it meant to know that someone had my back. With widened eyes, Raul looked like he had seen a whole circle of ghosts. I could even make out a band of sweat forming across his forehead. Abruptly Raul turned around and started walking away. He didn't even look back at us. After about seven or eight steps, Raul broke into a frantic trot, looking all at once like a frightened colt. Watching the scene, we couldn't hold back the hoots and chortles. If I had had access to the word *surreal* at the time, I would have thought it was the perfect description of the entire encounter—especially the ending. I had started the day terrified about what was to unfold, and here I was watching Raul's retreating back with a group of laughing, incredulous classmates.

Needless to say, I didn't have to worry about Raul again for the rest of the semester. In fact, he refused to make eye contact with me. He didn't even seem to be as big anymore, like his shame had taken off thirty pounds. But while you revel in the gall of Nina, the fourth-grade spitfire, come on over to my side for a minute. How do you have a long-lasting love affair with a woman who had to protect you from a bully when you were in fourth grade? Of course I'm no longer the cowering nine-year-old hiding in my room from Raul Orosco, but does that even matter at this point? If ever she's inclined to wonder about her safety and security in my presence, her mind must inevitably make its way back to the fall of 1981. How could she ever forget it? I can't (which may be a huge part of the problem). And when she gazes over at me, her lover, does she have maybe just a little doubt about whether she'd have to protect her damn self if ever the situation arose? And then there's the childhood fiction factor. In my previous relationships, my younger self was always an impressively strapping figure in the informational fill-in-the-blanks childhood discussions I'd have with my lady. I once even told a flight attendant from Harlem whom I was actively bedding that I was a member of the Jamaica, Queens, chapter of the Crips. I'm not sure whether Jamaica, Queens, ever had a chapter of the Crips—my childhood was thankfully free of detailed info about the local gang community—but I was certain my flight attendant for damn sure knew nothing about the Crips in Queens. (So enthralled was she by my detailed descriptions of my childhood depravities that I almost convinced her to give me head on the A train as it sped uptown on a Saturday night.) There was absolutely no embellishing available to me during childhood discussions with Nina. No gang stories, no tales of ball field triumphs, not even a greatly exaggerated listing of all my erotic conquests. Nothing but the painful, unvarnished truth. Sure, there were so many shared joys and common interests that we could spend hours on the past, but I missed the elevated status that a new boyfriend was allowed to enjoy in his woman's eyes. I was her best friend and I had no doubt that she had loved me for the better part of two decades, but I could never be a superhero to her. I'd always be just a man—and one with many flaws, at that. That thought filled me with sadness and doubt and a whole bunch of second thoughts.

her

Let me start off first by making something crystal clear: Aaron is *all* man. He may act all sensitive when you least expect it, like when he's admiring aloud the way flecks of moonlight bounce off waves crashing against the sand, or when he's watching the little girls sing their double-Dutch songs just beyond our front stoop, and giggling as hard as they. On a couple of occasions, I came home from work only to find him outside on the stoop, practically hypnotized by their little feet weaving at lightning speed through the spin of ratty jump ropes. They'd be chanting their silly singsong rhymes, and he'd be singing them almost as loud as they—*"When she's up, she's up/When she's down, she's down/Don't mess with Angie, 'cause she's all around/You go zig, zag, zig, kicka one/Zig, zag, zig, kicka two . . ."* Nobody would think that normal of a thirty-one-year-old guy—that he would actually get a kick out of watching little girls jump rope, and even try, on occasion, to do his own little black-girl double-Dutch jig. They thought he was doing it just to make them laugh, but the boy really likes jumping rope. On many an occasion, Aaron's mom had to call him into the house during our more intense, straight-into-the-night double-Dutch sessions; often, he'd be the one trying to get us to stay out just a little longer. Aaron was a good turner, but when it came time to jump, his big, awkward Chuck Taylors would always get tangled in the ropes. He never seemed to care that we'd collapse in laughter at his expense, or that, today, people quietly considered whether he was a perv for watching a bunch of little girls double Dutch. I just chalked up his fascination to his being a sweet man.

But I'm rudely reminded every day he skips out of our front door for work just how much of a boy he can be. He's just a little too damn giddy about bartending at the stripper-ho club. I'm sure there are some women who aren't bothered by the idea of their men sitting around a ratty, nasty, musty bar with a bunch of old-ass men, watching a succession of pockmarked women bounce their breasts and finger their G-strings for loose change. I'm not one of them. I find it to be humiliating, disgusting, and about as funky as a subway bum on a hot Fourth of July—figuratively and literally. And the person who actually works there? Well, I'd say they're just as bad in my book—if not worse—because they're profiting from the degradation of women (the ones shaking their behinds), and disrespecting the hell out of the ones sitting at home, thinking their men are out doing something more constructive than watching a bunch of girls get naked.

I'd always pretended to understand why Aaron was working there, but I made no bones about clowning him for it. "I know, I know—you need the money, right?" I'd said on more than one occasion, as he'd hurry away from our dinners to get to work (he bartends during the late shift—from 7:00 P.M. to 2:00 A.M.—when the club is good and funky and everybody up in there is hot and bothered. "You know, there's always a job at the post office."

"Ha, ha, ha," he'd said, sarcastically.

"And if you were really good at assembling burgers at Mickey D's, you'd be on fries in no time. Before you know it? Taking orders. The register!"

"Oh, no—Nina's got jokes. But you know what?" he said, peeling bills off a wad of cash he pulled from his jeans pocket. "All I'd be able to afford to feed you is free Mickey D's cheeseburgers if it wasn't for my gig at the club. And before you know it, you'd be getting all fat and nasty from the grease and carbs. So the way I look at it, working at the club is helping your driving just as much as it is mine."

"Oh, you're looking out for me?" I said, wide-eyed.

"Yes, you."

"How you figure?"

"I work, I make decent money. I make decent money, I can pay rent. I can pay rent, I can let you come over to the crib, maybe take you out to dinner, show you some things—you know, do things for you that you can't afford with your forty-five-thousand-dollar gig."

"Ah, but therein lies the rub: My forty-five g's are clean. My money don't smell like p-funk!"

"Yeah, well then how about your sweet-smelling dollars pay for that sweet steak salad you just swallowed!" he said, getting up to leave.

"Negro what? You better pay the lady!" I said, pushing past him to get to the front door. "Unless you're intent on washing dishes tonight!"

Still, I got a kick out of hearing all the soap opera stories Aaron would regal me with over our pre–strip club dinners. There was the owner, Shane Hooks, a white cowboy from Texas who struck gold on the East Coast by starting up a string of fairly clean-looking clubs that catered to men who loved big-booty black girls. Aaron told me once that Hook—that's what they called him, because, like the sweetest-talking pimp, he could "hook" young black girls into working there without much effort—had single-handedly tapped the ass of almost every woman who'd ever worked in his club, "because they all think he's a sweet white boy who actually cares about them." But let them not shake it hard enough, or miss their lap dance quota. Massa gets to trippin' real quick on that; Aaron told me he was good for firing chicks and replacing them with a quickness—usually with someone from the herd of high school girls who stood at the ready to make some easy change up in the Honey Pot. Me? I thought it was disgusting enough that he was making his cash off the asses of little girls and young women—but add to that the fact that he was a white man actively putting sistahs up on a stage to be ogled and bid over, and the implications behind that became just too much for me to want to consider.

Then there was the dj, Connects, who was always trying to get Aaron to hook him up with the newer, younger dancers—"Nothin' like some new booty," he'd say to Aaron whenever fresh meat hit the stage. Usually within a week, Connects would have a new girlfriend—some girl who looks like she's all of twelve when the lights are up, she's fully dressed in something other than what looks like her mama's nightclothes and heels, and her fresh face is void of all that Maybelline. "I swear," Aaron once said, "the younger they look, the harder he falls. He's definitely got some R. Kelly tendencies." I'd laugh, and make a mental note to keep Connects away from any children I knew.

And then there were all the juicy stories about the women themselves—the ones who really were dancing for tuition dollars; the ones who were strung out and shaking their tails for their next high; the single moms who were sneaking out in the middle of the night while their kids slept in order to put food in their kids' bellies. And the stars of the stage, who apparently created a stripper-ho hierarchy of dancers who had a clear run of the place—customers in particular. I do remember at some point Aaron telling me about some hooker named Cocoa he was considering asking out on a date. I clowned him over that so hard he stopped talking about it, and refused to give me any more details about her after that—no matter how much I told him I wouldn't make fun of him. Okay, so I always laughed when I said I wouldn't make fun of him, but my boy thought he was in love with a chick who takes her clothes off in front of strangers for a living—jeez.

"Wait, let me get this straight—you're thinking about dating some stripper at the club? Boy, have you lost your mind?" I yelled at Aaron through the phone line. I tried to fight off the pangs of jealousy that I felt in my gut. I thought about my oft-stated mantra: Who Aaron brought home with him was his business. But the roiling in my stomach was telling me otherwise.

"Well, uh, not like, uh, *date*, exactly," he stuttered. "That's not what I said. What I had said was,"—I started to laugh—"that she's real nice and smart. And, uh—"

"And you're thinking about meeting her for lunch or something. That's what you said, Aaron. Remember who you're talking to, okay? I know damn well it's not this woman's brain and personality that has your head all spinning. I'm guessing that there probably is a little more to it than that, right?"

"Well, of course the woman is attractive," he said. "She—"

"She probably is about my complexion, with long straight hair, juicy lips, and a big ol' butt, right?" I said.

He paused; I could hear his breathing.

"Aaron, I didn't hear you. What did you say?" I asked, teasing.

"What I *said* was, I like all types of women, and I've dated all types of women." I could hear the annoyance in his voice. I could even picture the look he had on his face, the brow furrowed, that slightly chilly stare.

"What makes you think you can guess what this woman looks like?" he asked.

"But am I wrong, Aaron?" I said. "That's all I'm asking." I giggled audibly. I heard more breathing. Wow, I must have nailed it.

"Aaron, I'm just messing with you," I said, finally. "I don't care if you go on a date with a stripper. But I'm warning you, don't even think about bringing her home to Josefina Simmons—you probably should avoid even being seen by someone who knows Josefina Simmons. And you should probably tell your girl to leave the G-string and pasties at home." I laughed again. Oh, I was enjoying this immensely.

"Cocoa is a very classy dresser, actually," he said. Before he could continue, my roar of laughter jumped through the phone line.

"Aw, you should have let me guess her name!" I said, still laughing. "Cocoa would have been pretty close to the top of the list! After Ecstasy and Passion and—what else? Oh yeah, the black magazine names—*Ebony* and *Essence* and *Honey*. Any girls named *Jet*? *Black Enterprise*? That one would be appropriate, right?"

"What you know about stripper names?" he said, trying to turn the focus. "You been spending a lot of time in some clubs I don't know about? Maybe I should be guessing your name."

"Ha, not funny. Aaron, honey, you can be sure if I take my clothes off for somebody, I'll be getting a whole lot more than a stinky little dollar bill in return."

He let that last one sit there for a minute. He was probably afraid to even risk a rejoinder.

"Thanks for all your help, Nina. Bye."

I heard the phone line go dead. Oh, this man did not hang up on me! I tried redialing his line about five times in quick succession. But he knew me too well—surely he had left it off the hook.

I leaned in toward the phone. "Coward!" I shouted as loud as I could.

If I couldn't abide by his employment at the club, I figured I'd do something about it. I got a subscription to the local newspaper, and started going through the want ads for my boy. Shit, the city was full of jobs, if you looked hard enough. Office clerk. Telephone technician. Telemarketing executives. Delivery services. The options were endless.

"What's this?" he said early one morning, shoving the paper onto my lap as I took a swig of hot coffee. A small amount trickled out of my cup and into my lap, splashing a few drops onto my silk skirt.

"Ow! Did you have to throw it? You made my coffee spill," I said, dabbing at my legs with my napkin.

"Sorry," he said, and then, without missing a beat, "What's that?"

"What does it look like? It's the want ads," I shot back. This was not the way I wanted this conversation to go down—I'd intended for it to be a much calmer, friendlier discussion about his need to seek a new career path.

"Why would I need to see the want ads, Nina?" he said, folding his arms. He was standing over me, clearly annoyed.

"So that you can find a new job, Aaron," I said with attitude to match his.

"Why would I need a new job, Nina?"

"So that you wouldn't have to be sweating it out with a bunch of butt-naked hos every night, Aaron."

"I'm not sweating anything out. I'm serving drinks in a reputable establishment, Nina."

"You call a place where women go to take their clothes off for money reputable?" I said, forcing a laugh. "*Reputable* isn't necessarily the word I'd be reaching for, if I were you."

"Right, because if you were me, you'd know that this is just a way for me to make money—not some kind of sinister plot on my part to see naked women."

"Well then if it doesn't mean anything to you to go up in there and see naked women, then why don't you quit and get a job somewhere else?" I said. I grabbed the newspaper and thumbed through the pages, looking for the positions I'd circled. "See? Right here, there's a job at McCleary's Publishing. Mailroom clerk. You could do that."

"I'm not going to somebody's mailroom, Nina."

"Okay, then how about this one," I said, flipping the page. "Telemarketing. With commissions. You're good at selling stuff. How about that one?"

"I'm not going to be calling and harassing people on the phone all day," he said, exasperated. "Look—what's the problem? We've been through this a thousand times. I work at a strip club. I'm doing it because it pays decent money, the hours are conducive to my photography schedule, and I like interacting with the people because occasionally, I make some good connections. Why are we talking about this, Nina? And more specifically, why are you trying to find me a job when I already have one that I actually like? I've said it before, I'll say it again: I'm the bartender at the Honey Pot. I like my job. I'm going to keep it. End of story."

And then he stalked into the bathroom and shut the door. He was still in there when I left for work.

But that wasn't the end of it.

So curious and angry was I about the pull this club had on my man that I secretly made plans to check the place out. Now that I look back on it, that may have been my grandest mistake. But that's called hindsight.

"Kenya," I said into the phone, the moment I heard her pick up. "What you doing tonight?"

"Um, there's this party I was going to fall through after work—nothing big. Why? What you got planned?"

"Come with me to the Honey Pot."

There was silence. And then Kenya started laughing. "The Honey Pot? What the hell would I want to go up in the Honey Pot for?"

"To help me figure some things out," I said back quickly.

"What you need to figure out, Nina? I mean, the Honey Pot is a strip club and men go there to watch women take their clothes off. Pretty basic."

"Uh, thanks for the update, Kenya," I said, my exasperation clear. "I know that's what happens in there. But I want to see what it's like—how the women act, how they interact with the men, what they look like. . . ."

"Ooooh," Kenya said, cutting me off. "I get it. You're trying to see what your man be doing up in there, huh?"

"I know what he does," I snapped back. "He serves drinks. I want to know what everyone else up in there does."

"Well, if you're so confident your man is just serving drinks, why you checking up on him?"

"He won't be working tonight, so I won't actually be checking up on him, per se," I countered. "Look, you coming or what?"

"Damn girl—I don't really want to get caught up in no strip club with another woman. You know what that'll look like? I'd get kicked out of training for sure."

She had a point. Kenya is in the police academy, trying hard to become a New York City cop. She had her morals clause to protect, and I didn't want to stand in the way of her getting the gig of her life—even if I thought it was crazy for a woman to want to wear a gun and chase criminals. Aaron had told me once that a lot of the black cops hung out at the Honey Pot, which I always found odd, since one would think that they would be there to shut the shit down, rather than shove dollars up those girls' G-strings. The last thing she needed was for her training sergeant to find her up in there. "Right, right— true. I forgot about that."

"Yeah, well, you're gonna have to go solo on this one, love. But you can call me on the celly if you need some support."

"Okay. And if you should happen to talk to Aaron, remember, I was hanging out with you tonight."

"Ooooh, scandalous!" she said, chuckling. "I got your back, girl— irregardless of how trifling it is."

My first problem was figuring out where the club was located. I knew it wasn't that far from my apartment on the fringes of the East Village. (I say *fringes* because my salary could only get me close enough to smell the East Village fumes, but most East Village residents would claim I lived in a neighborhood not so fondly called Alphabet City. It was one of those areas that the Yuppies had only recently discovered, which meant that you'd still find a strong element of seediness among the run-down tenements crammed together on these avenues. The main thoroughfares were known as Avenues A, B, and C, which is how they came to be known as Alphabet City. In a nod to the large percentage of Latinos who resided there, it was also called Loisaida, which was just the Lower East Side in New York City Spanglish.) But as I walked out of my apartment and stepped into the balmy late spring night, I was still unsure where I was going. I had left Aaron behind in the apartment watching television, enjoying his night off. He had always told me that Monday nights were slow anyway, so I wasn't sure what I would find inside the Honey Pot. But somehow I knew I'd walk away much better informed than I was now.

I pulled out my cell phone, hoping to get the address from dialing 411—but the damn place wasn't even listed. Goodness, what kind of hole-in-the-wall did my man work at? So what now? I paused in the middle of the sidewalk, contemplating my next move. I saw two fairly well-dressed black men about twenty feet ahead of me, in deep conversation as they walked along at a slow crawl toward me. This might prove to be embarrassing, but I didn't see what other options I had. I took a deep breath as they drew nearer.

"Um, excuse me?" I said. I wanted to sound needy, but I couldn't let myself lay on the damsel in distress too thick. "Would you gentlemen happen to know where I could find a, uh, club called the Honey Pot?"

The two guys threw each other quick glances that I couldn't read, then they both got the same goofy smiles on their faces. "Yeah, as a matter of fact, we're headed there right now," said the taller of the two. He appeared to be about my age, in his early thirties, and he wasn't bad-looking. But something about his grin made me uncomfortable. Then I caught his partner, who was a bit pudgier than he appeared from twenty feet, slowly pass his eyes over my body, pausing way too long at my chest. Wait—these Negroes thought I was a stripper! If darkness hadn't fallen I'm sure they would have seen the bloom that flushed over my face. God, I felt so stupid—why wouldn't they assume I was heading there to dance? And I had spent nearly a half hour in my bra and panties, staring into the closet and asking myself what in the world I should wear to a strip club. I had glanced into the living room at Aaron several times, wanting so much to seek his counsel. He even caught me once and gave me a winning smile when he saw that I was almost naked. I settled on a snug—hopefully not too snug—short-sleeved sweater and dark slacks. It was conservative but not corny. It was supposed to prevent this very occurrence—me getting mistaken for a stripper.

"You are?" I said tentatively. I had no idea what to say next. I wanted to explain myself, to throw some kind of explication out there that would remove me from the stripper-ho category.

"If you'd like, you can walk with us," said the tall one. He had a nice smile; something about him gave the impression of openness and warmth. Instantly I liked him much more than his fat little nasty friend.

"Oh. Um, uh, okay," I said, still tentative.

I fell into step with them, flanked on both sides. There was a slightly uncomfortable silence hanging in the air for about ten steps or so. I was trying to think of a way to tell them I wasn't a stripper. I couldn't even venture a guess what might have been on their minds.

"Soooo," said the talker. "My name is Trey. My friend, who is usually not this quiet, is Warren." .

I smiled shyly at the two of them. "Hi, Trey. Hi, Warren. My name is Nina."

"Hello, Miss Andrews!" The voice came from out in the street. I looked over and saw the big round head of Little Tony, the pizza delivery boy from Angelo's Ristorante. Tony was a little slow, but he was a sweetheart. Whenever he delivered pizza to my apartment, I always gave him a big tip. He never failed to call out when he saw me on the street, but at this moment I wasn't in the mood to see somebody I knew. All I needed was for one of my nosy neighbors to see me walking down the street in between two well-dressed black men. After all, I was only about six or seven blocks from my apartment.

I gave Tony a little wave, which was enough to prompt a big grin and a wave back. I glanced up at Trey, wondering how that little scene was being decoded in his head. He had an attractive, closely cropped beard that I now noticed was sprinkled with a little gray. Maybe he was a bit older than I thought.

"You, uh, live around here and you don't know where the Honey Pot is?" It was Warren who had worked up the nerve to ask the question. Warren's voice was much higher in pitch than I thought it'd be. It was higher than any man's voice had a right to be. I almost wanted to laugh at the chunky soprano man. I decided that I should come clean and tell these guys what I was up to. Almost.

"Well, I don't live that far from here, but I never had any reason to know where the Honey Pot was," I said. I was hoping that my voice didn't betray my quickly formed dislike for Warren. "But I have so many male friends who hang out at this club that I got real curious. I want to see it with my own eyes."

Warren and Trey both nodded. We walked along for nearly a block in silence. Apparently my admission had lessened their interest in me considerably. They seemed more accommodating in their body language toward me when they still thought I might be a stripper.

"Well, it's only a couple of blocks ahead," Trey said. I picked up on something in his tone.

"Okay, fellas. I can find it from here. You can go on ahead now."

Trey threw me a quick look, probably wondering how I guessed what he was thinking.

He opened his mouth: "No, that's—"

"Okay then," Warren said, interrupting his friend. "We'll check you out inside maybe. Come on, Trey. Let's hurry up. She said she was going on at nine."

Trey glanced at me before he followed behind his friend, who had quickened his pace considerably. I thought I saw his shoulders shrug, but I couldn't be sure of that. As I watched their suit jackets moving away from me, I purposely slowed my step a bit. I wanted to create as much distance as possible between us. I tried to tell myself otherwise, but I was a little perturbed that Trey had dumped me so quickly to go sprinting toward the stripper-hos. What kind of pull did this place have over grown men that it could tug them along like driftwood caught up in the tide? I was about to find out.

When I saw the cheesy little neon sign out front announcing the Honey Pot, my first thought was, "No way in hell I'm going in that dive!" The windows were all darkened and there was absolutely nothing inviting about the place. It was on a corner with nothing around it except a large abandoned warehouse next door and what appeared to be a lumberyard on the other side. These sorts of businesses were tucked away on the outskirts of Manhattan all up and down the island and I never even gave most of them a second glance. I felt my stomach churning and my legs felt a bit shaky. I wasn't ashamed to admit to myself that I was terrified. But something rescued me from the fear and propelled me forward—no, not the knowledge that my man and best friend strolled into there five nights a week and managed to make it home in one piece. You would have thought so, but that wasn't it. What helped me immensely was knowing that my new friend Trey, he of the pretty beard and warm eyes, had just walked through those doors and was now inside. Trey wouldn't let anything bad happen to me. Somehow I was sure of that.

I glanced around me—no one was watching. Thank goodness for this barren neighborhood. When I swung open the heavy metal door, I was surprised to find myself staring into the face of a large, rather ominous-looking Chinese man. Oh, Fong. I had forgotten about him. Aaron had told many tales about this place over the two years he had worked here and Fong was a feature player in many of them. How could I have forgotten about Fong? Except for the karate flicks my father used to watch on Saturday afternoon, I had never seen a Chinese man who looked like he could kick as much ass as Fong. Wouldn't want to tangle with this dude. Fong eyed me closely.

"Can I help you?" he said. I was relieved that he didn't think I was there to dance. But then again, was that a compliment? Maybe he thought I wasn't dancer material. Maybe I wasn't sexy enough in his mind.

Just as I was about to succumb to my insecurities, the inner door to the club swung open and two young white men exited. I got enough of a sight line into the establishment to see a black woman on stage, wearing nothing but a G-string and a look of considerable disinterest. The woman was—how could I say this kindly?—not exactly svelte. She was big and flabby and, as she turned on her ridiculously high heels, she had an enormous ass. Her face had the look of someone who had been worked over with a couple of heavy combat boots and had lived to talk about it. Homegirl was *not* cute. She was the perfect elixir for my insecurity.

"Yes, I want to go in the club," I said.

Fong looked into my face again. I wondered what he was looking for. But then I remembered another Aaron story, about the wife who had marched into the club with the toddler on her hip. Perhaps Fong was trying to assess whether I was another crazed wife, here to put my foot in my man's ass—or maybe pull out an AK and take out the whole club. So I gave him a kindly smile.

"Okay. Five dollars," he said. He didn't smile back. I reached down into my purse and pulled out a $5 bill. He unceremoniously motioned toward the door.

As soon as I stepped into the club, the first thing I noticed was the smell. It brought me back to my high school days, back to the locker room where the girls' dance team used to change after practice. Female funk, smelling faintly of pubes and sweat and the cheap perfumes that teenage girls liked to douse their bodies in. The funk here was mixed in with the unpleasant remnants of cigarette smoke. When my eyes adjusted to the room's gloom, I looked around for a seat as I tried to take in as much of the club as I could without attracting any eyeballs toward myself. I grabbed a stool at the bar and surveyed the scene. I saw a few of the men glance in my direction and quickly avert their eyes. I happily decided that meant they had concluded I wasn't a dancer and thus they had to follow the societal norms that existed outside the club—namely, they weren't allowed to stare.

Somehow the club managed to be far different than I imagined while it was almost exactly what I imagined. Let me explain. The men were a surprise to me, but the women were not. As the flabby dancer I saw through the doorway pulled some ill-fitting spandex back over her big fat ass, I noticed that there were at least a dozen women scattered around the club, most of them leaning on men or—I looked closer—bouncing on their laps. They were mostly black, or at least nonwhite—a few were of an indeterminate ethnic origin. I spotted Trey and Warren sitting at a table in front of the stage, clutching beers and looking around with grins. There were other men who looked a lot like them, well-dressed, well-groomed, solid-looking guys, the kind I had seen on all too many occasions at black singles-circuit hangouts like the Shark Bar and the Supper Club, leaning against the wall, nursing their Hennessys as their eyes undressed every decent-looking woman in the joint, knowing that their steady employment and disease-free bodies made them hot commodities on this open market. But they didn't look so cool and calm and in control here—they looked like eager little boys, waiting for Santa to pile a load of Christmas presents on their laps. I had been holding onto a very healthy hatred for the idea of the stripper-ho club, but for the first time I was able to see it from a man's perspective: All they had to do was have some dollar bills in their possession and they could sit down and have all the ass they'd ever want pressed against their hungry body parts, no questions asked, no promises made, no commitments expected. It was a strings-free, all-access, unmitigated bootyfest. If you were a dude, what was there not to like? I felt like I had been given a rare, almost secret, look into the male mind; I was being handed the kind of revelation that women like me almost never come across, information that I could use for years to come. The picture wasn't pretty and it certainly wasn't flattering to the male species, but it cleared a lot of things up, like the chilling view of the meat-packing industry Upton Sinclair presented in *The Jungle*. I gazed around the club, at the range of men represented, young and old, black and white and Latino and even Asian and Indian, a virtual United Nations of lustful grabs and erect penises, and I realized that men truly were motivated primarily by the care and feeding of their dicks. It was a remarkable unifier, bringing together guys who wouldn't ever be likely to even spit in each other's direction outside the club. Now they were side-by-side, their faces wearing the same pathetically excited expressions, as if the air were filled with manna from heaven. Outside the Honey Pot, a man like Trey, smooth, good-looking and obviously gainfully employed, wouldn't be apt to give a second glance to a woman who looked like the dancer whose ass he was currently caressing. The dancer had been introduced by the dj as Cherry (how unoriginal!) and though she probably wasn't any older than, say, twenty or so, her body looked like it'd been through years of abuse—by unhealthy eating, perhaps a baby or two. There were stretch marks down the sides of her belly, her breasts, her thighs. She was gyrating to some hip-hop song, alternately cupping and rubbing her titties, and every once in a while, absentmindedly licking her tongue at them as if she were considering pleasuring herself—but not really. Then, with a one-two step, she dropped down onto her knees and gyrated her vagina, to the delight of the men sitting in the front row, including Trey. Fistfuls of dollars lunged toward her G-string, which she'd hooked her thumbs into and was playfully pulling back and forth over her pudgy belly. The moment the dollars stopped coming, she rolled over (quite ungracefully), pulled up onto her knees, and threw her back in it—bouncing her ass to the rhythm of the beat. Trey was about to reach his fingers toward her ass again, but for some reason he looked behind him and his eyes met mine. I could see the momentary hesitation on his face, the dawning of a self-consciousness. In his eyes I could see the realization of how he must have looked to me. He turned his head back to the stage—but he retrieved his hand and sat back in his chair. He was embarrassed. My presence had chastened him. No, Cherry and her ilk would not be making it home to meet any of their mamas, but now I saw that from their perspective that was far from the point. I had always heard about how men put women in different categories—the Madonna-whore dichotomy—and now I saw it manifested before me like a one-act stage play. Cherry was for entertainment only, a way to escape the complexities of life with the Madonnas in their other world. I was a Madonna. Never were the twain supposed to meet—Cherry was supposed to stay inside the club and be groped and fondled; I was supposed to stay out of the club and ignore what happened inside. If the two came together, only bad things could come of it. That was spelled out on Trey's face, in his body language when he sat back down. I saw him lean over, whisper in Warren's ear, and throw his chin in my direction. But Warren wasn't trying to be pulled outside of the club—he shook his head quickly, clearly rejecting Trey's suggestion, and he made another lunge toward Cherry's ass.

The bar stools were a good vantage point to view most of the action in the club, but I couldn't get an adequate look at what was going on in the far corner, where I saw men sitting while dancers writhed on top of them. This is where the private lap dances were going on. I eyed a table off the side of the bar that was unoccupied and still somewhat unobtrusive—but much closer to the nasty corner. I slipped off the bar stool and headed for the table, fervently wishing I could disappear when I saw several sets of hungry eyes stare in my direction.

"I'm sorry, did you need a drink, miss?" It was the bartender, calling out to me, drawing even more curious eyes. Aaron had told me about the bartender who worked on his off nights, but I had forgotten his name. I glanced at him—a young-looking, cute Latino guy. His name came to me: Victor. Aaron called him Vic.

"Um, what kind of white wine do you have by the glass?" I said. "You have Pinot Grigio?"

I saw Victor grin and look over at one of the older white men whose ass hugged a bar stool.

"Nah, honey, we don't have no white wine," he said with a chuckle. Apparently I had just showed my cluelessness about strip club amenities. Well shit, I wasn't going to be ashamed for not being a stripper-ho expert.

"Okay, give me a rum and Coke," I said, keeping it nice and simple for Vic, whom I had quickly decided I didn't like. I brought my drink, which tasted like Vic had forgotten the Coke, over to the table and settled in to watch these lap dances. From this point of view, I could see clearly all the moves the dancers were using. Most of them were facing away from the guys, pressing their booties in the guys' faces, down onto their crotches or just rubbing their asses all over the guys' bodies. I focused in on one dancer in particular who was particularly energetic. She appeared to be Puerto Rican, or maybe just a very light-skinned black woman, and she had an incredible body—large round breasts that appeared to be natural, a small waist, big round hips, and an exceedingly big sexy ass. She was pushing her G-string–clad ass into some brother's face; I could see his hand wrapping underneath her crotch and stroking her pubic area outside the material of the panties, almost as if he were masturbating her. Her hands were reaching down between her legs and in his lap. It looked like she was squeezing his dick through his pants. Her eyes were closed and she wore a contented smile, like she was truly enjoying herself. Up to that point, based on comments Aaron had made about the dancers and my perceptions about stripper-hos, I assumed that the women were there simply for the cash and that they looked on their work with about as much pleasure as an attitudinal waitress or a girl working the register at McDonald's. It had never occurred to me that a dancer might actually enjoy hours of sex play every night with strange men. But clearly this woman was well down the path of ec-stasy. She let go of his dick and stood upright. Her hair hung behind her as she flung her head back. She ran her fingers from her scalp, over her face and neck, over her breasts, down her belly and then, fi-nally between her legs as she gyrated her hips. The man was sweat-ing. Strangely, I found a familiar tingling in my lower abdomen that signaled arousal. I was getting turned on! I felt my face flushing and glanced around to see whether anyone was watching me. Of course no one was. I was alone at my table, in my thoughts. I looked back at the dancer, who was now grinning, and I could feel moisture forming between my legs. I wanted to resist, to deny the warm feelings that were emanating from my pubic area, but the more I watched the less power I had to tear my eyes away. I was brought back to my child-hood, to the night when me and Aaron caught sight of my parents in the throes of sex. I had been mortified but also fascinated—and mor-tified by my fascination. Something about seeing such obvious evi-dence of two other people's passion, their intense connection to each other, was incredibly exciting to me. It wasn't so much about the physicality of it, watching the grinding of sexual organs, but more about seeing their bare emotions so plainly on their faces—and them not realizing that they were on display. When I watched a few porn tapes on occasion or came across the awful soft-core movies on late-night cable, I was turned off by the fakeness of it all—silicone-laden women being paid to moan on cue as they were impaled on some big horse dick. That was supposed to do something for me? But I realized that seeing it live was another matter entirely, especially if they didn't know I was watching all that passion play out on their faces. I could remember my father's face on that night, the grimace of pleasure, a light in his eyes I had never seen before or since. It dawned on me then that there was this whole other side to the man that I'd probably never meet, and that fascinated me and maybe even frightened me at the same time. Watching people having sex was like getting a secret peek into their intimate souls, the side of them they usually tried to keep hidden. I found myself wanting to reach my own hand down under the table and touch myself—and then I almost gasped at how hypnotized and shameless I had quickly become. I took another drink and watched the woman finish her lap dance just as the music stopped. She turned around and said something into the man's ear, giggled, and then disappeared into the backstage area. The man, a black man probably in his early forties, looked spent, like he had just had an intense workout. I wondered whether he had had an orgasm. But that thought grossed me out—eww, it would still be in his drawers! Just then, the dj made an announcement: "The one you want to pour into your cup in the morning, and cuddle up to every night—Cocoa!"

The room broke into applause and every man in the place slid up in their seats in anticipation. And then she appeared—the dancer who electrified the room just with her name. Aaron's Cocoa. The woman he'd once told me he was considering taking out on a date, until I clowned him so hard he stopped talking about her. There she was, a vision that, from my seat, appeared to be as close to perfection as I would ever find in a place like this. She was beautiful—caramel skin, long expensive–looking weave, big almond-shaped eyes that weren't even crusted over with too much makeup like the other girls. Her body was outrageous, the prototype of the female hourglass. She moved across the stage with a feline's grace—her appearance caused the men immediately to quiet down, to sit back and watch in what appeared to be awe. I saw her profile as she moved directly in front of where I was sitting; her ass was very big, way bigger than mine, but it still sat up atop her thighs like it had been attached to a winch. A quick succession of emotions raced through me, starting with awe, then moving from jealousy to hatred and, finally, to anger. I sat back and crossed my arms involuntarily, trying to keep a firm hold on my temper. But I glanced away and saw another unwelcome sight and this one put me over the edge. The light-skinned/Puerto Rican dancer who I had just seen pantomime sex with the middle-aged black dude was now behind the bar, flirting with Victor. As she walked by him, she pressed her nearly naked ass against his jean-clad behind, then she dipped down and ran her hands up his leg, stopping at his crotch. She giggled and moved away. Victor wore a sheepish grin, but he had made no move to stop her. So, that was the nature of the bartender-dancer interaction, huh? Flirting and groping and fondling? I had no reason to believe that things would be any different with Aaron, who was every bit as cute and sexy as Victor. With a loud expelling of air, I snatched up my pocketbook, took a long swig of my drink, then marched toward the exit, suddenly not caring who was looking at me. I caught another peek at Cocoa on the way out and saw that she was looking at me, wearing a curious frown. I was going to head straight to the apartment, tear Aaron a new asshole, then demand that he never return to this dive.

But as I walked through the dark streets of Alphabet City, expecting a rapist to jump out at me from behind every tree, I was so focused on my trepidation that my earlier outrage lost much of its edge. This was a good thing, for it gave me time to think a little about the implications of what I was about to do. If my love for Aaron were going to have any chance at building into something long-lasting and strong, I had to be extremely careful about how I handled this. Aaron was my best friend, but he was first a man. And I knew that no man responds kindly to his lady demanding that he quit his job. He had argued and argued with me about how his gig at the Honey Pot was ideal for a photographer. He said he had improved his craft so much over the past year that he felt like he was on the verge of signing with one of the big photography agencies that all the big dogs used, one of those places that filled the pages of the nation's top magazines with their clients' work. I was shocked to find out that once you were with one of these agencies, you could just scour the streets taking lovely pictures of whatever you wanted, and the agencies would be able to sell them to magazines and advertising agencies and whoever needed images of various things. They were called "stock photos" and the publications were always desperate for them. How would these prospects be harmed if he had to quit this gig and get a day job? But knowing what I now knew, how could I let him leave me every night to spend hours in the majestic presence of Cocoa, or get felt up by that little Puerto Rican stripper-ho? I couldn't abide by that, not for my man.

When I walked into the apartment, I wondered if I carried that cigarette odor that clung to Aaron's clothing with a vise grip when he returned home. I didn't see him in the living room, so I assumed he was in bed. It was only 11:30—this was early for him. I walked into the bedroom, trying to muffle my heels as they clacked against the hardwood floor. I saw his familiar form under the covers. I was glad that I would have more time before I confronted him. I had to figure out how to do this without causing an irreparable fault line.

The next day, after we had finished my roast chicken dinner, I brought up the club as he was putting away the dishes he had just washed. I wanted to come right out and tell him that I didn't want him to go down there that night or any other night. But I wanted to do this with some sensitivity, to not sound like the typical angry nagging girlfriend trying to control every aspect of her man's life.

"Aaron, I've been thinking about this club and it really makes me uncomfortable that you work around naked women every day," I said. I was leaning against the counter with my arms folded, trying to look strong and resolute but not overly angry.

He turned around quickly, nearly dropping the slippery plate he was holding. He eyed me more closely, probably wondering what had prompted this.

"Nina, damn, I thought we had resolved this. We've been over it like a thousand times. The club is harmless. I make a lot of money there. What's the big deal?"

I wanted to shout in his face that the big deal was named Cocoa, that the big deal was every little hoochie in the joint feeling like she had the right to touch all over the body that was supposed to belong just to me.

"It's a big deal to me, Aaron! Shouldn't that be enough? Last week somebody asked me what my boyfriend did for a living—and I had to lie to her." I had a scowl on my face, but right away I knew that it had been a bad tactic to so immediately talk about the outward appearances, about my embarrassment. That was hardly my strongest argument. Damn.

"Oh, so it's about how you look in front of your friends, huh? It's not about us at all." I knew he was going to go there.

"It has everything to do with us, Aaron. How would you feel if I was a waitress at the Honey Pot, letting men feel all over me while I served them drinks? Wouldn't like that, would you?"

His eyes narrowed a bit. "But that's not the same, Nina. I stand behind a bar. Nobody's feeling all over me," he said, sounding a bit exasperated.

"What about the dancers?" I asked.

"What do you mean?" His eyebrows lifted.

"Are you saying that none of the dancers ever laid a hand on your body?" I said, my voice rising. I was infused with the righteousness that comes from knowing you're right.

I saw Aaron glance away for just a fraction of a second—but it was long enough for me to know he was lying. I remembered a psychology class I had in college, when we learned that people will look up and away when they're lying because they're searching in their brain for the right fib for the occasion. So whatever Aaron was going to claim next was bullshit.

"This is ridiculous, Nina!" Aaron said, his face covered with a big scowl. He didn't even try to lie. He glanced at the time on the kitchen microwave and abruptly turned around. "I gotta go to work now, Nina—I don't have time for this bullshit!"

Without turning around to give me another glance, Aaron headed straight for the front door and disappeared with a slam. I felt the heat forming around my neck. I wanted to pick up a plate and smash it against the wall. That had not gone at all as I hoped it would. But I was sure of one thing: Aaron was lying.

Nina and Aaron,
Part IV

A aron could hear the water running through the bathroom door, but still he waited. He had an urge to kick the door down and demand an answer, but he knew she was to come to him. He couldn't force the issue. These things had their own time schedules—the urgency of needing to know had no influence on when your answer would come. So he sat forward on the couch and put his head in his hands.

"Aaron?" Nina called out through the door.

"Yes?"

"A couple more minutes, okay?" she said, trying to sweeten her voice.

"Okay," he responded flatly.

"Aaron?" she called out again.

"Yes?"

"You think it's going to be okay?" Her voice sounded much more hopeful than Aaron felt. But he didn't think this was a good time to reveal his profound doubts.

"Yes, Nina. I do."

him

I think I need to clear up any misperceptions that might be lingering about my employment at the Honey Pot. It's unfortunate that
this is even necessary—after all, no one would doubt my character if
I tended bar at a sports club or a high-priced restaurant. But because
I was in the company of women who remove some of their clothing
for money, their unsavory choices are supposed to rub off on me? I'm
shady or sleazy by osmosis? What does that say about attorneys who
spend their days around the most morally repugnant characters our
society has to offer? Okay, maybe attorneys aren't the best examples
of non-sleaze. How about plastic surgeons, peddling a corrupt fantasy
of the perfect human for a stack of cash? Are they greeted with the
same series of frozen grimaces or questioning frowns as I got when
they inform strangers of their chosen profession? At least I didn't go
to college with the intent of staging daily hijackings against the vulnerable and imperfect. I was just trying to pay the rent.

Let me take you inside the club so you can get a clearer picture.
First of all, you need to let go of any notions you might have formed
of such establishments based on one drunken visit or what your nasty-
ass cousin Junebug might have told you. From the outside, the Honey
Pot looked like a hundred other less-than-glamorous dark little bars

on the Lower East Side of Manhattan, frequented only by people very familiar with their insides. In other words, you wouldn't wander in off the street out of curiosity or even if you had to pee so bad your bladder was about to explode. A big scary Chinese dude named Fong sat sentry just inside the front door, poised to bar any characters who looked too shady—not an easy job at the gates of a strip club—or to remove anyone who got too friendly with the young ladies. Once you got past Fong and sauntered through the doorway and around a curb, your senses would likely be overwhelmed by the smells and sights— the odor of cheap perfume, stale beer, and a faint tinge of ever-present femaleness and all its attendant parts, like a girls' locker room that hadn't seen a hint of Mr. Clean in months; women scattered about, on chairs, onstage, standing around and watching, all mostly naked and most wearing fake smiles. The Honey Pot was decidedly a black club, which was a fact that affected virtually everything about the club and its clientele. At a white club, the saintly icon was the breast. It was the magnet that drew patrons into the club like mice to cheese—or, perhaps more accurately, mice to a cheese-laden mousetrap. A dancer's earning power was inextricably tied to the size of her rack—the bigger, the firmer, the more balloonlike, the more bills she'd be tugging from her G-string at the end of a set. Sure, it helped if the girl had a pretty face and was fairly shapely in the hips and leg, but her cup size was really what mattered. To fatten their take-home, the white dancers were forced to go under the knife and enhance whatever God and the gene pool had provided. The result was a tableau in a white club that might resemble a kiddy birthday party— when you looked around all you saw were balloons and teeth.

A black club was altogether a different world, starting with the object of worship. It was all about ass—big, round, jiggly, fleshy behinds that could hypnotize brothers so powerfully that they wouldn't even know how much cash they were dropping. The dancers at a black club didn't need to be overly blessed in the face or even the chest—what they needed were acres and acres of ass, served up to the male patrons in a thong so small that you'd need a magnifying glass and tweezers to retrieve it. In calling the Honey Pot a black club I am in no way implying that its patrons were black. In fact, that was far from the case. Its patrons were just men who spent many hours fantasizing about ass, men who couldn't draw their heads away from a bountiful behind that passed them on the street even if their wives were standing guard over every inch of their eye movements, men who needed to touch and fondle and attach themselves to as much ass as possible in order to be happy. While societal influences render it likely that the majority of the black club's patrons would be black men, there were always a sizable number of white and Latino men perched on the bar stools and chairs. In fact some of the older dancers had told me they'd been noticing in recent years—perhaps spurred by the influence of MTV and rap videos and hip-hop's worship of the booty—that the numbers of white boys in the black clubs had been steadily growing.

A curious outgrowth of the object of worship was the means the dancers used to make extra money. In white clubs, the table dance or lap dance or touch dance all featured prolonged thrusting of the breasts in the patron's face. Whether the patron could lift his hands and touch the breasts was another matter, usually connected more to the skittishness of club management and their popularity with the local vice squad. In sleazier clubs, breast touching was in no way discouraged. But there was usually a word of complaint that the patron would hear in the white club if he dared to raise his hands and caress the ass. That was considered far out of bounds.

In the black club, the dancers didn't even bother with the breast-to-face move—their assumption was that if they turned and presented their behind to the patron and bounced up and down on his crotch for two minutes, he'd be one happy camper—even if he never even saw her breasts or her face. Ironically, she might tell him that she wasn't even allowed to turn around and face him—it was against club rules.

Another key difference: In the white clubs, you'd be likely on occasion to see couples patronizing the establishment—a man and a woman, clutching her partner's hand in earnest, would enter, trying not to notice the questioning stares from all the patrons who couldn't imagine what might possess a man to bring his lady into such a place. But in a little corner of their minds, if they could manage clear thoughts in the midst of their groggy, lustful haze, they might secretly long for the type of partner who would join them in a strip club. The couple would search for a seat, the woman wearing an excited and slightly dazed expression plastered on her face, the guy giddy and just a bit embarrassed. There were no couples in the black club—no dudes who had managed to convince some sister to join them in their romp through the male version of Six Flags. The only girls you might find in a black club who weren't wearing a thong packed with dollar bills were the crackhead friends of dancers—who had wandered in to pick up their girl so they could go score another high.

These were the pieces I'd picked up over two years of spending my nights behind the bar of the Honey Pot. While many clubs preferred using exclusively babes behind the bar, the Honey Pot's owner thought that hot bartenders distracted the patrons from focusing on the stage girls and thus lost them money. I think the girls also preferred having me around—one less big-assed competitor for that almighty dollar.

"If there's one thing I hate, it's another muthafuckin' dancer," Essence, one of my favorite dancers, had told me one night with a big grin. "That's why I like you, Aaron. You ain't got no tits and hardly no ass."

Ah, the girls. Where shall I start? There were some that had become almost sisters to me over time. Sweet, vulnerable, passionate girls who I worried after and tried to persuade to walk out of the Pot and never come back before the life broke them with its unyielding and vicious assault on their self-esteem. Imagine how secure you'd be if your livelihood depended on a stranger deciding in an instant whether you were worthy of chunks of his paycheck, if you had to suffer through a never-ending sale on the auction block? There were a few I lusted after in a very passive way—they were strippers, after all;

how hard could it be? They were the ones with the crazy bodies, overabundant asses, mammoth titties, wildly proportioned vehicles built by a sex-crazed god with a sense of humor—they oozed sex so dramatically that their mere sight could make my dick swoon. But then again, I'd not want to imagine what it might be like to walk down the street holding the hands of a sexual billboard—like wearing a white sheet at a NAACP convention; just begging for trouble. A couple of the girls were so nasty and spiteful and full of hate that I steered clear of them whenever I could. I didn't even understand how these girls managed to eke out a living—their hatred for the patrons and for their jobs and themselves seemed to me to flow from them in waves, making it hard to see any man actually enjoying even two minutes of their presence unless he had a severe case of masochism.

And then there was Cocoa. It may sound like a cliché, but I always felt like Cocoa didn't belong in the Honey Pot. Possessed of a quick mind and piercing wit, Cocoa also had a certain sweetness that one wouldn't expect to find in such an establishment. I detected it right away, from my first hour on my first night in the club. I was trying to look tough and unfazed by the sights and sounds swirling around me—dancers jokingly disparaging the patrons and, most of all, each other; patrons propositioning dancers with perversions so strange that I found myself blushing; dancers placing immediate price tags, some big and some small, on the forehead of each customer who walked through the door, probably to a far greater extent than the customers realized. A couple of the cruder, nastier dancers had stationed themselves next to the bar, teasing me about what they called the frightened look on my face and trying to come up with something shocking that would rattle me. I didn't let on, but one of them succeeded when she contributed the wholly unnecessary tidbit that she was on her period and hoped that she didn't mess up anybody's slacks during a lap dance. They cackled like irredeemable hens, enjoying their shared disgust for the whole of the male gender. I was struggling to keep down my dinner when I happened to turn my head in time to see Cocoa prance through the doorway.

Her difference was evident right away by her clothes. Most of the dancers, in choosing outdoor attire, seemed to pick clothes that were merely extensions of their dance outfits, perhaps with just a bit more material. It looked to me that they didn't mind signaling to the world what they did for a living, as if they had given up long ago on hiding their occupation—or maybe they were actually proud of their chosen profession. Spray-on, low-cut jeans with thongs visible above the waistline, daring halter tops that simultaneously bared jiggly midriffs and acres of fleshy breasts. Dark ugly tattoos with obvious verbiage like "sex goddess" or "sexual chocolate"—talk about your sexual billboards!—etched across their bare backs or thick, fleshy arms. I think many of them wouldn't even know where to buy respectable clothes if a $100,000 office job was dangled in front of their eyes. But Cocoa marched into the Honey Pot wearing attractive gray cotton slacks that weren't tight but still managed to hug her scandalously curvaceous hips in the right places, black pumps only about two inches high, a white cotton button-down shirt that showed just enough cleavage to make you take notice, and carting a black leather Coach bag that wasn't intended to draw attention. She looked like a businesswoman heading to her midtown office in late summer. My eyes finally drifted up to her face and I almost gasped. The woman was breathtakingly beautiful, light-brown skin that appeared to be gleaming like burnished oak, big almond-shaped eyes that carried a curious intelligence, and lovely full lips that could set the male imagination racing. She glanced behind the bar and gave me a warm smile when she noticed me staring at her. I guessed that she probably went through her days fighting off stares—what had I done to deserve a smile? What was *she* doing here—she must be lost, was my immediate thought. But my two harassing hens let me know that this perfect creature did, in fact, belong.

First they both sucked their teeth, loud enough for not only me but our lovely lady to hear. "Oh, great, here comes the queen bee, her royal fuckin' highness," one of them said, prompting her partner to giggle.

"Yeah, I was hoping maybe she had gotten run over by a truck," the other one said, eliciting more giggles.

I expected the woman to pretend obliviousness, but she actually turned to the hens and gave them another smile. "Good evening, ladies," she said as she swept by. "I see you're still holding up your end of the peanut gallery."

The two women looked at each other, both frowning. "*Peanut gallery?* What the fuck is she talking about?" one of them said.

The other shrugged. "I never know what she's talking about," she said.

I choked back a laugh. They heard me and quickly swung their heads in my direction. But I had anticipated their looks and had already cast my gaze down at the sink, pretending to clean a mixing canister. Suddenly, with the entrance of this caramel goddess, the place had gotten even more interesting. When she emerged from the dressing room a half hour later and sauntered onto the stage, I saw why she was such a hated figure—every male eye in the room was locked in like a guided missile. She looked like she hailed from a different planet than the other dancers. Her body was simply outrageous—large (natural) breasts, very large ass, tiny waist, quarter-moon hips, and a tummy flat enough to play dominoes on. She obviously had the right body for the profession—watching the male patrons proffer $20s and even $50s in a steady stream over the next hour, she clearly did quite well in this particular profession.

I'd soon discover, however, that all the beauty and perfection that Cocoa exhibited on the outside was dwarfed, quite amazingly, by her personality. When she finally made her way over to the bar after accumulating impressive stacks of cash—I watched her out of the corner of my eye as she went off to the side of the club to pull the bills out of her G-string and her pocketbook and smooth them out—she started a conversation that was a first for me in the Honey Pot. She asked me about my educational background. The clear assumption on her part was that I actually had one. I told her that I had graduated from the University of Connecticut with a degree in sociology and a minor in art.

"UConn, huh?" she said, surprising me that she would even know my school's nickname. "That's a pretty good school. So what do you do during the day? Tending bar at the Honey Pot is clearly not a career. I bet you're doing something artistic."

I smiled. I was still flattered that she was talking to me. Flattered that she would even try to guess what I did during the day. Being the center of this woman's attention was not the worst thing in the world. I imagined that she could likely make every man in the club empty his wallet in minutes—if I was another dancer, I'd probably hate her, too.

"Well, I'm trying to get my photography career off the ground, mostly," I said, suddenly feeling shy.

"A photographer, huh? I knew it. An artist," she said, grinning. "Well, maybe you can take some sexy shots of me one of these days. I need some new pictures."

She watched my face closely. "Are you blushing?" she asked, smiling. "Aren't you a cutie. I want to just eat you up. What in the world are you *doing* in this place?"

"That's funny, I was going to ask you the same thing," I said.

She shook her head. "I ask myself that question at least ten times a day. I've been dancing for about two years. I know it's not the most respectable job in the world, but I make a whole lot of money. And the schedule works for me, the nighttime hours."

I felt like I could push for more info. "What do *you* do during the day?"

She looked down at the bar, shifting on the stool. She was still wearing the G-string, bikini top, and sheer little skirt that I, along with every other male in the club, had just watched her painstakingly remove. I could smell the faint scent of light and fruity perfume coming from her—not like the heavy, cheap stuff I had already gotten used to on the other women.

"You're not going to believe me—it sounds like such a cliché," she said. "I'm in school, a grad student at NYU."

That sat there between us for several seconds before I could get my reaction straight. Never did I consider not believing her.

"Wow," I finally said, nodding my head.

"It's funny, but you're only like the second person in this club I've ever told that to. I don't like giving these witches in here any information about me. I learned quickly that they will try to use anything they can get their hands on to destroy you. I've seen it before."

By the time Billy, the club manager and the bane of the dancers' existence, came over ten minutes later to break up our conversation, I had fallen halfway in love. Gorgeous, smart, funny, ambitious, sexy as hell, and preciously sweet—what was I missing here? But I got my answer five minutes later, as I watched a fat greasy white man slide his right hand underneath and inside Cocoa's ass cheeks as she bounced on his lap. She didn't bother to move his hand away as he tugged at her G-string, pulling it aside. I was transfixed. His hand appeared to move frantically back and forth, as if he were sliding fingers inside of her. She closed her eyes, but the expression on her face didn't change. It was a sight that proved helpful—this perfect woman was in fact a dancer who got groped and fondled and invaded every night for cash. I shook my head violently. Whatever I was feeling earlier during our intoxicating conversation had to be shaken off in a hurry.

But of course Cocoa continued to haunt my dreams. Five or six nights a week I stepped into the Honey Pot wondering what she would be wearing, how her hair would be styled, what she would smell like, and, most of all, what kind of flirtatious dance we would have. She let me know that she was attracted to me and that if I just said the word we could explore whether there was more than a workplace game at stake. I was unsure of how to proceed, so for six months I did nothing except torture myself in her presence. She'd stroll over to me and turn on the charm with thinly veiled sexual innuendo; at times she grinned at me like I was a cute little puppy grabbing for the string she held in her hand. I'd be on the verge of asking her to meet me for coffee or lunch or a picture-taking session, anything to be in her presence outside of the club. But then she'd scoot away before

Billy saw us, and less than five minutes later I'd look up to see her precious ass bouncing on some loser's piece. Quickly deflated, I'd vow to myself that she must be avoided, no matter how juicy the body and entrancing the mind. I was so perplexed that I even sought outside counsel—Nina's. In retrospect, as you probably guessed, even mentioning Cocoa's name in Nina's presence turned out to be a huge mistake. I'm not trying to beat a dead animal here, but I want to be sure you understand my fundamental point. Throughout my life I have acted toward Nina in a way that is completely in concert with her status as my best friend. Change her from best friend to lover and I've got enormous problems on my hands. A man simply does not tell a lover that he is developing a crush on a big-butt stripper with a winning personality. Just isn't done. So where did my foolish revelation to Nina leave me? With a suspicious girlfriend who turned into Sherlock Holmes every night when I left for the club, hounding me so feverishly that I eventually had to quit and find a new gig.

I have to admit, however, that when it came to Cocoa, Nina did have reason to be jealous. Especially after one particular night of freakiness that I'm almost embarrassed to tell you about. It happened months before Nina and I fell into our love affair, but the whole topic makes me nervous because I had to lie to Nina to cover it up. Not a complete lie—just a partial one.

"Did you ever fuck Cocoa?" Nina asked me one night as we lay in her bed. We were only weeks into our new relationship, when we were still so enthralled with the state of our newfound passion that we could hardly get through the day without floating nasty calls or e-mails in each other's direction. Because I had a roommate and she didn't, we spent a lot more time at her downtown apartment than my uptown one. Let me be honest—Nina was thoroughly grossed-out by my apartment in every way imaginable, from its (lack of) size to its (nasty-ass) neighborhood.

"Come on, Nina! How you gonna mess up the mood with some bullshit like that?" I tried to use volume and tone to disguise my unease. These were the moments that could doom relationships. Nina had no business asking me such a thing and it was my honor-bound duty as her lover to protect her from mental images that she'd find disturbing. At least that's how in my calculations I justified my response at the time.

Nina was unmoved by my tone and volume. How could I ever scare a woman who had threatened to beat down a bully on my behalf?

"Uh, easy—'cause I want to know the answer. That's how." She was propped up on an elbow, staring at me. I continued to look up at a spot on her ceiling. I saw evidence of previous water damage. I saw a fat mosquito darting in the rays cast by the street lamp outside her window. But nowhere up there did I locate the appropriate response to her question.

"Damn, Nina, of course I didn't! How did you even get to that question—when was the last time we talked about Cocoa?" I risked a glance over at her, to see how seriously she would treat the question. I needed to know the winding route she took to find Cocoa—so that I could bar her from that route in the future. Nina shrugged.

"I don't know. When we were doing it, I got to thinking about that thing you do with your tongue when you're down there." She giggled at her reference to oral sex—or perhaps at the fact that a reference to oral sex still made her giddy. "Then I started to wonder how much practice it took for you to learn how to do that. Then I wondered about other women you've done it to. Cocoa was the last woman you really told me about before we started seeing each other."

Could that be right? I wasn't sure, but now that I had her focused on her route to Cocoa, I wanted to keep pushing this line of inquiry to keep her away from the original question.

"Maybe I never did it on anyone else but you," I said. I was trying to sound bold and strong, but my statement sounded much too timid, weak. She made a noise and waved her hand in my face.

"Yeah, right, Negro," she said with a laugh. "Why stop there? Why don't you just tell me you were a virgin before we got together?"

Now it was my turn to laugh. "Uh, because you'd know it was a lie," I said.

"That's right, Mr. Simmons." She took her index finger and pressed it against my forehead. "I know everything about you. Or at least everything worth knowing." She giggled. "I know that Liz Coffey got there first. And Sharonda Reynolds was next, followed by Janet what's-her-name, and a long line of trifling hos up in Connecticut."

"Janet who?" I said, now rising up on my elbow. "I know you not talking about Janet Traynor! I did *not* have sex with that crazy girl!"

Nina laughed at my indignation. "Come on, Aaron. She told me herself!"

I shook my head. "Like I just said, the girl was crazy. When did she tell you that we did it?"

"I dunno, I think it was a few years ago. I ran into her at a party in Queens."

"She told you this just a few years ago? As a grown-up? And you believed it?"

Nina shrugged again. "Why wouldn't I? I knew you were a ho back then, so why not crazy-ass Janet? You telling me that her being a little, ah"—she encircled her right ear with her index finger—"*off* would be enough for you to turn her down?"

This was not an area that would offer me any benefits, debating with my lady which girls I had sexed more than a decade earlier. Especially if the debate would bring us back to Cocoa. Instead, I had a better plan. I turned to her and fastened my mouth onto her left nipple, which was peeking out from under the dark-red sheet. She moaned obligingly and fell back onto the bed. I felt her legs slowly spreading underneath me and smiled inwardly at my successful switch. As my mouth left a trail down her torso, I chuckled. Oh, the sacrifices a man must make to keep the peace.

Though I should have known better, I couldn't fight off Cocoa when I needed to. Every time I had convinced myself that I'd be much better off keeping her locked in the club, I'd look up and see her onstage, her eyes boring a hole through me as she unwrapped her deliciousness for my benefit, making it feel like the most intimate public striptease a man had ever received. I should have known better—in fact, I had already considered the lesson received, thanks to a close friend from college, Gerald Smithers.

Through Gerald's eyes, I had discovered that getting together outside of the club environs with a stripper was likely to be a huge letdown. My boy Gerald had talked for weeks about his blossoming affection for a woman he had met in a strip club. I believe her name was Sweetness, though outside the club she could be summoned by a much more prosaic moniker—Ann. Gerald told me over the course of several ebullient phone conversations about the specialness of their many lap dances and how Sweetness seemed to light up whenever he came in the club. I asked him whether her sudden light upon his arrival had anything to do with the large bills he carried around in his wallet—Gerald was a Wall Street trader—but he swore that his money had nothing to do with it. It was tempting to mock his naïveté, but Gerald had always been a fairly sensible guy. My experience in strip clubs was quite limited at the time; who was I to challenge his claim that this girl had feelings for him? They were going to meet for dinner; Gerald was thrilled about the possibility of the evening concluding with a session of wild circus sex, beyond anything he had ever dared to dream. Several days passed after their "date" with no call from Gerald providing details. I figured that either the date had been a hellish disappointment or the boy was so in love that he was now practicing girlfriend blocking, meaning he was reluctant to share what could now be called intimacies.

"So what happened with Sweetness?" It was the first question out of my mouth. A whoosh of air tickled my ear through the phone line. A heavy sigh couldn't mean good news.

"*Maaan*, it was like watching Dr. Jekyll turn into Mr. Hyde," he said. "She didn't even seem like the same person from the club."

"So I take it that she's Dr. Jekyll in the club—or is she Dr. Jekyll outside the club?" I asked.

"Huh? Man, what the fuck you talking about?" Gerald said, not even understanding my attempts at literary humor. Gerald—called Smitty by his friends—wasn't exactly the literary type.

"Nothing, man. Just go 'head, Smitty."

"Anyway, she didn't want me to pick her up at home. That was cool—she didn't know me that well. So I go to the diner where we're supposed to meet and she shows up about an hour late!"

"Wow, you stayed there for an hour?"

"I was hungry, so I ate some dinner," he said, his voice rising a bit. I didn't mean to embarrass him. That would have been too easy anyway.

"Finally she walks in," he continued. "The clothes were crazy, Aaron. Her breasts are almost falling out of this little shirt she's wearing—and of course she doesn't have on a bra. Her jeans are cut so low on the waist that you can actually see the top strap of her thong. And for some reason I had forgotten about the big-ass tattoo above her left breast. It says 'Pinto'—she had told me it was an ex-boyfriend, but turns out it's her son. Not that I was looking to marry this chick or anything. But anyway, it's about forty-two degrees outside and she doesn't have on a coat. Before she even got to my table I'm already thinking this was a bad idea."

I chuckled at the image he sketched. I was supposed to have accompanied him to the club to meet Sweetness, at his urging, but I had never pursued it. Now I regretted my apathy—I wished I had a mental picture of this woman to flesh out the vision. I was loving the Pinto tattoo. I wanted to press for details of the tattoo—size, color, shape—but I knew that would annoy Smitty. While he was a notorious coochie chaser, he was also quite exacting about the way his dates should look. His mom had been a celebrated clothing designer—he had been trained by osmosis to study the female appearance. He noticed things that other guys never even saw—or didn't care about. Smitty had once stopped calling a girl because she wore too much eye shadow. I shook my head and smiled at that particular college memory.

"So," I said, "in other words she looked like a stripper."

I heard his snort of disgust. Couldn't tell if it was meant for me or my comment.

"Exactly. Now don't ask me what I expected her to look like in public, but I guess I assumed she'd be able to distinguish stripper gear from, like, regular female clothes. You know what I'm saying?"

I nodded, but of course he couldn't see that. "And then what happened?" I asked eagerly.

"So we sit there through dinner, and homegirl hasn't said more than one or two words. I'm not expecting that we're going to be talking about the U.S. foreign policy in the Mideast, of course, but it would have been nice if she could have seemed even remotely interested to be there with me."

"Well, was she bored or was she intimidated by the situation?" I asked.

I could hear Smitty scowling. "Man, I really couldn't tell you. She was real talkative up in the club—though she wasn't really talking about nothing except sex. For obvious reasons I had never asked her to change the subject. But it never dawned on me that she *couldn't* talk about anything else.

"During this painful dinner, the one thing that keeps me going is knowing that at least I'm going to get some at the end of the night," Smitty said. "So that's what I kept reminding myself as I sit across from what has to be the dumbest woman on the planet."

"Why are you so sure you're getting some, because she's a stripper?" I asked.

Smitty gave me the silence of a man who has been presented with the obvious but would rather leave it unsaid. "Hey, that was kinda the whole basis of our relationship—if you want to call it that. I wasn't paying for all those lap dances for the companionship and the stimulating conversation, you know?"

At this point, I was tempted to ask Smitty exactly why he *did* spend so much time in the strip clubs. As I said earlier, this was before my strip club employment, so I had very little insight into their nature. Gerald Smithers was a good-looking, wealthy bond trader who had never met a female he didn't adore—and usually their feeling was mutual. His evenings were filled with jaunts from one end of Manhattan to the other, slurping down whiskey sours and diving into the toxic air of the big city's mating dance. More often than not, he didn't go home alone, at least based on the regular Monday reports I got, leading me to conclude that he wasn't likely to need strip club visits to find nighttime company. Yet Smitty couldn't seem to stay out of them. He admitted to me in a brief moment of rare candor that there was something addictive about them, the lure of uncomplicated eroticism. As opposed to the singles bar, thick with the confused thrusts and parries of desperate loners, the strip club's purpose was clear: offer males access to female flesh without nuisance. The twin currencies, all that was required for entry, were lust and money. I had plenty of the former, usually not much of the latter, which could easily explain my previous inexperience in the clubs.

"When I go to the clubs, I feel like a kid at a carnival," Smitty said to me one night after we had met for a late dinner. "Everywhere I turn, I get the thrill I used to get when I'd go the carnival and see all those rides and the lights and the cotton candy. Ladies, ass, breasts, everywhere, smiling at me, trying to please me. You walk out of the club and all you get from them are scowls, nastiness, fever. The club is like an antidote to real women, like a cure for the hatred most of us feel from them."

I laughed when he told me that one, thought it sounded like a bullshit rationale for sleaziness. But now I can feel exactly what Smitty meant. I saw the men every day in the Honey Pot, just so thrilled to be there, claiming that the club and its eagerness to please protected them from the seductions of adultery.

"Women can never understand this," Smitty said. "I guess it would be like the thrill some of them get from shopping, being up in the mall. The strip club is the male mall." He giggled for about ten minutes after coming up with that one.

But Smitty's "date" with the stripper revealed the club's deception. I learned quickly that through the stripper's eyes, the worshipful patrons were just big fat dollar bills who the dancers often viewed with thinly veiled contempt. Some of the dancers were better actors than others—they were usually the ones who accumulated the most cash, luring the clueless dollar bills into believing there was something real going on between them, that the law and club management were the only thing stopping them from ripping open pants and imbibing members.

Smitty and Sweetness did, in fact, find their way to Smitty's Upper West Side apartment—and immediately to Smitty's bedroom. He figured he would get his compensation for suffering through the agony of a dinner conversation virtually with himself.

"I was tempted to ask her to take off her clothes while I sat on the bed and watched, but I figured that would somehow be rude or something, like inappropriately reminding her of her job and the real reason we had gotten together," Smitty said.

"My, aren't you the gentleman," I said with the dry tone of sarcasm. But Smitty let it go. He was too far into his story to be halted by my childish mockery.

"She's not letting me kiss her on the lips. I guess it's like some kind of stripper code or something. I thought that was with prostitutes, though—which actually should have been a big red warning flag. But my dick is too hard and I'm too stupid at this point to do anything except forge ahead. So we take off our clothes and get into the bed—and homegirl just lies there, looking up at me like she's bored out of her mind. I mean, the boredom is like all over her face. Or maybe it's contempt or hostility—it's hard to tell exactly what her problem is. But it's the first time I've ever gotten this look from a woman lying in my bed. Maybe you get it from the sister on the elevator when you step on and say Hi, 'cause she thinks every brother she meets is trying to mack. Or you get it from the black girl behind the counter at the McDonald's who despises her job so much that she wants to abuse you for having the nerve to step up to the counter and ask for a damn hamburger. But a naked woman in your fuckin' bed? Are you kidding me?"

I tried to suppress the laugh, but it came anyway. I couldn't tell whether Smitty was trying to be funny. But he didn't even notice.

"Aaron, man, she might as well have just laid there. It was like fuckin' a corpse. She didn't move at all. It was like she was just doing me a favor, like it had never occurred to her that sex was something a woman might enjoy."

I shook my head. It was amazing to me that act that women and men could put on, the public face, and how drastically it could differ from the truth.

"But you want to know what the absolute worst moment was?" Smitty asked rhetorically. "When we were done, homegirl sat up in the bed, looked over at me, and asked me how much money I was going to give her!"

"Oh shit!" I said. "Damn, Smitty. She was just ho-ing? So, did you give her any money?"

There was a pause. I could tell he was ashamed of the answer.

"Yeah, I did. I gave her a hundred bucks. I felt like such an idiot."

"Don't sweat it, man," I said, trying to be encouraging. "I'm sure any dude would have done the same thing. I would have."

"Thanks, Aaron."

One might surmise that the adventures of Smitty would have taught me a lesson. But one would be wrong.

Andrew Murphy and I had been best friends since our sophomore year at UConn, when I put my cafeteria tray down at a table next to a skinny light-skinned black boy with a quick smile and, within about fifteen minutes, knew I had found a permanent sidekick. Andrew had been working as a bartender at various clubs around the city for years as he tried to make it as a freelance writer and sell his first novel. Unfortunately he was a much better bartender than writer, at least in my opinion. He got a few assignments from lesser-known magazines every year, but it didn't seem like the novel was any closer to happening than when he first told me in college that he was going to write books. One of our pipe dreams was for him to become a famous travel writer and me his photographer companion, darting off together to the far reaches of the globe for the fancy travel magazines. The closest we had come to that vision was me taking Andrew's head shot for a short piece that was supposed to be humorous that he wrote for a local weekly newspaper. I read the piece over about a dozen times, trying unsuccessfully to find something that was even remotely funny.

It was Andrew who taught me how to mix drinks and then hooked me up at the Honey Pot, an opening he had heard about through his bartending grapevine. Some of my warmest memories of our postcollege friendship were the nights we spent standing at our kitchen counter for Andrew's "bartending school"—using liquor he had absconded from various gigs.

I wasn't expecting Andrew to be at home at 10:00 P.M. on a Wednesday, but he had surprised me before. I had to weigh several factors in deciding whether to sit on the living room couch with Cocoa or make an early path to my bedroom—would she be offended if I suggested the bedroom; would Andrew possibly walk in on us if I decided to set up camp in the living room; was my room in a clean enough state for Cocoa not to be distracted? Within seconds, as my eyes swept down over Cocoa's body, which was encased in impossibly tight jeans and a snug red sweater, I had my answers: No, Yes, Yes.

"I don't want my goofy roommate to walk in on us," I said, pulling her to me in a tight embrace. I leaned down and softly brushed my lips past hers. "Do you mind if we just go into the bedroom?"

"Not wasting any time, huh?" Cocoa said, a sly grin creasing her face. Cocoa gave me the sly crooked grin a lot, usually when she was amused by something I had done or said. She pressed her lips against mine with extra force and then slipped her tongue inside my mouth. Abruptly, she pulled away.

"An aggressive man—I like that," she said. She took my hand in hers and purposefully marched across the living room. I was giddy and nervous—so much so that I didn't notice her heading toward Andrew's bedroom. Before I could gather myself to stop her, she pushed open the door—and quickly stepped back, gasping.

"Damn—what happened in there!" she said, pressing her right hand to her chest. I saw her widened eyes and couldn't help giggling.

"It's okay, baby—that's not my room," I said. "It's my roommate's pigsty."

She exhaled dramatically and smiled at me, letting go her own giggle. My room would look pristine compared to Andrew's breathtaking nightmare. Ever since I had known him, Andrew always amazed me by the levels of filth and clutter he could tolerate in his presence. Like a tone-deaf singer who doesn't know when to stop squeaking away, Andrew seemed lacking an internal meter to inform him of when the grime had crossed the line. My biggest struggle in sharing this Upper West Side two-bedroom with him was trying to keep his filthy habits confined to his bedroom. For the most part it was a losing battle, but he *was* clearly trying to get better. On more than one occasion I had even started making inquiries and looking through the newspapers for another crib because I had reached the outer limits of revulsion at my living quarters—and I had to hold my breath every time I considered bringing someone to my place. Andrew didn't even bother to bring ladies into his room—he usually just went to their place or, in times of desperation, did his thing on the couch and hoped I didn't show up. I did catch a glimpse of him sucking on a white girl's breasts once, but they had jumped up so fast that I couldn't even be sure I had seen nipple. I believe they finished up the evening at her place.

"What's the deal with your roommate?" Cocoa asked as I led her toward my room.

I shrugged. "He's just nasty, that's all. What did you see, anyway? I haven't looked in there in a couple of months."

She shook her head in disgust and fought off a shiver.

"I don't know—it was clothes everywhere, even on the walls and ceiling, it seemed like. And I saw some crazy-looking posters."

I chuckled again. "The clothes on the wall are actually a few signed jerseys he's gotten from NBA players. He hasn't gotten them framed yet, so he just tacked them on the walls. But because he got so many clothes thrown everywhere, the jerseys just look like more craziness."

"How can you live with someone that nasty?" I closed my bedroom door behind her and shrugged again.

"As long as the filth stays in his room, he's not such a bad roommate," I said.

"What about all the porn pictures on the wall? Does he actually bring girls in there?"

I didn't really have an answer for that one. Andrew was obsessed with porn—he couldn't be in the house for more than an hour without popping in a videotape. He had even taken the step of convincing an old girlfriend to star in their own porn tape. I knew that one was his all-time favorite—he had started to worry that he was wearing down the VHS tape and needed to convert it to a DVD. He had told me of this worry on several occasions. He even tried to get me to watch it with him once, but I was just a little too freaked by the idea of staring at my roommate's erect penis. I declined.

"He likes porn," I said simply, without any elaboration.

"I like porn, too. I like it a lot. But pictures on the wall?" Cocoa cringed. "Just a bit tacky."

I was intrigued by her admission. "You like porn a lot, huh?"

"Yeah, I do," she said, grinning coyly again. "As a matter of fact, I get a lot of great ideas from porn." I could feel the air getting thick again, like a heavy gas was wafting through my nostrils and shortening my breathing. In one quick motion, Cocoa reached down and peeled off her sweater. There was no bra underneath—as she lowered her arms her breasts jiggled enough to announce their heft. Of course I already knew Cocoa was not shy about taking off her clothes. And I had seen the breasts more times than I could count—a few times even in some fat slobbering dude's mouth. But still I was excited about their unveiling, demonstrating that the mechanics of arousal was indeed contextual in nature. Cocoa stared at me like I was a juicy hunk of steak. I felt my stomach do a little flip-flop—I wasn't used to being on the receiving end of such a stare. I studied the look in her eyes as I tried to decide whether I too should begin removing my clothes. She couldn't possibly be faking, could she? Hers was not the look of a woman who worked in the sex trade. I reached down and began unbuttoning my shirt, but Cocoa held up her hand.

"Wait, that's my job," she said. She sauntered over to me slowly, her round hips working extra hard, and she planted her lips on the hollow between my neck and shoulder blade, just as she started fumbling with the buttons. She made several failed attempts to loosen the second button, then she snorted audibly, grasped the sides of my shirt, and wrenched the buttons away. I looked down to see my buttons tumble to the ground; on the way back up, my gaze was halted by an almost crazed look in her eye that startled and perhaps frightened me a bit. Where Smitty's Sweetness had become bored and in fact somewhat repulsed by sex, my Cocoa was exhibiting signs of sexual hunger that would be more appropriate on a furloughed prisoner.

After yanking off my shirt, Cocoa shoved me onto the edge of the bed, grinning wickedly at me. She reached down and fumbled with my belt buckle—I decided to help her finish unbuckling it, afraid of what she might do if she got frustrated with that piece. She forcefully tugged my pants off my legs and tossed them into a corner, her heavy breasts bouncing and her breath heaving from the effort. She made another animal-like noise and dropped down to her knees, reaching for my boxers. She pulled them down too, though she couldn't even wait for them to get past my knees before she plunged her head toward my thickened penis. She took it into her mouth with such a frantic energy that I had a moment of worry, wondering if she was perhaps a bit out of control. She was not at a place where you'd invite someone lacking in control. She pushed her mouth down over it with force. I was too taken aback to feel pleasure. In fact, she pushed it in so far that I heard faint gagging noises coming from her throat. Damn, the woman was literally making herself choke on my dick. If she had decided at that moment to look up at my face, she would have seen an expression that might have resembled fear. She worked her mouth back and forth, still using a frantic energy with which I wasn't entirely comfortable—though I was able to sit back a little and start to actually feel enjoyment. She reached up with both hands, apparently searching for my nipples. She found both of them at the same time and squeezed so hard that I grunted in pain.

"Owww!" I said, not able to hold back. As the sound fell from my lips, I briefly panicked, not wanting to signal to Cocoa that she was doing something I didn't like. But her response to my yelp scared me more than anything she had done so far—she pulled her mouth off my dick and grinned broadly, even wickedly, like a bloodthirsty hyena, making it clear that she had intended to inflict pain. I'm sure a shadow crossed my face. What had I gotten myself into here? I was as sexually adventurous as the next guy, but pain? *Sheeit.* Aaron doesn't like pain.

Still, I was curious as to where this would go. If this was Cocoa's idea of foreplay, what fireworks might she have in store for the main event? Abruptly, she pushed herself away from me and stood up. All of her movements had a frenetic, herky-jerky quality to them, almost like she was drugged. For a fleeting second I wondered if perhaps that might be the case. But I dismissed that one—I knew Cocoa better than that. Maybe this was just her body's curious way of exhibiting her excitement. She kicked off her shoes and stripped off her own jeans in one swift motion. I found myself staring at her neatly trimmed bush; Cocoa wasn't even wearing panties. I would have found that sexy as hell an hour earlier, but now it just increased my panic. I was fighting a sinking feeling that this whole encounter was no longer in my control. If I had thought hard about it, I might have realized it probably was similar to what a rape victim might feel.

I figured that I'd have the opportunity to reciprocate the oral attention she had given me. I certainly assumed I'd have time to reach over into my nightstand and grab a condom. But with stunning haste, Cocoa hopped onto the bed and impaled herself on my penis, sliding it inside of her without comment or contraceptive. She wrapped her arms around my neck and bobbed up and down in my lap, her feet planted firmly on the mattress on both sides of me and her ass rising and falling in a steady tempo. It may sound pathetic in hindsight to claim that I felt helpless, but at the time I wasn't sure if I should tell her to stop—and even if I wanted her to. Without a condom, with nothing to bar me from the hundreds of men who might have been in this exact same position, I was screwing a stripper. Like a massive weight resting on my shoulders, I felt the heaviness of guilt and shame. Sheepishness and stupidity. I couldn't even remember the last time I had had sex without using a condom—I was a child of the AIDS generation, schooled in sexuality well after the disease cut a swath through huge sectors of American society, and I had learned my lessons well. I could even recall one drunken occasion when I halted the sex act only seconds before insertion because we weren't in possession of a condom. I had always been proud of that moment, thinking it one of my finest—strength of character even in the face of eagerly spread thighs. But after all those years of discipline, I was now exhibiting the classic weakness of the flesh, unable to summon the will to withdraw. If I fixated on the dangers I had thrust myself into— or, more accurately, that had been thrust upon me, I might have run from the room shrieking in terror. So unless I was going to end this now, I had to move past fear. Once I did that, I closed my eyes and settled into the powerful waves that were racing from my pelvic area, threatening to end this freakiness before it really had a chance to start. I struggled with the orgasm urge that was starting to build—the last thing I wanted was to end my first sexual encounter with Cocoa in disappointment.

Cocoa pulled back and stared into my face. She still wore that slightly demonic expression. I decided at that moment to reinterpret that look as extreme pleasure—this felt so good to her that it was driving her crazy. She slammed her hips down on top of me even harder, but she didn't lift them back up. Instead she kept grinding downward, forcing my penis deeper inside of her. She slowed her movements now, allowing her inner thigh and Kegel muscles to do all the work.

She threw her head back and stared up at the ceiling. She opened her mouth and let out a moan that sounded almost like a scream. I could smell her perfume, mixed in with the faintly pungent aroma of our two nether parts emitting evidence of their mutual exertion. It was a raw smell, musky and tart, one that could not be mistaken for anything other than what it was. I gave in to a few hearty groans of my own.

The next scene happened almost like a slow-motion shot in one of those high-tech action movies that feature a hero dodging actual bullets. Cocoa swept her head back toward me, but it was followed by her right hand, which swooped downward in a wide arc. The sharp talons on her hand tore into the flesh just above my left nipple, leaving a red streak about four inches long that immediately started oozing dark-red syrupy blood. I looked down at my chest and back into her face, so aghast that I was frozen. But she wasn't done yet. Staring into my eyes with a gleam in hers, Cocoa lunged forward, leading with her mouth, and fastened her lips onto my bleeding cut. I heard and felt the strong sucking motion of her mouth and I saw her tongue slip from her lips and lick whatever blood had started running down.

"Cocoa!" I shouted at her. "What the fuck are you doing?"

She glanced up at me, her teeth now pink, and ground her hips down onto my lap even harder, reminding me that my penis was wedged so far inside of her that I could have sworn it was knocking against her cervix. The throbbing that ran up my torso merged with the sharp pains coming from my chest, combining in a jumble of extreme sensations that almost made me faint. I could hear this woman continuing to suck the blood from my fresh wound, at the same time as she licked my left nipple and pressed me deep inside of her. So many different impulses were competing for attention in my confused mind that I couldn't show allegiance to any of them. Stay or flee? Pain and pleasure—or nothing?

As I drifted in my haze, Cocoa struck again. She lifted her left hand and jerked it swiftly downward, making a deeper but shorter cut above my right nipple. This time she fastened her mouth onto it before I even had a chance to see any blood. Looking down at her head from above and hearing her suck on my bloody chest like a hungry newborn, I started to emerge from my daze. The whole thing was surreal, getting fucked by a beautiful sexy woman who abruptly had turned into some kind of erotic vampire. But as she licked the surface of my abused flesh and thrust the tip of her tongue into the gash, my pain quickly overtook my pleasure and the flee response became dominant. Anger gave me a rush of strength; I forcefully shoved Cocoa off my lap. She landed on my thin, worn carpet with a thud. Her eyes, wounded and surprised, widened as her ass made contact with the floor. I stood over her, my bloody chest heaving, and stared down with all the malevolence my face could muster.

"Woman! Have you lost your fuckin' mind?" I screamed at her. "What were you doing?!"

She closed her eyes and seemed to sink into the floor. I couldn't read her expression at all. You work with someone for months, have deep meaningful conversations about everything imaginable, and then get the shock of your years when you discover you don't really know them at all. Cocoa didn't even try to offer explanations for her behavior—what could she possibly say? She slowly lifted herself onto her feet and began retrieving her clothes. Huffing, enraged, I waited for some form of *mea culpa*, something.

"Cocoa, why did you cut me up like this?" I asked, trying to soften my voice. I looked down at my chest, the eyebrows she had carved for my nipples, and saw that both wounds had started running blood again. And I could feel the hot pain starting to dash throughout my body. Cocoa turned around to look at me after she pulled on her sweater. I saw a tiny smile form on her lips.

"I'm sorry," she said so faintly that I was really just reading lips. Without another word, she was gone from my bedroom. I heard the front door slam seconds later. I caught a movement in the corner of my eye and looked down to see that the blood had started staining the rug. Damn. A few drops had fallen onto my penis. That sight was upsetting enough to send me sprinting toward the bathroom.

her

There isn't a person on the earth above age, like, five who doesn't have skeletons in the closet—big juicy bones we bury way in the back, past the winter coats we wrap ourselves in to protect us from other people's judgment, behind boxes full of memories that remind us of how far we've come, beneath the suitcases of baggage we lug around as testament to being hurt before, and promise that it'll never happen again. The coats, the boxes, the suitcases, they all serve their purpose in how we approach our relationships, and occasionally, we'll lend them to our lovers, always keenly aware of intent and outcome.

But skeletons? They are buried deep, snug, where no one is meant to find them, for a reason. Let one of the bones drop, and, no matter the strides you've made, no matter how lovely a person you are, that bone can taint perceptions, change minds, become the impetus for loss. We're all clear on the fact that we have them, but there is a "don't ask, don't tell, don't snoop" policy that lovers instinctively know not to violate—perhaps out of respect for the fact that people make mistakes and change, perhaps to protect themselves from heartbreak. The ones who violate the policy—well, they're dismissed with a quickness, with just cause. Because doing so denies the violated the right to put her best foot forward—to be all she can be (until, of course, she decides she doesn't want his ass anymore, and she starts beating him over the head with said juicy bones, with the express hope that they'll be so disgusted by your past that they'll run away. Fast.).

My Aaron enjoyed an open door policy when it came to my closet; he'd seen all my skeletons (hell, he was complicit in the formation of a few of them!)—my sexual misadventures, my twisted motivations, and, especially, my particularly embarrassing familial exploits. Indeed, I tended to talk to Aaron about my crazy parents more than I did my own sister, mainly because I knew that, even though she was directly affected, too, by their particularly bad brand of parenting, that she still had the potential to take sides and try to justify their behavior. What more could you expect from a wide-eyed daughter who, when it came to her parents, neither heard, saw, nor spoke of their evil? But Aaron always took my side, always instinctively knew to shut up, listen to what I had to say, and comment without judgment. Occasionally, he might even have some solid advice, too. That's what my best friend was best at.

Which is why the first person I should have run to when my dad called me from the Brooklyn correctional facility was my best friend confidant lover. After all, Aaron would have instinctively understood the history behind this particular bone and the embarrassment and anger that was sure to accompany it, seeing as he was the one who helped me discover the truth about Willy Andrews: that he was on the lam from the law. I was twelve when I found out about it. My Aunt Carena, with her drunken behind, was the one who dropped the news during a summer visit from South Carolina.

"Yeah, girl, your daddy was always some kinda special," she said to me between sips of muscatel. We were in the basement, she just talking about nothing, me trying to concentrate alternately between my homework, an episode of *General Hospital*, and my unique ability to tune out Aunt Carena without her even noticing (the latter of which wasn't all that hard since, even when she wasn't drunk, Aunt Carena didn't care much whether people were listening to her or not, so long as she got to drink and ramble, in that order). "I remember when he was your age—what you, 'bout ten, eleven?" (She didn't bother waiting for an answer.) "That boy sat up in the house one day marking up a piece of wood with house paint he stole from over to Mr. Martin's barn. It said, 'We deserve to read, too,' in red. And then he marched himself and that sign right on down to the library, talkin' 'bout how Martin Luther King didn't have nothing on him because he was about to integrate the library and he was going to do it without them sickin' the dogs or the hoses on him." I wanted to tell her to shut the hell up—*General Hospital* was getting good and I couldn't hear what Luke was hollering at Laura about. Instead, I gave her a "hmm," so that she would think I was really listening to her, and I could concentrate a little bit more on my show. Aunt Carena kept right on talking. "Chile, I tell you, by the time he was ready to march out that door, his daddy caught wind a what he was gone do, and put a whipping to his ass like he'd just marched to Selma with King and got caught by the police. Put a end to that nonsense with a quickness, I tell ya. Hmph. Integrating the county library in the middle of Orangeburg, South Carolina, all them white folks down there mad that black people were trying to read, much less trying to touch they books. I tell you, if Willy Sr. didn't whoop his ass, them white folks sho woulda. Mighta found his fool behind hanging from a tree out in front of the library." By the time she got to the part about hanging from a tree, a commercial was about to start, and so her words hung in the air—thick and ominous. Hanging from a tree? She had my attention then.

"He got hit for trying to read?" I said.

"Girl, it wasn't about him trying to read," Aunt Carena snapped. She took another drink and shook her head at me, like *I* was the dummy in the room. "It was about him bringing shame on the family and putting all our asses in danger. I tell you, the best thing that coulda happened to this family was him changing his name. Don't let them fool you little girl: There's still parts of the South that don't care for the likes of yo' daddy with all that black power business."

Changing his name? What the hell was this old woman talking about? She'd had my attention now, for sure. I got to asking a few questions for myself. "What do you mean, he changed his name?" I asked her, sitting up from my book and turning around to face her.

She took another swig and just stared at me, without saying a word. I could hear a Coke commercial playing on the television, but I didn't look at it. I just sat there, waiting for my aunt to get to the point. Finally, she offered it up. "What's my last name, baby?" she said, leaning forward out of her chair, closer to me. Thankfully, she was still far enough away that the liquor on her breath wasn't all that strong, but I could still tell, even from that distance, that she was good and sauced.

"Uh, is it, um, Andrews?" I stammered. I'd never really considered Aunt Carena's last name—that's how it is with families, particularly African-American ones. We'd go for years recognizing kin by the names we were taught to call them—most of the time, they'd be some jacked-up nickname you couldn't shake, no matter how old you were, without being bothered to find out what the person's mama named him. Like, I have a cousin named Tip (named for the way she walked on her toes) and an uncle named Hobble-Up (he got his moniker after he messed up his knee and was forced to hobble around the house until it healed), and I don't know either of their real names. Likewise, I knew that my aunt's name was Carena, but I just assumed her last name was Andrews. So that's what I told her. "Uh, Andrews?" I asked. Clearly, I was unsure about my answer. But my aunt had my attention.

Aunt Carena snorted, then rolled her eyes and leaned in some more. "Naw, baby, my last name ain't no Andrews. It's Carruthers," she said, then adding for emphasis, "Ca-Ru-Thers." She let that sit, like I was supposed to automatically understand what she was trying to get at. When she realized I was still in the dark and quite confused, she breathed heavily, crossed her arms, and said it again. "Carruthers is my last name. That was yo' daddy's last name, too, until he went and hurt them people up in the city and had to run from the law.

That's why yo' last name is Andrews. Woulda been Carruthers if it wasn't for yo daddy's foolish ways."

I didn't really know what to say, so stunned was I with this tidbit my aunt had let slip from her lips. I'd considered, however briefly, to ask for details, but I didn't want to give her the satisfaction; Aunt Carena seemed like she was actually getting off on telling me that my father had done something so incredibly sinister that he had to change his last name to duck the law. That's what she'd said, right? That he was ducking the law? I was all at once scared and fascinated; I needed to know more. What had he done? Did someone get hurt? When did all of this go down? How did he get away? If they caught him, would he go to jail forever? Would we be in trouble, too, for knowing he did something bad, but not turning him in? I excused myself from Aunt Carena—told her I had to go to the bathroom, then packed up my book and marched upstairs and right out the door and over to Aaron's house. He was in his backyard, ripping the wings off of bees.

"Aaron—you gotta come with me," I said, wincing and staring at the bug twitching between his fingers.

He looked down at his hands, as if this were the first time he'd noticed he was torturing insects. "What?" he said. He sounded like I'd accused him of doing something wrong. "I'm conducting an experiment. If I were doing this in school, it'd be called biology."

I dismissed him with a wave of my hand. "I don't care about your stupid bugs, Aaron. You gotta come with me and help me look for something."

"What?" he asked, finally catching on to the desperation in my voice. He tossed the bee on the ground and stomped it with his navy blue Pro-Ked. "What you need?"

I told him about what my Aunt Carena had said as I grabbed his hand and rushed him across the street back to my house. When we got to the door, I put my fingers to my lips to signal that he should be quiet, then slowly opened the front screen door, hoping that I'd done it gently enough so as not to disturb my aunt. I didn't want her to know what we were up to—didn't want to give her the satisfaction of knowing that her words had shaken me to the core. I tipped up the stairs, Aaron's hand in mine, and headed toward my parents' room. The door was locked—for some reason, my parents had decided that they needed to lock me and my sister out, probably because we'd gotten into my mother's makeup, perfume, and jewelry one too many times for her to trust us not to go through her things, or maybe because they didn't want anyone to see the mess that was their bedroom—but we'd learned almost as quickly as the lock went up that if you hit the door with your hip just so, it would pop open with ease. I gave the door a nudge with my butt, and watched it bounce toward the wall. I caught the doorknob before the door hit the wall, and then looked at Aaron. By now, he was looking at me like I had three eyes in the middle of my forehead. I still hadn't told him why I'd dragged him from his experiments, much less why I was busting into my parents' room.

"So here's the deal," I whispered, my eyes darting first behind him to make sure my aunt hadn't heard us breaking and entering, then around my parents' room. It was a complete mess—clothes hung from practically every piece of furniture in the room, newspapers and magazines were piled high, several dirty dishes were lazily laid on the dresser, a chair, the floor. I was, for a moment, embarrassed to have my best friend in their private space, exposing just how much of a set of slobs my parents were. As I surveyed their nasty room, I hurriedly started explaining to Aaron what my aunt had told me about my father. "I don't know what we're looking for, but I need to find some evidence of what Aunt Carena is talking about."

"How do you even know she was telling the truth?" Aaron asked, almost pleaded. I could tell he wasn't comfortable being in my parents' room. "You said yourself that she was drunk."

"She's a drunk but she's not stupid—just mean," I said. "Mean enough to actually want to hurt my feelings with the truth. Besides, you and I both know my dad's no saint, always talking all that black power stuff. What if he did do something really bad? Don't you think

I should know about it, in case . . ." I let my sentence drop. I didn't really want to consider what could happen to my dad, or my mom, or the rest of my family—me—over some nonsense my dad did. One thing was for sure, though: I needed to know the truth. "Come on, dig in. I'll take the dresser drawers. You look under the bed—my dad's got some metal boxes under there he keeps his papers and stuff in."

Reluctantly, Aaron dropped to his knees and slowly pulled out a box. I started snatching open drawers—there were jewelry boxes, underwear, some weird-looking pills in a circular aluminum holder (I'd later come to realize those were birth control pills), and a pretty worn copy of *The Joy of Sex*. I held the latter up and examined some of the pages, my mouth agape as I stared sideways at the two dirty-looking white people humping each other in near acrobatic positions. "You find something?" Aaron asked, popping his head up from the lockboxes under the bed.

"Just this really weird sex book," I said, frowning up my face. It didn't take Aaron but two seconds to register the word *sex* and jump up to see what I'd found. He rolled over the bed to get to the other side of the room more quickly, completely mussing the bedspread. "Aaron! Come on—don't mess up the bed," I said through clenched teeth. "My parents are going to know somebody was in here." Aaron absentmindedly looked at the bed and ran his hands across the covers, then looked back at the book in my hands.

"Wow, your mom and dad are freaks," he said, snatching the book out of my hands. He was turning his head sideways, as if he were trying to absorb and memorize each of the different sexual positions.

"I don't know why you so interested in that—it's not like you'll be getting any practice," I said, snatching the book out of his hands. "Anyway, we're not looking for sex stuff. We're trying to figure out if my dad's a criminal."

Aaron reluctantly walked back to the other side of my parents' room, dropped to his knees, and resumed his search through the boxes. I'd moved on to the next set of dresser drawers, and the next set. Nothing. I looked behind the heavy wooden furniture, between the mattresses, under the TV stand—still nothing. Aaron hadn't any luck either. We tackled the closet together, Aaron on the left side, me on the right. "Wow, your pops got a rifle? Does it work?"

"I don't know, fool! He doesn't exactly use it in the house."

"Ha, ha! You're so funny I forgot to laugh," Aaron said. I swear that boy sure could be some kinda cornball.

"Could you *try* to stay focused," I said, with another roll of my eyes, before leaning into the very back of the closet to feel around on the floor behind my mother's shoes. Just then, my hand hit something hard, like a book of some sort. I leaned in a little more, and pushed some of the shoes aside. It was an album of some sort, with a black fist drawn on the cover. I pulled it out, and then sat down on the floor. "Aaron, look at this," I said, opening it up. He pulled himself from beneath my dad's jackets, and leaned over my shoulder to get a better view. There were pictures—of my dad and people I didn't recognize. They were all dressed in black leather and sporting huge Afros, some with applejack hats hanging precariously from their dos. They were posed awkwardly, like they were in an army or something. In some of the pictures, the men were holding guns; in others, their arms hung easily around the shoulders of women similarly dressed. None of them were really smiling—the seriousness of their faces told me they were dealing with some heavy business. I kept flipping, past letters, and maps and more letters and pictures, until I landed on a news clipping. The headline—and the picture—sent a chill through my body:

Bungled Heist Leaves Toll Collector Injured
Police say black militants responsible

Just below that was a picture of three men. Two of them I didn't know. One of them I did. It was my father. The caption said his name was Willy "Baby Ruth" Carruthers. Aaron, sensing that I couldn't bring myself to read the actual story, started reading it aloud, but I barely heard what he was saying, so stunned was I by this piece of evidence that my Aunt Carena, through her drunken stupor, was telling

the truth. I didn't exactly know when Aaron finished reading the story; I just remember that after a few minutes, he was silent. I felt his hand rubbing my back, and then saw him shut the book and push it back into the closet. "Come on, Nina. It's gonna be all right."

But what was I to do with this piece of information? It wasn't like I could confront him with it; I wasn't supposed to be up in his room snooping through his things anyway. Surely, he'd whoop my butt if he knew. And even if I took my ass-whooping, what was I going to do after that? Call the cops? Hide? Ask him to turn himself in? Be afraid?

I settled on afraid, making a point to never tell anyone in my family—not my parents, my sister, my Aunt Carena, anyone—what I'd found. The only person I ever talked to about it was Aaron, who, after our initial conversation, didn't really bring it up much. Occasionally, he would jokingly call me Nina C—for Carruthers—but that was only when he was really trying to get my goat. I'd just smack him and tell him to hush up before someone heard him.

And now, almost two decades later, I was being confronted, quite possibly in a very public way, with my father's ghosts. All because he couldn't keep his penis in his pants. My mother? She'd finally had the last straw. After all the years of verbal, and sometimes physical, abuse, poverty, uncertainty, degradation, and rants, my mother picked up the phone and called 911 on Daddy's ass. The reason? She found out he'd been dipping out on her with some woman he met down at the gas station where he works. Funny how that goes, huh? He beat her, damn near starved her kids, went for months sometimes without bringing so much as a penny into the house, much less a decent living to take care of his family, and Mommy turned him in over what? Cheating with another woman. Isn't that the way it always goes down, though? I can remember hearing about stories like this on the news— women who were abused for years, and only got to trippin' after they found out their tormentors were tipping out on them. None of them ever really seemed to get that the ideal time to jet would have been when their mates tried to rearrange their faces; their excuses for staying would always be cloaked in some kind of martyr complex—you

know, "If I leave, what'll happen to the kids," and "If I go, he just wouldn't be able to live," and, "If I leave, then I will have denied him a chance to change."

All that changes, though, when they find out the dick's been somewhere it wasn't supposed to be. My sister tells me that Mommy turned Daddy in with a quickness—waited for him to leave the house, then walked (walked! My mother *never* walks!) over to ol' what's-her-name's crib to see if my dad's green 1982 Caddy was sitting out in her driveway (her girl, Thelma, had tipped her off to this phenomenon over a month ago, but Mommy didn't actually take heed to it until she started recalling how much time "overtime" he was putting in down at the shop) and sure enough, there it was, parked just beyond the gate. Apparently, my mother had considered walking into the house and whipping both their asses, but she did what she thought was even better: She calmly walked back over to our house, picked up the phone, sat in her favorite chair, put her feet up on the ottoman, and dialed 911. It took the police exactly thirteen minutes to hightail it over to ol' what's-her-name's house and cuff the long-elusive Willy "Baby Ruth" Carruthers.

Daddy sounded downright pitiful when he called my cellular phone. He was given the opportunity to make one phone call, and apparently, I was the only one he trusted to do something to help him, though I'm not clear why. If I were thinking with my mind instead of my heart, I would have let him rot right there in that cell until Bobby Seale himself bailed his butt out. Alas, I jumped into a cab and beat it to Brooklyn, talking to Kenya all the way there.

"Kenya, you think there's anything you can do to help me?"

"First of all, it wouldn't be you I'd be helping; it'd be a twenty-something-year fugitive," Kenya said quickly. "I'm not a cop, yet, but it doesn't take an oath ceremony and a law degree to see that a recruit who tries to help an accused felon probably wouldn't be looked upon favorably."

God, she sounded like some fake TV cop—using awkward police words much too big for someone with what was essentially a blue-

collar job. If she wasn't my girl, I'd have been insulted. I was about to be anyway. "Kenya. That's my father you're talking about."

We were both silent for a minute; I couldn't tell if she was hesitating to say something else, for fear that I'd be even more insulted, or if she was actually considering what I'd just said. Then, finally, she spoke. "Okay, look—I'll see what I can do. Meet me down at the courthouse. I'm going to see if my boy can meet us there. He's a legal aid attorney."

"Kenya, I can't thank you enough. Thank you, thank you, thank you!" I shouted into the phone.

"Easy, star—don't get too excited. They might have it in for him, seeing his history with the Black Panthers and all."

"My father didn't really hurt anybody," I said quickly, my voice growing dark.

"I know," Kenya shot back. "But he's a part of a group that systematically targeted, threatened, and, in some cases, killed police for their cause. Cops don't tend to forget those kinds of things, even if they did happen three decades ago." I was silent. I didn't want to say any more, because if I did, I'd lose a friend and any chance I had of getting my father out of jail. Perhaps sensing this, Kenya checked the bass in her voice, and softly asked me if anyone else knew about my dad's history. "I mean, we've been friends for years, and you never, ever, once told me anything about this," she said.

"I never even told my dad that I knew," I said quietly. "And I figure after all these years, why bother him with such things? The only other person I've ever talked to about it is Aaron."

"Hmm . . . how is he taking this?" she asked.

I was quiet again. I hadn't told him. I know, I know. Of all the people I should have told, Aaron should have been at the top of my call list. But I just couldn't bring myself to dial his cell phone. He was on his way to his parents' house to visit his mom, who was recovering from a sprained ankle she'd gotten during a Sunday school softball game. Can you believe that? A sixtysomething woman playing sports hard enough to hurt herself? "Well, what in the world was she doing sliding into the base?" I asked Aaron, all-at-once amused and incredulous. I was curled up on the lounge chair in our bedroom, half reading and half watching Aaron stuff underwear, socks, and a couple of shirts into his overnight bag. "She shoulda been somewhere getting ready to serve up the apple pie!"

"Yeah, well, she likes playing baseball, she's got a lot of spunk left in her, and she doesn't always have to be standing over a stove to participate in the church," Aaron said. He wasn't laughing, and if I had heard correctly, there was a bit of defensiveness in his voice (he wasn't facing me when he said it). But, following in the history of our age-old friendship, I seized on his defensiveness like a lion on a wounded antelope, and zoomed in for the kill. Hey, we never lost a chance to turn each other's unease with a topic into a prime joking opportunity—why stop now? That's what Aaron and I do.

"See, she should have stuck to showing off in the kitchen, instead of on the field. Everybody know your mama got skills when it comes time to stand over the stove. She don't know nuthin' 'bout sliding into no bases!"

"She probably knows more about sliding into bases than your dad does, seeing as pseudo–Black Panthers don't do baseball, apple pie, or Chevrolets," he said dryly. This time he was looking me dead in my eye. I wasn't sure whether I should have been amused; he called my dad an anti-American fake black militant, didn't he? How in the world did we get there? I admired that his mom was out on the field playing with the kids. I couldn't do that and I was only in my thirties. Besides, I was just joking about his mom's sprained ankle and her cooking—you know, trying to cheer him up, make a little conversation. I considered slinging a few zingers aimed directly at his mom, but instead I held my tongue. I couldn't count how many times we'd made fun of one another's family—I'd rib him over his mom's housewifery and his dad's laid-back persona, he'd wallop me over my dad's power-to-the-people antics and my mom's theatrics. Before now, neither of us really took what the other said personally—mainly because we both realized there was a whole lot of truth mixed into the jokes.

We loved each other so, and held our friendships so dearly, that it didn't occur to us to get offended by the insults, or remotely consider that we were judging each other's family and upbringing. Because that was something that we would just never do. We trusted each other with those skeletons, and instinctively knew that no matter when the other said them, it was all in jest—just jokes.

But something was different about this—something a little more sinister in tone. Maybe I was just reading into it, but I felt like Aaron was poking fun at my father for his beliefs—and, by extension, me, his child. Aaron had had a front row seat for the craziness that was my childhood—was privy to more information about my family than most of my family members, really. Never before had I once considered that Aaron would turn around and use what he saw against me, his friend. But I wasn't so sure if he could look past all of that now that we were together. Particularly now that my father had gotten busted. How, exactly, does one go about telling her man that her crazy daddy was an abusive cheat who once almost killed someone, and is now on his way to Rikers because his crazy wife called the cops on him? How in the world would my very own live and in-color incarnation of Theo Huxtable view his girlfriend, the product of a relationship so very distant from the ideal in which he grew up? Would he embrace me? Or throw his hands up in disgust, toss this one last bone into my closet, and walk away?

My guess? This news wasn't going to be met with a warm embrace and an "it's going to be all right, Nina." I had a sinking feeling that he would finally recognize my family for what it was—nuts—and walk away. I wasn't ready to say good-bye. This skeleton, I was keeping to myself. "Aaron's not here—he's at his mom's house and he's not answering his cell phone," I said to Kenya quickly, trying to throw her off the trail. I didn't much feel like explaining to her why I hadn't told my man about my dad's case. "But I need help now. So I'll see you at the courthouse," I said. I hit "end" on my cell phone, and then turned it off. I didn't want any more questions from Kenya or anybody else for that matter. I just wanted my father to come home.

Nina and Aaron,
Part V

"Aaron! I think I need your help!" Nina finally gave up and called out for him. She had been sitting on the toilet seat for more than fifteen minutes, waiting, sifting through a lifetime of images starring Aaron Simmons. She prayed that she wasn't about to get life-changing news. Not now. Not when they were in the midst of World War III.

Aaron rushed through the door wearing a worried look. Nina almost wanted to laugh when she saw his expression. What did he think, that she had fallen into the toilet? She handed him the box.

"Here, can you help me do this?"

To Aaron, as she sat there with her big sad worried eyes, she looked very much like the little girl he once knew so well.

him

There was a magic to Nina Andrews at age twelve, an indefinable quality that could exhilarate the kids around her, make them attach themselves to her like algae clinging to a whale. Try to think back to your childhood for a moment and imagine what it would be like if the toughest kid on the block and the prettiest girl in the neighborhood happened to be the same person. It was one of those biological impossibilities—like Nina's parents had unwittingly hit the genetic lottery when they laid down to conceive her. In retrospect it made some kind of sense—her father was undoubtedly a tough customer, albeit a major turd, and her mother was quite fetching—but the girl was still a preadolescent marvel, a person all of us kids knew even back then we would only encounter once in a lifetime.

So put yourself in my place as a twelve-year-old, spending most of my days and part of my nights with this confident, graceful, lovely creature, sharing my deepest thoughts and fears, putting my body in close quarters with hers on a daily basis—and watching with fascination as her body began to transform right there in front of the two of us. It was like having a close-up seat as Lon Chaney (or Jack Nicholson) turned into the Wolfman, seeing her longness and straightness morph into increasingly radical curves and swerves, the scars and rough edges smoothing out into supple womanness. And while most girls welcomed the changes with the poise of a trapped toddler, Nina stepped directly from girlhood to the verge of womanhood without as much as a stumble, like she knew exactly what was coming. At the age of twelve, head held high and proud, rounded hips twisting ever so slightly, Nina walked down the sidewalk like she was on a runway in Milan—and drew the stares of grown men at an alarming rate (at least alarming to me).

So now that you understand the context, let me tell you about my first wet dream. At the time it felt so real, so vivid, that I had to convince myself that it hadn't really happened. I can still recall every gory detail. Of course, Nina was the star. I guess you could say it was a one-woman show, in fact. As we had done since our earliest days together, we were engaged in a marathon tickle contest, seeing who would break first and give up. Usually it was me. In this dream, as I was tickling Nina, her blouse popped open, revealing naked breasts so new and ripe that they protruded at a radical ninety-degree angle, young mahogany nipples happily announcing their freedom. (I don't think Nina's breasts at age twelve were nearly as big as they were in my dream, but the breasts of a boy's fantasy world are rarely small.) I stared at her chest; Nina stared at me staring. Expecting a shriek and an escape, I averted my eyes. But I heard her soft voice float through my defenses and invite me to turn around and have another look. When I turned, Nina was now naked down to her slight little panties, which were black and lacy (I'm quite certain my twelve-year-old best friend did not at the time own a pair of black lace panties, but again, in a boy's fantasy world all panties were black and lacy—if they existed at all). I was thrilled and scared to death. It was then Nina's turn to stare—she gazed downward and smiled. I followed her eyes and saw that I was now completely naked—and as erect as a drill sergeant. She reached out, took my penis in her right hand and started squeezing.

At that moment, I woke up with a start. I sat up abruptly in my bed, more than a bit confused. My left hand touched something wet—I quickly pulled back the covers to discover several soggy puddles had joined me in the sheets. I was mortified. I had heard several boys talking about "wet dreams" several weeks earlier in gym class, but the particulars sounded so inconceivable to me that I had dismissed the talk almost immediately after hearing it. I was supposed to believe that after falling asleep, I would have a dream so spectacularly real and lifelike that my body would respond as if I was having sex? That's the way pudgy little Chris Lawrence described it—"you have sex in your dream and you shoot your stuff all over the place!" From what I could tell, most of my dreams up to then involved stickball games, baseball cards, and trips to Six Flags and Coney Island. They were never sexual—even though a few of them had been so real that I once remember being so convinced after a dream that I actually did own Dave Winfield's rookie card that I bragged about it to a few of my classmates. When one of them challenged me to present it, I was roundly embarrassed when a dozen trips through my entire collection failed to unearth it.

I climbed slowly out of bed, wondering how I was going to hide the soiled sheets from my mother. I hatched a plan to wash the sheets myself. But I had to make sure that my older brother Carney didn't see me doing it because it would arouse his suspicion. Carney's favorite pastime in the house, when not ignoring me, was looking for some reason to ridicule me. And he seldom failed to find something. Soiled sheets would be worth weeks of mockery from my idiotic brother. My main problem was that even if I could get the sheets in the washing machine before school, I wouldn't have time to dry them and return them to the bed. So I decided to hide them in my closet, behind the large pile of discarded old sneakers.

When I returned home from school later that day, Nina surprised me by inviting herself to my house. This wasn't unusual—she came to my house at least once or twice a week after school, but on this day my plan had been to avoid her. So shaken was I by the dream that I knew I'd feel uneasy in her presence. As we walked home, she detected my shyness but she misinterpreted it as anger.

"Are you mad at me, Aaron?"

I looked up at her in surprise. I shook my head vigorously.

"No, I'm not mad," I said.

"Yes, you are. We've been walking for almost ten minutes and you haven't said anything. You didn't even laugh when I imitated Mr. Felton. You always laugh when I imitate Mr. Felton." I saw the concern in her furrowed brow and I was touched that my mood could still have such a powerful impact on her. In fact, I was even surprised and somewhat giddy that Nina still treated me as her best friend. It was all about my insecurity—she never gave me any reason to think she felt differently about me than she did when we were seven years old and inseparable. But as I watched the world treat her like a star, I couldn't shake the inadequacy I had started to feel in her presence. I imagined it was similar to what happened to movie stars and musicians after they became famous: They didn't feel any differently about their old friends, but the friends certainly felt differently about their friendship—and closely watched for any tiny hint that the celebrity was downgrading them.

"Okay, do the Mr. Felton imitation again," I said. "I promise to laugh this time." Honestly, I had been concentrating so strongly on fighting away the memory of the wet dream that was trying to assert itself that I didn't even hear her Mr. Felton imitation.

"Okay, I'll do it once more," Nina said. "But only once."

She lifted up her shoulders in a decent approximation of Mr. Felton's turtle-in-his-shell posture. She thrust out her neck and let her bottom lip hang. The alteration of her beautiful face into Mr. Felton's added to the humor. It was the first time I realized that her beauty had something to do with my usual reaction.

"Now, Peter, you know God-darn well that six times twelve is not eighty-eight!" Nina said, nearly nailing the extra-fast cadence Mr. Felton used when he was upset. We both had Mr. Felton for math, but not at the same time. I opened my mouth and roared a little harder than normal to make up for my earlier goof. Nina grinned happily.

We were on our way to my room to listen to music and study when my mother stepped into the hallway to block my path.

"Aaron, what did you do with the sheets from your bed?" she asked accusatorily. She had her right hand on her hip, which was a clear signal that she was expecting something dubious to come out of my mouth. Somehow she had found me out; she knew! The import of the question made me feel queasy, maybe even a little faint. I felt a hotness on my leg and realized with horror that I had peed on myself, if just a little bit. Damn, what was wrong with me? I glanced over at Nina and saw that she was barely paying attention. Stupidly, my first thought had been that everyone would know what I had done that morning, but Nina's disinterest signaled that I was overreacting in a major way. I let out a soft breath and relaxed a little—enough to be able to finesse this mother encounter.

"Oh, did I forget to put them in the hamper? I'm sorry, Mom." I looked her in the eye, hoping she could sense my sincerity. "I spilled something on them this morning, I think it was milk, and I forgot to bring them to the washing machine."

Her eyes narrowed a bit. She didn't respond for a moment, like she was deciding whether there were several other layers of truth that she was missing. She had once told me, in a rare moment of candor, that the job of a parent with boys was trying to figure out how many layers beneath the boy's public statements did she have to dig before she got to the truth.

"Boy, how many times do I have to tell you not to eat in your room?" she said. But the reprimand sounded perfunctory in tone, missing the conviction to really sell it.

"Sorry, Mommy," I said. After enough hesitation to show my contrition, I slipped past her toward my room, with Nina close behind.

There's a reason why I went back and told you this story: One might think it would be ideal as an adult to ultimately wind up with the girl who starred in your first wet dream—but you'd be wrong. What it does is throw the whole carefully calibrated engine of an adult relationship out of whack. A true and mature adult relationship requires a certain freedom with our fantasy life, the realm of imagination. We need to be able to take trips of fancy anywhere our nasty little minds take us, whether it's with the woman on the subway, the secretary down the hall, or the first girl we ever had sexual fantasies about. How restricting on our imagination if that girl now happens to be our wife. Our past and our present all get mixed up in one big confusing mess. It'd be like having your wife work as your secretary, the star of all your porn tapes, and the headliner at your local strip club—all at the same time. That's what I had in Nina—the star of my first erotic fantasy, the real-life headliner in my sexual escapades in the here and now. I couldn't get away from this woman, even in the far reaches of my imagination. Now that our relationship had hit the rocks, this thought hovered over my head like an anvil in the *Road Runner* cartoon. All these links, these connections, these stories—it was all starting to feel about as comfortable to me as a coarse scratchy noose around my neck.

And let me say a word here about Nina's personality. More specifically, her loud, demanding, controlling way of dealing with the world. I should say dealing with *her* world—because she always acted like we were all just players in her world anyway. Having known her for virtually her entire life, I saw this egocentrism develop from its infancy and get fattened during those pubescent years I just spoke about like a lion cub feasting on fresh antelope meat. When you're as beautiful and magnetic as Nina was at age twelve, how can you not begin to have a warped sense of the world? And then add the nasty edge that living with Willy Andrews would bring and you have a fairly lethal brew.

As I've said before, I like peace. It's what I've known my whole life; it's what I seek in my relationships. During our friendship, Nina's toxic combustibility was entertaining as hell. I'd stand to the side and watch her aim her uncompromising directness at a pitiable sales clerk or waitress. And heaven forbid if this person decided to offer a view of the proper order of things that contradicted Nina's. There would be nasty zingers, pointed fingers, twisted necks, and eventually a choice curse word or two. It was comforting and even exciting to know that, even at her angriest, she would never direct her wrath at me, not really. I was her partner, meaning I had a special place inside the little cocoon that made up Nina's world.

But once she went from my best friend to my lover, her loud crudeness became a constant source of embarrassment and even humiliation for me. When it came to home training—how can I put this delicately?—Nina had some serious deficiencies. And I let her know about it probably too many times for our own good.

The low point for us came during an evening at one of our favorite restaurants—what was supposed to be a romantic night out for two young lovers. It was in February, about a month after I moved into her apartment. It was a Sunday night, so we didn't have to rush so I could run to the Honey Pot—which always managed to piss her off, no matter how much time she had had to get used to it. The restaurant, a popular seafood joint known for large, tasty servings at reasonable prices, was bulging with people. The hostess informed us that we probably would have to wait at least a half hour. I braced myself for thirty minutes of torture—Nina was not very good at waiting. This wasn't the most convenient character trait for a native New Yorker. As she usually did, she scanned every face in the waiting area to make sure she knew exactly who was here before us. When she was satisfied that she had the crowd memorized, she finally picked up the white wine that I had fetched for her. I tried to draw her into a conversation about her workweek, hoping it would distract her from monitoring the restaurant's comings and goings. It worked for a while, but about twenty-five minutes into our wait, the dam finally broke.

"Hold up!" Nina said loudly, rising up from the one stool we had been able to get at the bar. "Those people got here *waaay* after us!" She was pointing to a young white couple that was following the hostess to a table. The people in our vicinity, mostly young and white themselves, followed Nina's pointing finger. Almost all at once, they saw that a white couple was at the end of the point and, immediately understanding the sure racial implications of her sudden outrage, they all looked down at their shoes or away from the evolving scene.

But of course I didn't have that luxury. This was my girlfriend, and I was trapped.

"Are you sure, Nina?" I said, trying to lessen her ire. But that's not how she took my comment.

"What, you making excuses again for the white people?" she said to me, much too loudly. "Why can't you take my side for once, Aaron?"

I leaned toward her face, trying to demonstrate to her that this conversation could actually be held without the rest of the restaurant listening in. "Nina, that's ridiculous!" I said in a stage whisper. "I've been taking your side for twenty-five years."

"Maybe for twenty-four years—but for the past year you've been taking everybody's side *but* mine!" she said, still too loud. "I wonder what changed, Aaron?"

We both knew exactly what had changed. I felt my neck growing hot. But I had no answer for her when she got like this, brimming with the perfection of her outrage, unable to accept any competing notions. She looked away from me with a scowl.

"Well, I know one damn thing," she said, almost to herself. "It's past time for you to pick sides."

her

It wasn't really a good day. Not that anything happened, really. It's that nothing really happened. Aaron and I had gotten over the massive hump that was the Honey Pot (no pun intended), and finally had settled into our relationship. I think the key word here is *settled*. He was working at a comedy club on the Upper West Side. He was making pretty decent money (not as much as he made at the Honey Pot, but whatever). My job was going okay, now that my boss got the ax and they moved up another middle manager to take his place, a woman with a lot more experience and a much more even temper.

But Aaron and I had taken to coming home from work, cooking dinner, eating dinner, staring at the television without really talking much, then turning into bed and waking up the next day to start the routine all over again. The weekends weren't much better; we usually went to dinner, then caught a movie, then came home, stared at the television and then went to bed, and woke up the next day and—well, you get the idea. About every two to three days, we'd have sex. That was still good, but even that's becoming routine, too: oral sex, doggy style, missionary, climax, drink juice, pee, sleep.

My problem? It's not a problem really—just depressing. When we were friends, we used to have so much fun together, laughing,

finding eclectic things to do around the city, bonding with one another, flirting, and reveling in the sexual tension that we'd yet to act
on. Aaron my friend made me feel sexy and free, sure of myself,
cocky—even when things weren't working out with whatever boy I
happened to be messing with. "You are one sexy muthafucka," he'd
say to me often, particularly on the nights when I was dressed in a way
that warranted a little extra attention from my boy (shoot—I'd take it
where I could get it, since these trifling Negroes out here are so busy
pushing us women out of the mirror they can't fix their mouths to
give a pretty girl a compliment). There were some nights I'd put a little extra into what I was wearing—stilettos, curve-hugging skirts,
blouses buttoned for just the right amount of cleavage, even racy, lacy
underwear to encourage me to put a little twist in my hips while I was
stepping lively—just to see what Aaron would say. "Turn around and
let me see something," he'd say, playfully grabbing at my arm. I'd
shoo him off of me, but I could tell by the look in his eyes that he
really meant what he was saying; had that same look he got when we
were kids and I announced to him that I was "officially a woman."

"Huh?" he'd stammered, wondering what was about to come out
of my mouth. We were at his house, staring more at the television
than our homework notebooks, but our effort was evident enough to
keep his mom off our cases. I'd been itching all day to tell him about
how the night before, I'd gotten my period. His mom was far enough
out of earshot for me to give him some details. "Last night? Right before it was time for me to get in the bathtub? I got the most wicked
stomachache you could ever imagine! I mean, I was doubled over in
pain," I said, leaning in to him conspiratorially. He looked at me
wide-eyed, but didn't say anything. I continued: "I thought I had to
go to the bathroom, so I went to sit on the toilet, but when I pulled
my panties down, there was blood all over them!" I waited for him to
say something, but Aaron just kept right on staring. So I just kept
right on talking. "Remember in health class last year, when Mr. Abato
was talking about how girls, when they become women, they men-
struate? That's what it was: I got my period! I was going to scream be-

cause I was scared. But Shelly Parker and Sarah Mauro told me that when they got their periods, it wasn't a big deal, so I calmed down, well, a little, and called my mom into the bathroom and she just smiled and handed me a sanitary napkin. I was kinda waiting for a speech or something, but she didn't say anything about how if I have sex I could have a baby and stuff. I already knew it though, so it didn't really matter. It was kinda gross. But I'm officially a woman, and I can have babies and everything!"

I was just about to turn thirteen—a late bloomer by most standards. But I'd long had hips and breasts and other curves that made the boys—Aaron included—stare. Once, Aaron was staring at my breasts so hard I had to break his concentration by sticking them out and telling him to "take a picture, it'll last longer!" He didn't think that was all that funny. He turned a few shades of red and hurried away.

But when I told him my period story, I can't explain it—it's like he got a gleam in his eyes, a look I'd seen him give Michelle Richie (she had the biggest boobies in the entire seventh grade—you could even see them through thick sweaters!) when she passed. Had I not known my boy, I would have thought he was going to pounce on me and ravish my body. And for the first time in our long, innocent friendship, I didn't feel like we were so innocent anymore—that Aaron was looking at me in a sexual manner that was reserved for the upperclassmen and grown-ass men who often scared the bejesus out of me when they'd honk their horns and catcall out of their passenger-side windows. Except when Aaron did it, I wasn't scared. I was curious.

I can't say that Aaron's stare, or the feelings that I got from them, ever really changed. We'd had an almost silent agreement that sort of went, like, I dress up really sexy and fish for compliments, and you give them to me and make me feel hot, and we'll both give each other the attention we need so that we'll both always feel like the sexiest muthafuckas alive. And every now and then, we'd actually call each other that out loud.

But now that we were together, it was like we weren't even honoring that agreement anymore. I got the feeling that I could be standing in the most expensive, revealing, sexy La Perla bra and panty set imaginable, and I'd get the same treatment as if I were standing in front of him with my terry cloth robe. It's a nice robe. Just not sexy. Now, most nights, I felt like he'd hit it any ol' way he got it—it didn't matter what I looked like, he just wanted to get some, then move on. That's a clear violation of clause Number 1 in the agreement: Thou shalt make your girlfriend feel like a sexy muthafucka.

Desperate to snap out of the routine (surely, he felt it, too, because he did this without any nudging from me), Aaron suggested we take a trip to Jamaica. It would be the first trip we'd take since consummating our new relationship. "Let's just get away," he insisted. "You're tired, I'm tired, we both need a break." He was right. So we scraped our little cash together, made reservations and, three weeks later, we were laying up in Villa Olga, a beautiful private villa in Montego Bay that came with a cook, a butler, a cleaning staff, and access to an exclusive private beach far, far away from the tacky tourists who drank one too many Red Stripes and Guinness Stouts and Sex on the Beaches, and embarrassed the rest of us sensible, gracious Americans. So excited were we to be spending time with one another away from the hustle and bustle of the city, our jobs, all the things that surely contributed to early onset of gray hair and eye wrinkles, that we were practically boning before we boarded the plane. But we saved it for when we touched down in Montego Bay.

"Welcome to Jamaica," our driver boomed as we walked up to him. He tucked his sign bearing the villa's name under his arm and grabbed our bags just as another man, this one in an airport uniform, made a bold dash for them. "No no!" he yelled at him. "I have this!" He then turned his attention to us, and explained that he would be our personal escort for the rest of our trip, courtesy of the villa. "Wherever you want to go, just call on Henry. I'll be there," he said, slamming the trunk to his van and dashing to the driver's side. "Will you be going to the beach today?" he asked, peering through his rearview mirror as he carefully pulled out of his parking spot. Aaron had his hand on my thigh—my upper thigh, practically under my skirt. I squirmed a little—partly because he was making me wet, partly because I was afraid that Henry would see that I was flush.

"No, we're going straight to the villa for some much-needed relaxation," Aaron said to Henry. But Aaron was staring at me. "We'll do the beach tomorrow."

Well, needless to say, we didn't get around to doing much of anything for the first two days, except each other. We'd emerge from our spare but tastefully decorated suite long enough to eat meals, catch a few rays while flipping through magazines by the pool, and eat the meals prepared by the staff (oh—a word about them: When we'd booked the place, I thought it would be cool to have a staff there to wait on us hand and foot, but nothing could be further from the case. Our unease with one another was palpable; the cook, who was supposed to know how to cook the country's best dishes, didn't at all seem comfortable serving us anything other than typical American foods—pork chops, fried chicken, spaghetti and meatballs—until we begged her one night to cook us some curried goat and stew peas. We were, all at once, elevated from the screwy, tasteless Americans who didn't appreciate the beauty of Jamaica, into old friends on which she could try out new dishes. We ate good after that. The morning that I begged the butler to stop changing into his uniform and join us for our breakfast of *bami* and codfish and ackee, instead of serving it to us, we didn't see much of him anymore. But that was all well and good, because I didn't feel comfortable with a grown black man shuffling to the table to serve me anyway) and then head back into the room for some more mind-blowing sex. So amorous were we that we didn't even care if the staff heard us boning. We'd even both romped carefree out onto the pool deck after dark to screw under the stars, mosquitos be damned. We spent the next day nursing our bites, drinking, and watching the beautiful, clear water lick the beach's white sands. A few times, while I stared at the ocean and the sky and watched the fish dance in the tide, Aaron wandered off with his camera, pointing his lens at everything in sight—the band, the waitresses, the boatmen, with their locks mingling with the water that sprayed from the engines of their rickety charges. In fact, he took that camera everywhere we went, and even requested a special trip of Henry up into the mountains of Jamaica to "see his country" with his camera. It was, indeed, a sight to behold—these beautiful people, who looked just like us, living in squalor but amidst some of the most breathtaking sights imaginable. Henry delighted in showing us the orange fields that rolled over the hills as far as the eye could see, and the tiny stands where one could get anything from a paper bag–full of fish to the most elaborate hand-carved wooden sculptures one could lay her eyes on. There were fishermen, catching crabs as big as our heads and cooking them in rudimentary stoves buried in the sand, and goats wandering the streets like strays in a neighborhood of an errant dogcatcher. Aaron delighted in watching it all through his camera—would make Henry screech over to the side of the road every few miles and just disappear with his Pentax, taking it all in.

That night, we went to a nightclub and took turns laughing at the white folks who were trying to keep up with us as we danced to all the American rap songs that'd found their way into the Jamaican dj booth, and marveling at the Jamaican women who moved all that ass they were carrying with such rhythm that even I felt like I didn't have any serious moves. When the wack-ass electric slide came on, Aaron instinctively knew to lead me off the dance floor, order me a Melon Ball, and find us a cozy seat to enjoy our drinks while we watched the white folks bold enough to take on the national black line dance trip over their feet.

"You know, I remember that you were into photography when we were in school, but when did you become so passionate about it?" I asked. I felt the Melon Ball kicking into my system, and made a mental note to order another one, fast, because I liked the way it felt. "I mean, is there anywhere you don't go with that camera?"

Aaron laughed. "Nah, not really. It's funny, but I can remember being really little and always wanting my dad to let me take pictures.

I never wanted to be in them, but I thought it was so cool to look through the lens and see people's moods change the moment you told them to say *cheese*. Usually, it didn't matter how mad they were, or sad, or whatever, they'd always have a smile for the camera. Thing was, even if you thought they were smiling, you could always tell someone's true feelings when you got the prints back. The smiles said something different in each one of them—I'm sad, I'm mad, I wanna fight. I don't know, I guess it's my way of reading into people. There's so much more to see in a picture than you could ever imagine. There's stories there. I love telling the stories."

When we got home, Aaron didn't waste any time developing his film—he got the prints back, and sat down at the dining room table like a kid on Christmas, about to unwrap his presents from Santa. But it was I who was moved even more than he; there was majesty in his pieces—sweeping landscapes and desolate shacks, women with desperate looks, begging passersby to buy their wares, and children, barefoot, clothes tattered, playing amidst ruins as if they hadn't a care in the world. One picture, of a mother hugging her child from behind, he crying, she looking off beyond his little head—at what, I don't know—actually moved me to tears. And all at once, I looked at Aaron—specifically, his passion for his art—in a whole new light. He was talented, for sure, and he needed to have his craft nurtured in a way that I, his girlfriend, had neglected to embrace.

Until just then. And in that moment, I became much more like the white French ladies in the fifties and sixties who took care of the black jazz musicians, feeding and mothering them because they were awed by their talent. I'd taken on the spirit of the little French man in the movie *Round Midnight*, who does everything for Dexter Gordon and explains, "I just think the best saxophone player in the world should be happy and have food to eat."

"You know what," I said, carefully placing down his pictures and staring at him. He didn't respond; he was too busy admiring his work. I paid his inattention little mind; I had to tell him what was on my heart. "You don't have to do the bartending thing anymore. You need to concentrate on your passion."

He looked up, his eyes quizzical, almost as if he were trying to process what I'd just said.

"What do you mean, 'I don't have to do the bartending thing'?" he asked. "You mean quit my job?"

"Yes. I mean quit your job. How else is my man going to become an award-winning photographer? You can't be mixing drinks with a camera in your hands."

"Baby, are you serious?" he said, his smile widening.

"Yeah, I'm serious," I said, though, inside, I wasn't so sure I hadn't spoken too fast. I mean, what was I signing myself up for here? In essence, I was telling Aaron—my best friend—that I would support him while he pursued his dream. Yeah. I did.

"I don't know about that, Nina—we got bills and rent and . . ."

"Come on, baby. We can save up over the next few months so that we'll have a little cushion, and if you're doing your photography thing full time, you'll get money for your work anyway. What have you got to lose?"

He grinned. And then there was that gleam in his eye again—just like when we were in Jamaica. You know what happened next. And there wasn't a single thing routine about it.

Nina and Aaron,
Part VI

A aron reached out to take the box and the plastic stick away from Nina, but he was so distracted by the sadness in her eyes that he wasn't paying attention to where his right hand was going. His finger hit the stick and knocked it out of her hand—and straight into the garbage can. They both looked down in horror, aghast at the implications. Nina put her left hand over her mouth. Aaron wiped sweat from his forehead.

"Damn!" he said, mostly to himself. He reached toward the can, prepared to dig, but she interrupted him.

"It was supposed to stay flat!" she said, her voice rising to an alarming pitch—either tears or a nervous breakdown were on her heels. "Now we have to start all over again!"

Aaron watched her slowly reach back into the box and pull out the second stick. Her hands were shaking. He was glad his were now safely at his sides.

"I need another glass of water to do this," she said. She sounded weak, resigned. "And probably another twenty minutes."

him

Lest you get the impression that my early life with Nina was one endless string of days and nights with us attached at the hip, I should tell you that things changed for us when we got to high school. In good ways and in bad ways too. It was inevitable that the dawning of puberty would start to create some separation. Separation was certainly helpful for my male ego, to step out from Nina's considerable shadow and sprout in the rays that I didn't even realize had long been denied me. For an adolescent boy, those rays of course come in the form of attentions from the opposite sex. When I moved through the corridors as Nina's twin, any girl inclined to pay me extra mind had to think about it long and hard. Did she want to risk an entanglement with the queen bee, the cockiest, coolest, sexiest girl in the entire school? Very few girls were secure enough to take the chance that Nina might be bothered if they stepped to me, so they all stayed away. Dumbfounded, devastated, but also perhaps a bit flattered, I learned about this whole dynamic about halfway through our freshman year from a girl who worked up the courage to move closer to me.

Her name was Stacy German. I had known her since third grade and generally had good thoughts about her, if not overwhelming ones. She was cute in a bubbly pixieish sort of way, like Janet on

Three's Company, a show to which Nina and I had long been obsessive devotees. It wasn't even apparent to me what was occurring between me and Stacy until Nina pointed it out to me one day during a chilly walk home. I had started to stay after school for the photography club and Nina was trying out for the school's dance club, so we seldom had a chance to walk home together anymore. But the dance club tryouts were now over and my photography club was taking a little hiatus while the school was doing repair work in our darkroom.

"I still can't believe they didn't pick you," I said to her, shaking my head to demonstrate my disbelief. "Those girls must be incredibly stupid."

Nina shook her head and grimaced. "No, they are incredibly jealous is what they are," she said. "I can dance better than everybody on that team except maybe two other girls. But the decisions were made by these two ugly trifling little seniors who were threatened by me."

I looked at her, blinking. Even though I saw evidence of it on a regular basis, I was always startled by Nina's extreme confidence. One might want to call it arrogance or conceit, but she carried it with enough grace that to an outsider it just looked like strong self-belief. She noticed my expression.

"I'm not trying to be conceited—all the other girls told me that. They even told me that before the decisions were even made. Marisol said that they were jealous of me and probably would keep me off the squad. She said the same thing happened to her when she was a freshman. There was a senior captain who was jealous of her too. But they have tryouts again in the spring. Those are conducted by the juniors who will be taking over when the seniors graduate. Marisol will probably be a captain, so she told me to try out again. Then I get to dance at the football games next year."

I nodded happily. I had seen the dance squad at a couple of the football games and I would not mind seeing Nina in the tight little spandex outfits they wore. They made the cheerleaders look like nuns. Our school, Middle Borough High School, was lucky to have a dance squad. Not many high schools in New York City had such squads—Jamaica High School, the other high school in our area and our archrival, certainly didn't have one.

"So what's up with you and Stacy German?" Nina asked in a stunningly abrupt change of the subject.

"Huh?" I said.

"Don't play dumb with me, Aaron. Y'all been spending a whole lot of time together lately. Seems like whenever I see you, she's always somewhere close by, like your own little puppy dog." She giggled at her little crack at Stacy's expense. "I'm just playing. She's cute."

I was about to object, to tell her she was way off-base, but something held me back. Stacy in fact did seem to often find me, to make a point of being in my presence as much as possible. She had even joined the photography club a few weeks back. Up to that point I hadn't made anything of it; I was still far too young to possess any interpretative skills when it came to females—not that the years have brought any improvement in my skills. But it wasn't until Nina's observation that I even did the math.

"We're just friends," I said, waving my hand in dismissal. But in my head, I was staring at Stacy's comely heart-shaped face, flicking my gaze over her big soft eyes as they followed my every move. Yes, she *was* cute, wasn't she? And she did seem to like me. Why the hell hadn't I figured that out on my own? And how could I put this information to good use?

A few days later, Stacy and I found ourselves squatting together under a tree outside the school, our cameras trained on a squirrel inspecting a potato chip wrapper. We both clicked simultaneously; the sound of the shutter caused the nervous animal to leap in the air and scurry away.

"Damn, I need a quieter camera," I said.

"How much do they cost?" Stacy asked.

I shrugged. "I don't know. I think Nina's dad has one. Maybe I'll see if I can borrow his."

At the mention of Nina's name, I saw a shadow pass over Stacy's face. Her shoulders even appeared to tense. What was that all about? I didn't dare ask.

"Do you ever get through the day without thinking about Nina?" Stacy said, her voice noticeably shaking. Turns out I didn't have to ask.

"Huh? Of course I do, Stacy—what's *that* supposed to mean?"

"Well, sometimes it seems like you two are attached at the hip," she said, without looking at me. "It's always seemed that way. I know a few girls who even liked you but were scared to say anything to you or approach you because they were, uh, intimidated by Nina."

I had no idea what to do with that. Nina had been scaring the girls away from me? So my love life could have improved by a couple of magnitudes if not for my friend's scary presence? That was a thought that brought me a pleasant shiver—but also a shred of worry. It was flattering to think that there was more interest in me out there than I ever suspected, but I would have to ditch my best friend to take advantage? That couldn't happen—could it?

"Girls like who?" I asked.

Stacy still avoided my gaze. She shrugged. "Like, um, that girl Teresa Matthews from middle school."

I flashed on the image of a chubby girl with glasses who now went to Jamaica High School. Was that the best she could do?

"*Ooookay,*" I said, signaling that I was less than impressed. "Teresa Matthews, huh? Anybody else?"

Stacy shrugged again, still looking away. "There were a few others, Aaron." She looked through her camera, pretending to focus on the potato chip wrapper.

I took a deep breath. "How about Stacy German?"

For a long second she didn't move, hidden behind her camera. Finally she lowered it and turned to me. She stared, her expression a mixture of fear and tenderness. I wouldn't have thought it was possible for one look to transform a relationship, but I felt my stomach flip and my heart triple its pace and I knew that something had just happened between us. I reached out an unsteady hand toward her, not

really sure what I expected her to do with that hand but hoping she
might have some ideas. Stacy took a step toward me. She put her soft,
small hand inside mine. I wanted to bend down and kiss her on those
perfect little lips, but I needed some type of signal from her that it
would be all right. She reached up with her other hand and slowly
moved it across my cheek. That was surely my signal. I moved my lips
toward her slowly, giving her plenty of time to reciprocate the approach. She did, meeting me halfway in the softest, sweetest kiss that
I had ever had up until that point. A strong tingle raced up and down
my spine, weakening my knees just a bit. We held the kiss for several
long juicy seconds, neither one of us wanting to be the one to break
it off, to let it go. I opened my eyes and saw a few classmates watching us and pointing. Embarrassed, I pulled away a little too abruptly.
Stacy appeared startled and a little hurt.

"I'm sorry," I said. "We got an audience over there." I gestured
with my chin. Stacy turned around and saw the grinning faces of a few
classmates, none of them familiar to me, standing near the school
building about fifty feet away.

"I know one of those guys," she whispered. "He's in my algebra
class, even though he's not even a freshman. He's an asshole."

I nodded. That much was clear—I mean, how unusual was it to
see a couple kissing on the grounds of a high school? I saw it practically every day, and not once did it ever cross my mind to stop whatever I was doing and start laughing and pointing. I won't deny that
the sight sometimes got me excited and maybe even a little jealous.
But no more. Now I was one of the kissers.

That kiss was the beginning of my first semi-serious romantic relationship. Stacy and I spent many after-school hours engaged in lip-
lock in various hidden corners of the school, our cameras quickly put
aside so that we could explore the depths of this newfound adolescent
passion. Once you start down that path, very soon you start encoun-
tering signposts, points on the road where you must decide how close
you're going to get to actual intercourse. After a few weeks of just
kissing, Stacy let me slip my hand inside of her bra and stroke her

breast and nipple. The feeling of her soft velvety bare skin and her hard pebbly nipple against my fingers transported me to another level of arousal. For a minute I thought I was actually going to ejaculate in my drawers, I was so excited. I forced myself to calm down by focusing on the pungent smell of cleaning products and dirty mops inside the janitor's closet where we were tucked away. I could feel my erection start softening—until Stacy reached her own hand down and slowly pressed it against my crotch. That was a first for her. I drew in my breath sharply, almost letting out an audible moan. The idea that my new girlfriend was now bringing our intimacy to new heights through her own initiative electrified me. I desperately wanted to reach my own hand down and open the zipper for her, but I was still too afraid of scaring her away to make such a bold gesture. The escalation of contact during these adolescent make-out sessions was a delicate operation, fraught with the risk of moving too fast and having the whole thing blow up in your face. I was learning that I had to earn increasingly larger sums of trust in order to gain access to another door, to convince Stacy that I loved her and respected her and had more important things on my mind than a feel of her breasts. One of my most exhilarating discoveries was that, though her jeans and skirts and pants looked exceedingly tight, I could actually slide my hands down her back and then underneath her clothing without any objections from her. She would even let the hands move beneath her panties, giving me total access to her booty, which I could squeeze and caress and stroke for long minutes at a time without her protest. After three or four extended booty-stroking sessions, I felt that I had earned the right to move up to a greater level of intimacy. I tried to slowly slide my right hand around from her backside to her front, all the while keeping it under her panties. But I hadn't cleared the hip before she grabbed my hand and yanked it out of her pants.

"No, Aaron," she said, looking up at me and then quickly averting her eyes in embarrassment. But I was the one who felt the true shame, for getting slapped back, for being told I hadn't earned entry yet to that sacred ground.

"Sorry," I mumbled. Though I tried to pull her back to me, the sexual energy was gone—I had chased it out of the storage closet with my eager grubby paws.

But a week later, inside the same closet, Stacy took my breath away when she grabbed my hand, which had been squeezing her booty inside the panties, and dragged it around to the front. Led by her bold direction, I had skipped over the hip and hopped into the warm and mysterious region that had become the focus of my latest obsession. I had found a copy of a human biology book in the library and, casting my eyes warily about me to make sure I had no witnesses, dove into the clinical but fascinating discussion of the female vagina and its attendant parts. I can remember staring at the diagram, trying to commit it to memory but experiencing deep frustration because the book told me not a word about how a woman would feel if I happened to stroke each of the many parts with a curious finger. I had a thousand questions that were still unanswered—the only person I could think of to approach for information was Nina. But the thought of that conversation—even the question of how I would phrase my initial query—paralyzed me into inaction.

My fingers moved as slowly as I could manage, opening, probing, wondering exactly where I was in relation to the map that I had memorized. Once I struggled through Stacy's pubic hair, I felt warmth and moistness, but I had no idea where anything was. So I softly stroked everything in my path, closely listening for any change in Stacy's labored, terrified breathing. After about thirty of the most intense seconds I had ever survived, I touched something that felt knobby and harder than everything else. Stacy gasped and nearly punctured my left arm with her grasping fingernails. Her breathing quickened considerably, grew a bit ragged and uneven. I knew I was on to something here—it must be the clitoris. The one fact that had come through loudly in examining the biology book was that most of a woman's sexual pleasure was connected to the clitoris. It appeared to be buried beneath lots of flaps and folds in the diagram, which elevated its importance in my mind. It was so special a part of the woman that it deserved its own special place. You get there and you get special rewards. That's the way I looked at it. Dudes were just so much simpler in every way. Nothing hidden on us.

"Oh God, Aaron!" Stacy whispered sharply in my ear. Her voice sounded different than I'd ever heard it—there was a reckless quality to it, like she had let down her guard a bit.

I touched the knobby protrusion tenderly, running my finger back and forth over its soggy squishiness. Stacy clutched me even tighter, her claws hurting my arm and back—but I wouldn't have protested if she had been tearing off a layer of skin. The only sound in the room was the drip of the faucet in the large slop sink and Stacy's breaths, which had now become moans. I felt my own erection straining against my crotch and I wondered if a guy had ever had an orgasm from the excitement of fingering his girlfriend. I wasn't even sure that I was still taking breaths—so hard was my concentration on the three longest fingers of my right hand. I don't think it had even crossed my mind at that point that the denouement of this fingering might be an orgasm for Stacy. I was aware of the connection between the clitoris and the female orgasm, but I thought somehow rose petals and silk sheets and Luther Vandross's sweet voice had to be employed to bring about such a treat.

"Aaron, oh Gooooddd!" Stacy moaned into my chest as she pressed her mouth against me. I heard a high-pitched squeal that seemed to come out of the top of her head. Her body tensed up, her shoulders and arms and fingers grew taut. Stacy was actually having an orgasm. As she slowly came back down to Earth, a huge grin spread across her face. Next to my first Little League home run, it was my proudest moment up to that point. When Stacy finally pulled her face away from my chest, she smiled weakly up at me, her eyes distant and dreamy. Right away, my next thought was of my penis—I wondered whether I could convince her to return the favor?

The rest of that day is a bit hazy in my memory, but I do have one vivid recollection: About three or four hours later, as I sat in my family's living room staring absently at the television, I wasn't even aware of my mother's suspicious eyes trained on me until I heard my name, which came out of her mouth like a vicious bark.

"Aaron!"

I jumped and looked up, seeing her for the first time. Her tone brought Carney out of the kitchen to investigate.

"What is wrong with your fingers, boy? You been sniffing on them for the past twenty minutes."

Thanks to Nina, the fingering session in the closet turned out to be the highlight of my relationship with Stacy German. Things turned one weekend afternoon, when Nina wandered over to my house after spotting me on the front stoop. She wore a sly grin on her face, which signaled to me that something unpleasant was about to happen at my expense. It was late March and winter had finally been banished, the sun stretching its legs after months of frigid temperatures and spreading a warmth through the air, sending most of my block out of their houses to verify the apparent seasonal change.

Nina wore just a long-sleeve T-shirt and very snug jeans. Her jeans had grown increasingly tighter over the past few months—a subject that had led to many boisterous verbal skirmishes with her mom. I connected the fit of her new wardrobe to the attentions she had started to receive from the more celebrated members of our student body—the football and basketball teams. But I hadn't had the nerve to share that observation with her. Besides, I was too busy stalking our school grounds looking for new hidden corners to make out with Stacy.

"Sooooo, Aaron," Nina said, plopping herself down next to me on the stoop. I watched her carefully, not comfortable with that all-too-familiar grin. "You and Stacy *do* it yet?"

I held back the gasp that almost spilled forth. Nina was trying to incite a reaction like that. She looked at my face intently, no doubt hoping to see the payoff from antagonizing me. I refused to give her one. In all the years Nina and I have been together, the middle school and early high school years were by far the most awkward between us.

But then again, kids at that age were awkward with everybody—even themselves.

"No, Nina—not that it's any of your business," I said, forcing out a laugh. I knew it probably sounded forced, too. But it was infinitely better than a dramatic gasp.

"What y'all waiting for?" she asked. "You scared?"

I repeated to myself again and again to remain calm, to not give her the overreaction she was looking for. Nina was a pro at agitation. I had proved myself to be a pathetic amateur at resisting.

"Why do we need a reason, Nina?" I shot back. "Have *you* done it yet?"

"I'm not the one sneaking around the school all day long, making out all over the place. Y'all acting like you'll die if you go a whole day without sucking face." There was just a tinge of nastiness to her voice, an edge that I hadn't detected at first. I looked at her more closely, wondering if she realized that she was sounding a little upset—jealous even. She saw that my gaze had changed, had locked in a bit more. So she looked away from me. Perhaps she had realized how she sounded. I was tempted to ask her if she was jealous, but such confrontations rarely worked with Nina. She'd just find a way to turn it around and make me feel silly.

"And if you must have an answer—it's NO! I *haven't* done it yet." She said that last sentence with a saucy twist of the neck. This was the kind of conversation that got playacted in high school sex-education classes across the country, illustrating to the impressionable youth how to rebuff negative peer pressure. At this point, the earnest instructor would have stopped the actors and bored the class with a lecture on why it's okay to admit to your friends that you don't want to have sex, or even that you're scared.

But only three weeks later, Nina and I had a reprise of the sex conversation. Only this time her tone was much different—she was on the verge of tears. She had tracked me down as I walked home from school with Stacy, who lived a couple of blocks away from us in a section of Jamaica that we had long been told to avoid by our parents. Stacy's neighborhood was technically in South Jamaica, though the more upwardly mobile residents in the southern section tried to avoid using the "south" tag. Stacy was one of those residents.

"Hey, guys!"

Nina's voice came from behind us. She sounded out of breath, like she had been running. As Stacy and I turned around, I saw Stacy roll her eyes. She was not a big Nina fan. But as soon as I caught the obvious distress on Nina's face, I immediately forgot about Stacy's eye roll. Something was wrong with my friend.

"Nina! What happened?" I asked, instinctively reaching out a hand toward her. She took the hand and pressed it against her cheek. It was an impulsive gesture, and it touched me deeply. I was conscious of how troubling this would look to Stacy, but I figured I would have time to make it up later. We were on a main street, in front of a row of businesses, with cars and pedestrians streaming by. Nina stepped toward me and rested her head on my chest. I don't even think she glanced at Stacy once.

"Aaron, I need to talk to you," she said in a hushed, secretive voice. Her face was buried in my down jacket so that Stacy couldn't hear her. I looked over at Stacy just to make sure. She shot me back an icy glare that startled me with its venom. Whoa, I was going to have some serious making up to do later. But it was Nina who worried me more than Stacy's jealousy. It had been years since Nina had sought me out like this when she needed consoling. This had been my regular role during our childhood years, usually when she was distraught over the crazy drama that regularly raged in her household. But as we grew up and slightly apart, Nina seemed to need me much less. Well, Nina didn't in fact seem to need anybody—so I guessed I shouldn't feel too bad.

"Tell me what happened," I said softly to her, hoping my voice was soothing.

She buried her face even further in my jacket. "I can't talk in front of her," Nina said. Her voice was muffled, but I heard her as loudly as if she had shouted in my ear. She was forcing me to ditch my girlfriend, playing the ultimate friend gambit—and knowing she would win.

"Get rid of her." Nina said this a bit louder—loud enough for Stacy to hear. Surely she did that on purpose.

Stacy wore a stunned expression, as if she couldn't believe Nina's nerve. She looked up at me questioningly, no doubt waiting for me to tell Nina that Stacy wasn't going anywhere. But Nina's pull over me was too strong, like the moon tugging at the tide. I was powerless to resist a decade of coexistence, of our two lives at times being lived as if it was the same one.

"Uh, Stacy, can you give us a minute?" I asked softly, hopefully. I prayed that she'd extend to me just a tiny bit of understanding, to see that I couldn't very well turn my back on my friend, even if she was making an unreasonable demand.

Stacy sucked her teeth loudly, provocatively. "Aaron, you know what? I can give you more than a fuckin' minute—a whole lot more. I've had enough of her. If that's the way it's gonna be, then you can keep that bitch!" She turned on her heels and stomped away. Stacy was not a big scene-chewer, not fond of drama, so I knew it must have taken a monumental dose of rage to inspire her to present her little speech.

Nina pulled her head back from my coat long enough to watch Stacy march away. Satisfied, she rested on my chest again, then she started talking, softly at first.

"I was with Boobie, who kinda had asked me to be his girlfriend last week. So we were making out and stuff, in that janitor's closet in the basement that I saw you in one time with Stacy. That's how I knew about it. But Boobie starts trying to take my clothes off. I didn't want him to, I just wanted to kiss. But he wouldn't stop."

Her voice grew thick; I could tell she was on the verge of tears again. "It's okay," I said. "Take a deep breath." I took both of my arms and wrapped them around Nina, enveloping her in a bear hug that she seemed to appreciate, judging by the tender way she looked up at me. I saw the manager of the grocery store eyeing us. His store was a frequent hangout for the high school students and was often the launching pad for scurrilous school gossip.

"He started opening my pants and trying to pull them down," she continued. "Luckily I was wearing these tight jeans and he was having a hard time." I shook my head—how ironic that her fashion rebellion that so incited her mom had protected her.

"What a fuckin' asshole—those guys think they can do anything they want and get away with it!" I growled, getting increasingly agitated. This was an important moment for me. It was clear to me that Nina expected me to do something on her behalf—otherwise she wouldn't have come running to me.

"What should I do, Aaron?"

Her question, spoken at a near whisper, sat out there like a big flashing neon sign, like the ones on the New Jersey Turnpike that told you to slow down because there was an accident up ahead. She was placing the resolution of this potentially catastrophic situation in my hands, essentially giving me the license to possibly snatch Boobie's future away from him in an instant. If she told the school authorities, there would be hell for him to pay—but also for Nina, too. Her hell would start at home with her parents and follow her all the way to school, leering at her every time a student glanced in her direction and whispered to a friend or pointed at her. I had seen enough after-school specials and reports on the evening news to know that it was almost a societal cliché for prominent athletes to be accused of rape or sexual assault. But because it was so commonplace, there wouldn't be many who would doubt its veracity. Nina *was* beautiful and mature and poised beyond her years, but she was still a high school freshman who had been trapped in the clutches of an eighteen-year-old junior—I had picked up Boobie's age by reading the *Daily News* sports pages. No, I didn't think the official report was the right move for Nina. And as quickly as I rejected that one, another idea started to bloom, one that was almost insane and suicidal in its implications—but perhaps for that very reason, because it was so far out of my character, it had a certain appeal to me. It was almost Shakespearean in its melodrama; it would forever cement my bond with Nina.

"I got an idea," I said excitedly. Nina heard my excitement—she drew back to look up at my face. I could see the anticipation in her eyes.

"I'm going to confront him and tell him to leave you the fuck alone."

Nina's eyes widened. She peered at me more closely, perhaps to assess whether I still had all my faculties. I imagine that this wasn't an easy moment for her—she had to convey to me the ridiculousness of the idea without totally mocking my emerging manhood, my toughness.

"Aaron, are you crazy? Boobie will kill you!"

Well, maybe the moment wasn't as difficult for her as I thought.

I grinned. "Why do you say that, Nina? Just because he's about eight inches and sixty pounds bigger than me?"

I had sprouted several inches between seventh and ninth grades; I was hovering somewhere near six feet now. I was still a bit thin, about 165 pounds, but I was trying desperately to pack on more weight, which I had decided a few weeks before that I'd transform into muscle with a strict weight-lifting regimen. We already had the weights in the house, left over from Carney's ill-fated plan to join the football team. He got hit during tryouts so hard that he suffered a concussion—and then he suffered even more when he got cut from the squad.

Nina shook her head. "You know I'm not trying to hurt your feelings, Aaron, but you can't be serious. Why don't we just tell the principal or something?"

I noticed how she had used the first-person plural, indicating that we were in this trial together. I wasn't sure how she would accept my argument, if she might consider it a bit insensitive, but I plunged forward anyway.

"Because if you tell the principal, Boobie will get kicked off the basketball team, maybe even arrested, and everybody in the school will despise you forever," I said, hoping it sounded at least a bit gentle. She stared at me, looking deeply into my eyes, but she didn't react right away. I was relieved that she didn't gouge out my eyeballs.

"Why should I care what happens to Boobie, after what he did to me?" But I could tell that she was only saying that because she felt she must. There was little conviction behind the words. I waited, silently, for her to go on.

"You think he could get arrested?"

I nodded. "You're only fourteen. He's eighteen. He'd be arrested."

She stared at me some more. Then she looked away.

"Damn," she said softly. It occurred to me that maybe she needed to report him anyway, despite what it would do to her standing in the school, in order to keep her sanity.

"But if you want to go ahead and report him, Nina, I'll be right there with you." I squeezed her a little harder to show that I meant it. We were being watched by more than the grocery store manager now. Several streams of students had walked by, eyeing us suspiciously. A few of them looked familiar, but nobody spoke to us.

"I don't know, Aaron. I need to think about it. I don't know what to do."

It never occurred to either of us at the time to bring in an adult, to get another opinion. We were going to handle this on our own because that's what we had always done, the two of us, making sense of the world as a team.

I avoided Stacy the next day, staying away from the lunchroom during sixth period, not just because I didn't want to talk to her, but also because I didn't want her to know about the bold and insane move I was planning. But I did want Nina to know. I tracked her down after the lunch period was over. She was headed toward English class.

"Nina, be at the front of the gym at three thirty today," I said to her as soon as I approached.

"Huh? The gym? Aaron, what are you going to do?"

I placed my right index finger over her lips to hush her. "Don't worry, just be there." I started to walk away.

"Aaron!" she called after me. "What are you going to do?"

I had stayed up most of the night, running through scenarios, ways that I could embarrass Boobie, get revenge for Nina, and not get hospitalized in the process. I failed to think of anything that would accomplish the first two and still insulate me from harm. So I concluded that I would have to face the probability that I'd get my ass kicked. The worst thing that could happen to me? Pain. That was really it. Once I accepted that there would be pain, like a visit to the dentist or a nurse taking blood samples, I could calmly step right past the terrifying visions that were haunting me. Years later when I rented the Brad Pitt/Ed Norton movie *Fight Club*, about a group of men who are transformed by the bloody brawls they secretly participated in, I was taken back to the calculations I made that night, when I vowed to conquer the fear of physical harm that handcuffed so many males and crept into so many aspects of their personalities, often keeping them from becoming the bold, confident, successful people they could be.

The basketball team usually gathered outside the gym at about 3:20, lingering before they went inside to practice. Because they seemed to draw students wherever they went as if they had their own mobile fan club, I knew there'd be plenty of cheerleaders, dance team members, student government types, and several other movers and shakers from the school somewhere in the vicinity of the gym at 3:30. This was the time and place if I was going to do something memorable and I wanted the whole school to know about it—the news would have swept the hallways by the following morning.

As I approached the gym, I saw most of everything I wanted to see: the basketball players, including Boobie's tall, hunched frame, and a crowd of other students. But I didn't see Nina. This gamble would have only a fraction of the desired impact without Nina's presence. Not only did I want her to see me in action, but I needed her as a visual prop. I moved to within thirty feet of the group and paused, partly to collect my nerve, mostly to see if I would be joined by Nina.

"Aaron!"

The shaky voice came from behind me, unmistakably Nina's. And clearly frightened. She was partially hidden by one of the school buildings, standing with her arms folded like she had been waiting for me. I knew she was expecting me to rush to her, but I didn't want to give her any chance to make a last-second appeal. I headed toward the throng of students.

"Aaron! Where are you going?" I heard her say behind me. I could hear her footsteps. She was following me, as I knew she would. With Nina at my heels, I walked through several small bunches of loitering students. I had a purpose to my step and I was heading straight toward Boobie. A few of the students noticed my curious gait, along with the beautiful girl at my heels, and they followed me, too, albeit much slower than Nina. Finally I reached Boobie and stood motionless in front of him, trying to remain calm as my heart expanded and threatened to push up through my throat. Boobie was sharing a joke with his buddies, his shoulders shaking from the laughter. His back was to me, but he noticed that his teammates had stopped laughing. Slowly he pivoted. This was the moment I had been passing through my mind for the past twenty-four hours, ever since I held Nina on that busy sidewalk the previous afternoon. Officially, it was now too late to back down.

Boobie looked down at me quizzically, a half-smile on his face. Of course he would expect that this was about anything but a physical challenge. Six-foot-seven basketball players rarely got physical challenges. His eyes scanned the people behind me—suddenly his brow furrowed. He must have caught sight of Nina.

"What *you* want, boy?" Boobie said contemptuously. The newspaper articles always described Allan "Boobie" Richmond as a big, sweet kid, a good-natured charmer always quick to smile. But the students at Middle Borough had many reasons to doubt his good nature, having seen him accost and berate far too many classmates for minor or nonexistent insults upon his person. If he was quick to do anything, it was to take offense if any of his classmates showed him anything less than a worshipful respect. I knew all this about him far too well.

I reached down inside my jacket and pulled out a piece of paper that I had carefully rolled. I unrolled it and thrust it in Boobie's face. He pulled back and looked at me before he looked at the paper.

"Boobie," I said, surprised by the calm in my voice, "this is a contract I want you to sign. What it says here is that you will pledge not to molest any more girls."

There were a few gasps in the crowd, and also a few titters. I noticed that the gasps were of a high pitch. Boobie glared at me with menace. I saw him try to locate Nina, but I think he failed. I saw the calculations being made, could see the way his eyes shifted. Then a smile crossed his face.

"Boy, what the *fuck* are you talking about?" He looked around his circle, seeking support. He got back a few smiles as fake as his own.

I still held the paper in his face, about a foot away from his nose. After Boobie attempted the laughing dismissal, the paper in his face quickly became a gesture of impudence that he had to quash. He snatched it away from me and, staring down at me with a snarl, began ripping it up.

"I think you better get out of my face. *Boy*," he said. He balled up the torn pieces and tossed them at my head, as if he were flicking water at me. But I was prepped for Boobie's fists—balled-up paper was not going to give me pause.

"I ain't never molested shit," he said with disdain. His eyes scanned the crowd again. I knew what he was looking for. Or whom.

"Oh, so you're calling Nina Andrews a liar?" I said with the exaggerated volume of an amateur actor trying to project to the back row. Nina stepped out of the crowd. She didn't say a word, but she moved closer to me. I threw a glance in her direction and saw that her eyes were locked in to Boobie, sending him one of the iciest glares I had ever seen on her face. Boobie, weighed down by the import of that look, dropped his eyes.

"He did the same thing to me."

All eyes shifted to that voice. It was one of the girls from the dance team. She stepped next to Nina. She also glared at Boobie. I saw her right hand reach down and grab hold of Nina's left. I didn't know her name, but she certainly was familiar to me, a fresh-faced ebullient Latino girl whose spectacular curves drew hungry stares whenever she switched down the halls—or when she donned the dance team's tight little spandex numbers. She was an upperclassman, a popular member of the student body—no inconsequential new-comer like Nina. There was only silence in the crowd now, a tense, expectant silence. Like one big eye, the crowd turned slowly back to Boobie. A grimace crossed his face; he looked confused, unsure of his next move. Then he spotted me; his eyes bore in on me as if he were seeing me for the first time. I could see the thought forming: This was all my fault.

Boobie moved swiftly toward me, stiffening his hands and shov-ing me hard in the chest. I had seen it coming so I was braced. I took a few steps backwards, slightly stumbling, but I didn't fall down. I heard Nina's gasp. I stepped forward and pushed him back, probably not as hard as he pushed me. For a second he lost his balance—I sus-pect he didn't expect my retaliation—but he gathered himself without falling. His eyes were slits now, I couldn't even see the eyeballs. I no longer could hear the ambient sounds of the group—I was zoned in on his next move. He stepped forward, gathered himself, and un-leashed a vicious right hook. I saw the punch coming long before it reached my head, almost as if I was getting the super slo-mo replay. I ducked my head down, bending at the knees like I knew what I was doing. The punch grazed the top of my head, not hurting at all but leaving enough of a sting that I could assess its ill intent. The punch told me one thing—I couldn't let him get in another one. Before he could wind up again, I brought my body together in a tight little ball, bent a bit at the knees again, then propelled myself toward Boobie. I believed that my feet might even have left the ground as both hands connected with Boobie's chest, like a football player hitting the tack-ling dummy. When his back made contact with the pavement—with my 165 pounds on top of him—I heard a sound escape his lips, prob-ably involuntarily: "Ughh." There was the usual flailing of limbs when two teenagers are twisted together on the ground, a confusing jumble of denim and bright urban gear. I saw Boobie's grimace as he tried to both push me off and to inflict pain. He forced his left arm up in a violent motion and his hand connected with my throat. I felt a sharp pain that spread out from my neck, but it didn't slow me down. I forced the full brunt of my weight down into Boobie's mid-section, leading with my elbow. I heard him cry out. I sensed that my knee was somewhere in the vicinity of his groin, so I whipped it forward and down, feeling a softness at the end of it when it made contact. To this, Boobie moaned. I felt something on the back of my collar—could Boobie's arms really be that long?—and suddenly I was being lifted up and dragged away.

"Let go of me!" I yelled out as instinct. I twisted my neck around, trying to wrench free. But then I saw who it was—Coach Harrow. Boobie's coach. That meant the fight was over. I had survived. I let my body go limp, felt the tension and the adrenaline draining away. Nina rushed toward me, literally stepping over Boobie, who was writhing with his hands clutching his crotch. She was crying, but she wasn't overly emotional.

"Aaron, I can't believe you did that . . . for me," she said softly. She reached up and hesitated when her hand approached my neck, as if she were afraid to actually touch it. For the first time, I noticed the throbbing in my throat. I looked down at her and saw something I couldn't remember ever seeing on her face when mine was the reflection in her eyes. I saw admiration.

her

The only person I've ever trusted is Aaron. Not my mom or my dad or my sister (they tend to make mountains out of molehills with whatever information I bother to dole out to them, so I spoon it to them with great caution). Not any of my girlfriends (you know what they say about women, right? They're catty, catty, catty—turn against you in a heartbeat, and put all your business out in the street in the next one, this much I *know* is true). Definitely not any of my trifling-ass ex-boyfriends (I heard enough halfhearted *I love you, babe*'s, and *She doesn't mean anything to me*'s to last two lifetimes, for real).

But Aaron, I could trust with anything—and I mean anything. Like, the time when my sister and I had that knock-down, drag-out fight over the purple Bubble Yum gum I lifted from the store. See, what had happened was, my mom had taken us to the drugstore with her so she could buy some cough medicine for my dad. He had a cough something terrible, and he was in no mood to so much as hear my sister and my mouth, much less entertain us while he tried to sleep off his cold. So Mom piled a bunch of clothes on us, hustled us into the car, and stepped on the gas, bitching all the way to the store about how she was tired of doing all the work while Daddy was "laying around on his ass." Clearly, she was in no mood to deal with kid foolishness, but that didn't necessarily cross my "don't get on Mommy's nerves" radar, so I started begging before she'd even strapped us in. "Mommy, can I have gum at the store?"

"No."

"But, I want some gum—the grape kind."

"You don't need no damn gum."

My sister was snickering now; I knew her laughing wasn't going to help my case any. "Shut up!" I sneered, rolling my eyes at my sister. "Make me sick."

"You shut up," my sister shot back.

"No you!"

"No you!"

"Both of y'all shut the hell up before I put you both out the car," Mom yelled, practically stomping on the brakes and turning her body around to shoot us that "I'm about to beat the black off you" look my sister and I feared most. Guess what? We both shut the hell up.

But we hit and pinched each other all the way out of the car, all the way into the store, and up and down every aisle. Just as she made a run toward the lotion, the wrapping on the grape Bubble Yum caught my eye: It was a jumbo pack with my name written all over it. I stopped in my tracks (bonehead kept running), mesmerized by the idea of having ten pieces of the sweet stuff all to myself. But Mom said she wasn't going to buy it, and I knew if I asked again, I ran the risk of getting popped, hard. I sure as heck didn't have any money to buy it for myself. And then, just as quickly as my fingers were wrapped around the package, I was shoving it down my pants. Don't ask me what I knew about stealing; I was seven. I wasn't really thinking ramifications—I just wanted the darn gum.

And then, my sister asked me what I was chewing. We were out on the porch; she was playing hopscotch by herself, while Aaron and I ignored her. I was pretending to read a superhero comic book Aaron had brought over to show me; I didn't really like all that boy stuff, but I hadn't the heart to break it to my best friend, seeing as they were practically, like, his life, for some reason. But the flimsy book provided what I thought was good cover for the big-ass bubble I blew just as the savory sweet-and-sour confection I'd been gnawing achieved the perfect consistency. "Ooooh!!! Where you get gum?" she said, as I tried desperately to scrape the lavender sticky stuff from my nose and top lip. "I'm telling Mommy!"

Aaron looked at me, I at him, all at once frantic. My mind raced from scene to scene: Mommy whipping my ass, Nikki laughing at me, Daddy marching me down to the station house, them throwing me into a jail cell, where I'd eat mush for the rest of my life. Just as my sister ran into the house (she was yelling, "Mama!!! Mama!!!") I frantically pushed the gum into Aaron's hands. "Here—hide this," I said. Aaron had a confused look on his face, but his body did what it was supposed to: He took the pack of gum, shoved it into the front of his shirt, and trotted across the street without saying a word. Moments later, just as my mother was making her way to the front porch to rip my head off my shoulders, Aaron reappeared with more comic books in his hand, just as cool as you please. "Hey, Mrs. Andrews!" he said, excitedly.

"Uh huh," she said, dismissing him. "Nina—where'd you get gum from?"

"What gum, Mom? I don't have any gum."

My mother looked at my sister, raised an eyebrow, and then stared at me as she listened to my sister rat me out. When the girl finally stopped running her mouth, my mother broke her intense stare into my eyes long enough to direct her eyes to my mouth: "Open it," she said.

I did. There was no gum in there; I'd put the wad in the pages of Aaron's comic book and shut it really tight so that neither my mom nor my sister could detect it. "See?" I said, with my mouth open wide. "No gum. I don't know what she's talking about. Maybe she heard Aaron chewing gum."

"I had a piece of gum, Mrs. Andrews, but I threw it away. It was getting hard," Aaron said with conviction, like it was the God's honest truth. My mother rolled her eyes, first at him, then at me, then my sister, before she stomped back into the house, mumbling under her breath. "I know one thing," she said as the door slammed. "Y'all are getting on my last good nerve around here."

I looked at Aaron and snickered. He smirked. My little sister stomped her foot and followed my mother into the house.

"You stole the gum from the store?" Aaron said, his eyes wide.

I was a bit embarrassed relaying this message to him—I was supposed to be above common thuggery, and I didn't want Aaron to think I was some petty thief. But I knew that chances were he'd think that what I did was more cool than anything. At least that's what I was hoping. I wasn't so sure he'd be as pleased, though, with the my putting the gum in his comic book. "I have something to tell you," I said, looking down at the paper book. "You're probably going to be mad at me, but I didn't know what else to do with the gum."

Aaron looked down at the comic book. I saw his whole body deflate.

"I'll pay you back for it, I swear," I said. "You can even keep the gum I gave you. And as soon as I get the money, I'll buy you another one."

Aaron was silent for a moment. He looked over at the cover of the book, and then back at me. A smile grew across his face. "I didn't really like that one that much anyway," he said. Then he held up the book that was in his hands, with two overly-buff cartoon characters, one obviously good, the other obviously evil, locked in a furious struggle. "Now this one? This is the best. You have to read it!"

And just like that, my best friend was all good with me. What's more is that two days later, when I asked him about my gum (which I was sure he'd eaten because what seven-year-old can resist chewing up a whole ten-pack of grape Bubble Yum, especially when the owner ruined your best comic book?), he pulled it out from between his mattress, all nine pieces a little smooshed, but still intact. He hadn't eaten one piece.

I knew from that moment on that I could trust Aaron with *anything*. And time after time, Aaron proved me right, including the day

I ran to him with the news that Boobie had tried to molest me in the janitor's closet. Honestly, it hadn't occurred to me that he would kick the boy's ass—Aaron was a little bit of a 'fraidy cat, and it was clear to anyone with eyes that Boobie could raise a pinky and send Aaron packing. Still, there wasn't a person on the Earth whom I could possibly tell that I'd invited Boobie to the janitor's closet, invited him to kiss me, invited him to touch my budding breasts and booty, invited him to press his body against mine, but that I really, truly, had no intention of having sex with the boy, except Aaron. He wouldn't judge, wouldn't name-call. I knew he'd assume that Boobie was in the wrong. I trusted, though, that my best friend would help me to make it right again—to help me figure out what to do. That he kicked Boobie's ass was a bonus; I didn't know the boy had it in him. I guess I should have trusted him to find the Herculean strength it would take to knock Boobie on his ass. That single act made it crystal that Aaron was my go-to guy—my friend, my confidant, my protector. Even when I wasn't the easiest friend to have. He recognized and happily accepted his role, and I, confident that my boy would never hurt, deceive, or embarrass the shit out of me, happily let him.

Which is why I was trippin' over my obsession with Aaron's daily activities, now that he was concentrating less on bartending for cash, and more on his photography. He was working at the comedy club part time, but spending an extraordinary time outside the apartment, (he said) going to photo shows and visiting galleries to check out the competition and "making connections," whatever that was. I had his connections, all right. I wanted to know what connections he was making that he was able to afford the brand-new digital camera he'd brought home one day. Where on earth did he get the money for that thing? The photographers that shot the wine ads for my company didn't even have digital cameras this snazzy—this I knew for a fact, because it was I who had to rent the more high-end equipment for the shoots, seeing as none of the photographers could really afford them on their own. And if a photographer that was working steady gigs and getting paid upward of $2,000 a photo shoot working for us, much less some of the bigger agencies and magazines, couldn't afford one, then how in the hell was my broke-ass boyfriend sporting the latest in cameras and accessories?

I was never one for holding my tongue, so it was a given that I was going to ask Aaron where he got it from. But I needed to do so with caution and care. The last thing I wanted to do was start a chicken fight—or, more accurately, let him know that I was going all through his stuff. I let it sit for a few days, then I saw my shot: His knapsack, with the camera sitting practically in plain view, was laying on the dining room chair—the chair that I conveniently decided to sit in to read the *Times*. "Wow, that camera sure looks expensive," I said, as I lifted his knapsack out of the chair and made the flap fall open. I reached in and pulled it out, holding it up to my face for a better view.

"Oh yeah," he said, a bit too uneasy for my taste. "A friend of mine hooked me up with a great deal. It's one of the newer models, with a zoom that's out of this world. I never really trusted digital cameras, and I still prefer my Pentax over them, but if I ever had to rely solely on a digital, that baby's it."

Of course, by now, I'd tuned him out. A friend? Got him a deal? What friend? How much of a deal? Here I was, working my behind off, paying most of the rent, paying most of the bills, buying all of the groceries, and foregoing buying myself cute shit so that we could scrape by on his part-time gig, and he was wasting money on "deals" from his "friend"?

I was livid. But I didn't say much, just, "Oh."

And then I launched my investigation. I started scouring camera stores, looking for a duplicate to see how much it cost. I scoured the circulars in the Sunday paper—Circuit City, Best Buy, Sharper Image, the Wiz, you name it, I looked in it for this camera, and I couldn't find it. Assuming that it was even more expensive than I thought, I stepped up my investigation a notch, and started checking out some of those photo stores that dotted midtown—you know, the ones where they have every electronic gadget one could ever imagine, piled up in the window with handwritten signs touting what the owners considered to be steals. I'd once heard on a television news investigation that most of the items in those places were refurbished, and nowhere near the money they were charging, but I was holding out hope that I would find Aaron's camera in the back, where they supposedly kept the better merchandise you couldn't find out in the window. Still, nothing. I was going to have to bring out the big guns.

"Hey Scott, I'm looking to buy a really nice camera for my boyfriend for his birthday, but I want one of the expensive ones that the photographers use. Where do you buy those?" I casually asked the photo editor at my job. He was bent over a layout, and barely listening to me.

"Huh?" he said, before finally looking up. "An expensive digital for a professional?"

"Yeah," I said, staring at him intently. "Where do I get one of those?"

"Well, there's a specialty camera store called Forty-second Street Photo, over on Ninth Avenue. That's where all the real photographers shop—like the newspaper guys and the magazine editors and people like that. You might want to try there. They're really expensive, though."

"Like how much?" I asked, leaning in.

"Oh, depending on what you're getting, at least a grand or so."

I made a point of fixing my face to make it seem like $1,000 was no big deal to me, but damn if it wasn't. One thousand dollars? Where in the hell did that Negro get that kind of money? And that's the least expensive ones? I made up my mind right then and there: I was going to slip that camera into my purse, and take it to this Forty-second Street Photo to see exactly what this man had wasted my money on.

That night when I got home, I put my workbag on the dining room table, too. (Usually, I put it in the closet in the hall entryway; that way, it wasn't cluttering up the apartment, which, thanks to Aaron's penchant for scattering his clothes/books/shoes/hats/bags/anything else under the sun all around, always managed to look messy despite my attempts to keep it neat.) The plan was to sneak the camera into my Louis Vuitton and steal it away to the photo store the next morning during my lunch break. I just had to get it, first. Aaron wasn't making it easy for me, though; he'd decided to camp his butt right there on the couch, where he usually sat and alternately stared at the television and read magazines and books. "Why don't you come over here and sit next to me," he said, patting the sofa. "Why you sitting all the way over there? Your man is lonely."

I jumped when he spoke; I'd been concentrating so hard on figuring out how to lift his camera that I wasn't really ready to hear the boom in his voice. For sure, though, I wanted to keep as much distance as possible, because the moment he turned totally around to watch the television, I was going to reach into his knapsack (which I was now practically sitting on), take the camera, and slip it into my bag. "Um, I have some work to do," I said, grabbing my bag and pulling out an assortment of papers and a pen. "I'll be over in a minute, I said."

"*Okaaaay* . . ." he said, making puppy dog eyes and an upside-down smile with his lips. "Can you hurry up, though? Your man needs some attending to."

"Sure thing, baby," I said hurriedly. "I just need to get a few things done, then I'll be right over, okay?" I said, forcing out a smile.

The moment he turned his head, I pounced on his bag, feeling around with my hands while I stared at him to make sure he wasn't looking. When I touched the metal with my fingertips, I wrapped my entire hand around the camera and fished it out of the bag and into mine in one quick motion—all the while scared to death that he was going to see me. He didn't notice a thing.

A few minutes later, I put my papers and pens and things back into the Louis, careful to push the camera way down into my bag, then closed it and shoved it into the closet. I walked slowly over to the couch and sat practically on Aaron's lap. Almost instantly, he grabbed my ass and pulled me closer to him still, his face coming straight toward mine. I wasn't feeling the scene, though; I didn't want to cuddle or kiss—partly because I was a little disgusted with him over the expensive camera, partly because I was ashamed of the fact that I'd just, in effect, stolen my man's belongings. Even deeper: The moment my fingers touched that camera is the moment I realized that I no longer trusted my best friend. I mean, I should have been just fine with what he said, right? His friend got him a good deal on a camera, and he bought it. Simple as that, right? Then why couldn't I just leave it alone?

Because not trusting Negroes is in my DNA, that's why. Because I'd learned from my mother and my mother's mother that the only person to be trusted is you and your womanly instincts, that's why. Because instincts just don't lie. They didn't lie when I found out about Wallace the Millionaire and his blonde, and they sure as hell didn't lie when I became Stephen's booty call and Liam's jump-off. Ninety-nine out of a hundred times, a woman's instincts about men's cheating and lying were on the money. It was a matter of "whether you choose to follow them, or you choose to be the fool," my mom used to always say to me and my sister.

I was choosing to follow mine.

But why did I feel so damn bad?

"Oh, this is a nice camera," the man behind the customer service desk said to me as he grabbed it from my hands and held it up to the light, like it was a diamond he was examining for clarity. "We just got these in. Where'd you get this one?"

"It's my father's—he's a photographer," I lied. I don't know why; it's not like this man knew me or Aaron or needed to be lied to about the circumstance behind why I was standing in his store moments after it opened asking him to price my man's equipment. But lied, I did. And I lied some more. "I'm thinking about buying one for my boyfriend, but I couldn't find it in any of the electronics stores I went to."

"Oh no, you won't find this in an electronics store," he said firmly. "This baby you can only find in the upscale stores catering to professionals. Your dad couldn't tell you where he got his?"

That was a good question. I wasn't prepared to answer it. Good thing I didn't have to. "Do you sell it here?"

"Yeah, we have a few that just came in a few weeks ago. Let me show you one," he said. He struggled to climb off the chair—I'd notice his chubby fingers as they felt all over Aaron's camera, but his face betrayed the fact that when he actually stood up, he was quite short (the seat was actually a stool), and extremely big. Making his way to the back of the store was laborious in and of itself, but reaching for the camera on the high shelf, next to a bunch of cameras so highly priced that they were in the "if you have to ask, you can't afford it" section of the store, was clearly torturous. He struggled to climb the short ladder, and, breathing heavily, pulled out a wad of keys before clumsily shoving one of them into the lock that stood sentry over the equipment.

"Here it is. This one is just like your dad's—it's a little over a grand, but if you take it home now, I can give it to you with a store warranty and a box of photo cards for an even thousand, not including tax."

A grand? This man had a $1,000 camera? Where in the hell did he get that kind of money? Here we were, foregoing $10 movies and cheap take-out dinners so that we could pay rent, and he was sporting a camera worth a cool G? My mind began to race: Maybe he was working at the strip club again. The comedy club didn't pay him shit, but he could easily double his pay working a few nights down at the Honey Pot, and I wouldn't even know it. Or maybe Cocoa the stripper bitch bought it for him. Why not? Maybe she's collected enough dollars in her stink-ass thong to breeze on down to the store and offer fatty fingers a lap dance in exchange for a discount on a camera for her work hubby. Or maybe she gave Aaron the money and a lap dance, and after he thanked her properly with a romp in the champagne room, he bought it himself. Who the hell knew where he got the money from?

I wasn't quite sure what I was going to say to Aaron about this.

The in-your-face Nina wanted to confront him with it, and demand details—about his paycheck, his relationship with Cocoa, the truth. But Nina the friend was hesitant to explain to my man that I'd stolen his camera and essentially played detective to find out its price, and figure out how I was going to get all up in his ass about it.

By the time I'd made it home that night, I'd decided I'd slip the camera back into his bag and find a way to ask him about exactly how much he paid for the camera without turning the discussion into a heated battle. But, stupidly, I didn't anticipate what happened when I walked through the door.

"Hey—babes, you seen my camera around? I was looking to go out and shoot this afternoon, and for some reason, it's not in my knapsack," Aaron said before I'd even rounded the corner into the living room.

I hesitated, and momentarily pictured the camera nestled inside the Louis, which was still dangling from my shoulder. The moment of truth: Should I tell him I took it and why, then get into a battle over it that'd clearly caught me off-guard, or should I deny, deny, deny, and figure out a game plan after I threw him off the scent?

Deny.

"Um, no babe. I haven't seen it," I said, squinting my eyes to feign concern. "Where could it be?"

"I don't know—I don't get it. It was in my bag yesterday, and I took some pictures with it and I thought I put it back. I had my other cameras with me too, though; I'm hoping I didn't leave it somewhere. That would be fucked up if I did."

"Yeah—jeez, I don't know what to tell you, sweetie. I haven't seen it," I said, walking slowly past him and toward the kitchen, where I paused to catch my breath while I casually flipped through the bills. "Did you go back to the places you were shooting?"

"Nah. If I left them there, they're gone now. I just can't figure it out. I have a clear vision in my mind of putting it back in my bag."

"I'm sorry, sweetie," I said, walking over to him, the Louis still on my shoulder. "It'll turn up."

Later that night, we lay in bed—both of us doing work. He, looking through some of the pictures he'd snapped during a trip to the mountains just across the river in Jersey, me pretending to look over some paperwork I'd fished from the bottom of my bag. I'd brought it into the room so that I could sneak the camera back into Aaron's knapsack, which, for some reason, he brought into the bedroom. Usually, it sat in the dining room chair like a piece of furniture in and of itself; it always disgusted me how he'd let it just lay around without ever thinking about how much neater the room would look if he'd just put it in the closet until he needed it. Tonight, though, it was in the room—which I counted as a blessing, considering I had to sneak the camera into it. The plan was to feign working long enough for him to fall asleep, so that I could sneak the camera into the bottom of the bag. I'd reasoned with myself that it was small enough to just kind of "appear" in one of the smaller pockets, and that I could somehow convince Aaron that he just didn't scour his knapsack hard enough for it. Dumb idea, I know—at least now I do. Because just as Aaron dipped into what I thought was a deep-enough snore to prove he was sleeping, I quietly and gently climbed out of bed, grabbed the camera, and sneaked it into his bag. But what I saw next made me damn near pee in my pajamas. There, under the glow of the streetlight, I saw Aaron's face. His eyes were wide open.

Had he been watching me the whole time? Did he know what I'd just done? Was he going to say anything?

I held my breath as I climbed back into the bed, waiting to hear the bass in his voice—what would surely be the accusatory tone, followed by the scowl and then the argument. He'd leave me for sure, once he found out I'd violated his trust. He'd leave me. We'd be no more.

Instead, though, Aaron was silent—didn't say a word. And we both spent a long part of the rest of the night staring at the ceiling. Quiet, save the sound of cars passing down our block and into the night.

him

I'm venturing a guess that every person in every relationship has se-crets. They're unavoidable, picked up over the years like lint balls on an old cotton shirt. In fact, the secrets actually help a relationship because they offer a welcome relief from the tedium that years and years of monotony can bring—going to the same job every day, com-ing home to the same place, greeting the same person, eating the same food, watching the same lame shows on the same TV in the exact same spot every night, having sex in the same positions for the same duration of time with the same urgency or lack thereof—then you go to sleep, wake up and repeat, like the directions on a shampoo bottle. Every once in a while, when one partner allows to drop a tasty little morsel of a secret, the whole tedious past is called into question, just a bit, as you discover that maybe you didn't know your partner so well after all.

Well, Nina and I didn't seem to have any of these secrets. We knew every factoid that was worth ever knowing about each other, from the first person we kissed to the first time we had sex to the exact spot we both were when we heard our first rap record to our precise location when the space shuttle blew up and Ronald Reagan was shot and Nelson Mandela came to New York and the Mets won the World

Series and the World Trade Center fell to the ground. Sure, there were undoubtedly little things we had done over the years that we had declined to share, but you can bet that if it was worth knowing, then we already knew it. This lack of secrets between us was now a problem. I mean, what guy really needs to have the gory details about the day his girl lost her virginity? And I was also there the day she found out the truth about her dad's mysterious background and that he was still wanted by the cops for some Black Panther foolishness. I could tell Nina was embarrassed when we first found out the reason he was skulking around the neighborhood all those years, but later, she and I laughed heartily. We both had the same thought: foolish man.

I also have some info that is starting to prove useful. I know all the dirty little tricks Nina played on previous boyfriends, sneaking around to find out things about them that they wouldn't want her to know. She'd call me up, confess to me some act of sneakiness that she had committed, then she'd try to get me to agree that she had done the right thing. Usually I took the guy's side—which is what she expected me to do and which is why she called me in the first place, but she'd still find my stance annoying. It was clear that Nina's distrust of her male partners, which she seemed unable to control even if she wanted to, was like a toxic virus that would eventually put the relationship on its deathbed. I believe they call it the self-fulfilling prophecy: If you start out not trusting your man, eventually he's going to do something to demonstrate he was unworthy of your trust. In other words, if you look hard enough for something, eventually you'll find it.

It's recently come to my attention that I've become the target of Nina's distrust. I guess it was inevitable. Once you decide you'll be Inspector Gadget in every relationship, it's kind of hard to turn it off and suddenly become the perfect trusting girlfriend. One might ask whether I gave Nina reason to be suspicious. But I can't think of anything I've done to warrant it. Her angst seems connected to my new camera. I'm a photographer—it's what I do in every spare moment and it's what I've always wanted to do. Every photographer's obsession is camera equipment. It makes sense—the quality of your pictures, of your work, is inextricably tied to the performance of your camera. The better your camera, the better your pictures. Simple formula. So when a photographer buddy of mine offered to sell me a fairly new high-quality digital camera he wasn't using because he had gotten a great deal on a newer model, I jumped on it with both feet. He knows I don't have a lot of extra cash on hand, so he was even willing to work out a payment plan with me. I give him $200 a month for eight months and the camera is all mine. And in the meantime I could use it all I want. So it was like a rent-to-buy agreement.

When I brought the camera home, I planned to show it to Nina, but I stopped myself. Something about her mood told me to wait until later. We had been arguing a little too much lately and me making a new purchase seemed ripe territory for a new battle. Already I had quit my gig at the Honey Pot, not willingly but to get Nina off my back. Her constant questions annoyed me to no end—always with the implication that I was messing around with every dancer in the club. At first I brusquely resisted her nagging and defended my employment there, telling her I couldn't make nearly as much money at night anywhere else. But she refused to let up, refused to see things my way. I even tried to use the Hugh Hefner argument on her, saying that he had become one of our society's most respected businessmen, and he published a porn magazine.

"How many times has his old ass been married?" Nina countered. I didn't know the answer to that—and that wasn't the point anyway. I shrugged.

"Now he's just a pathetic old man who has to surround himself with twenty-year-old silicone-implanted airheads to be happy," she continued. "Is that your role model?"

I shook my head. Women just would never understand the world of the strip club—unless they worked in one. Just as people who work in the porn industry claim, eventually you can become inured to anything—even being surrounded by naked women. But no amount of arguing and justifying was going to make the world any clearer to my girlfriend. So finally I just walked out of the Honey Pot one day and never looked back. When I got home that morning—I usually slipped into bed at about 3:00 A.M. and went to sleep without waking her up—I tapped Nina's shoulder until she stirred.

"I just wanted you to know that I quit tonight," I said. I made an effort to keep any kind of emotion out of my voice. I didn't want her to think I was asking for her gratitude or that I was upset about having to quit—though I was upset. "I'm not going back."

I saw her blink a few times through her grogginess, trying to comprehend what I was telling her. A small smile formed on her face. She dropped her head back on the pillow and within seconds was out again. About a week or so earlier I had started tending bar part time at a lame little comedy club bar on the Upper West Side. Even with their outrageously overpriced watered-down drinks I made barely half what I pulled in per night at the Honey Pot.

When I finally did show her the camera, Nina seemed to question its expense right away. She didn't say a word about how lovely it looked, just said that it looked expensive—then she walked away. I heard her in the kitchen banging around a few pots and I could feel the anger start to build. How dare she question me like that, with no justification whatsoever. It might have helped matters to explain the camera financing situation, but I quickly decided that she wasn't worthy of an explanation. If she wanted to think that I was still grinning at the naked girls up in the booty bar, then let her go right ahead and be foolish. I shook my head—why did all my relationships have to degenerate to the same point? Every woman I had ever been involved with eventually reached this impasse, where she so distrusted me and so expected me to fuck up that it was just a matter of time before she'd find something to latch on to, some piece of evidence that she had been right all along, and the thing would collapse in an instant. I thought matters would be different with Nina. My God, the things we had been through together. The sacrifices we had made on behalf of each other over the years. All that meant nothing to her? It was just tossed out the window that easily, dismissed with something as trivial in the scheme of things as a new camera. What had I done to deserve such disrespect from her? Where had my best friend gone?

After the new camera unveiling, Nina acted a little strange the rest of the week, a little bit distant. We still had our usual sessions of intense energetic sex every other night, but I could detect that something was slightly amiss. Every time I thought about it, I got angry all over again. One night as I stepped out of the bathroom after brushing my teeth and walked toward the living room, I could see her from a distance poking around inside my camera bag. I was barefoot so my footfalls hardly made a sound. With a scowl, I ducked into our bedroom before she looked up. Damn, she was still sweating the stupid camera? What was wrong with her? As I got ready for bed, I wondered what she could have been looking for. When she entered the room, I shut my eyes and pretended to be asleep.

h‹er

I think I've been fairly honest with you up to this point, so I won't start twisting the truth now. I really did *stumble* across the pictures. Granted, I probably should have just asked Aaron for what I was originally looking for: some photos that could prove he was worthy of shooting publicity shots for the new team of executives who'd joined the board of Golin Estates. But he wasn't around, and I needed to move fast if I was going to make it happen for him. We'd been struggling financially; my company, which had been suffering from poor sales and intense competition with foreign estates, was cutting back drastically on employees and perks, all of which put an end to lavish parties, expensive lunches, and confidence in one's ability to continue collecting a paycheck. Two people in my department alone had been laid off within the last month, and I was watching my back and pinching pennies in anticipation of my head being put on the chopping block next. None of this bode well for our humble household; Aaron was working only one day a week so that he could focus full time on his photography, so we were basically surviving off of my little bit of money from the job. So when the publicity firm that worked with Golin Estates came calling for a photographer to shoot the portraits, I (for selfish motives, more than confidence in Aaron's abilities, I'm now ashamed to admit) offered up my man for the gig, which was paying somewhere in the neighborhood of $1,200, plus expenses. All I had to do was bring samples of his portraits to the job.

Which led me to the photography booty he kept in these elaborate boxes he had stuffed into a corner of our office/laundry-sorting room. I'd snuck away from work during lunch to sort through them; I had to, after all, move fast if Aaron was to get picked. Besides, I thought that he'd be home, seeing as he didn't have to work and hadn't told me that morning that he planned to take his camera out to shoot. Alas, he wasn't. And, he wasn't answering his cell phone, either. So I rolled up my sleeves and got to sorting through his pictures.

Again, I was blown away by my man's talent; he was so incredibly gifted when it came to capturing the spirit of his subjects. There were pictures of the little girls double-Dutching outside—shots of their feet flying lightning-fast through ropes the camera could barely capture, shots of their determined faces, as they tried to keep their craft going. There were also shots in what looked like the Bronx Zoo— little kids looking in wonder at the animals. One was of a little girl screaming; she looked absolutely terrified—her eyes red, her mouth grotesquely widened enough to see clean back to her tonsils, her hands held up as if in surrender. Behind her, just beyond her shoulder, was a gorilla, staring at her intently—almost humanlike. In the animal's hands was a baby, hugging his mama's neck, his head nuzzled into her neck. The image was simply arresting.

There were more shots like this, as well as plenty of pictures of landscapes, flowers, architecture, and his specialty, portraits. Plenty of them. Of his family. His friends. People I didn't recognize. Me.

I guess I'd flipped through one box and was nearly to the bottom of the second when I came across them—stacks of contact sheets, featuring a woman that I at first didn't recognize. I picked up one of the sheets and pulled it closer to my face, and had the nerve to squint my eyes to make sure I was seeing correctly. My eyes did not mistake me: It was picture after picture of Cocoa the stripper-ho. Scantily clad in what I was sure was her best stage outfit—lace bra, barely covering her nipples, breasts perfectly round and plump and pushed up into a mountain of cleavage on their own accord. Her pants were black and shiny and tight, circa *Dance Fever*, except her ass wasn't at all flat like the white girls who strutted their stuff in the super-tight Gloria Vanderbilt and Jordache creations of their time; like her breasts, her ass, too, was plump and high and practically its own spectacle in many of the shots I saw on a few of the other contact sheets. I flipped through them—there must have been a good two dozen sheets—and picture after picture got me more heated than the next. I fully expected that I'd eventually hit the contact sheet in which she'd be completely nude, but those never materialized. Not that the ones in which she was clothed left anything to the imagination; in a few of the pages, Cocoa was literally center stage, working the poll and swinging her blonde-highlight weave as she stared seductively into the camera. The look on her face said it all: The moment you put that camera down, I'm going to fuck you like you've never been fucked before.

I slammed the contact sheets down on the floor and frantically ripped through the rest of the pictures in the remaining two boxes, looking for evidence of the two of them getting it on. But there was nothing but more of the same—landscapes, portraits, animals, people. None of the other shots, pictures of other women included, looked remotely as sexy and seductive as Cocoa's. My adrenaline rush still had me amped, but I got even more heated when I went back to the Cocoa shots. Whose idea was this? How did they arrange the shots on the stage? Were there more pictures in a private collection somewhere? Perhaps in her possession? Did they indeed sleep with one another? "How could they have not?" I asked out loud. And then, almost like a woman gone mad, I started turning each of the contact sheets over, looking for evidence of when they were actually taken. I mean, he said he wasn't working in the club anymore, but who's to say he wasn't? He had enough money to buy that expensive-ass camera—and I know he couldn't have saved up for it with that pittance of a salary he was making down at the comedy club. And that would explain his access to the stage, and Cocoa—maybe they took them in the early evening, right before the nasty old men started pouring themselves into the Honey Pot's musty seats. I remembered that when I was little, the pictures my mom took with her camera always had the date on the back, stamped there as a reminder of whatever memory you'd created with the snapshot. Alas, the only thing on the back of the sheets was Aaron's name.

"Hey—gotta question for you," I said, trying not to sound too excited or anxious about what I was about to ask Charles, the head of publicity and an amateur shutterbug who was charged with picking the photographer to shoot the executive portraits. "Can you look at pictures and tell when they were taken?"

He was distracted—looking through portfolios of other photographers and making notes, I assumed on the ones that he liked. He barely took his eyes off the picture he was studying—it appeared to be a beauty shot of some woman, her face all shiny and full of different shades of pink and green makeup. She was perfectly hideous—I'd seen clowns with less makeup than she. But the portrait was, indeed, high-end. "Uh, did you bring your boy's work samples? I'm close to picking the photographer but I'm still willing to look at his stuff if you have it."

His distraction annoyed me; I needed him to focus. "He had a few other jobs already lined up, so he asked me to tell you that he needed to pass this time, but to keep him in mind for future projects," I lied. "But answer my question: Can a lab photo technician look at a picture and tell when it was taken?"

Charles looked up for the first time, and raised an eyebrow. "Yeah," he answered slowly. "If you take it to a good photo lab."

"Well, what's the best photo lab in town?"

Charles studied me some more, and started smiling. "Oooh, trouble in paradise? Stumble across some pictures you weren't supposed to see, hmm?"

Did I mention to you that Charles is gay? And nosy? And rude? And quick to get all up in someone's business? I would have read him on it, but I was too busy trying to get to the bottom of when those Cocoa pictures were taken. So I ignored his catty stab and got back to the point at hand. "Come on, Charles, where do I take the damn pictures already?!"

"Manhattan Color Labs," he said simply. "Best in town. If it can be done, they can do it."

By the time he said the word *town*, I was already out the door, cell phone to my ear, dialing Information to get the address for the place that was going to help me figure out if I was going to cut my Aaron off forever.

him

I was deep into an article in *American Photo* when the shrill ringing of the phone startled me. I looked up at the time: 2:27 P.M. Damn, time to leave for the club. I wasn't working there steady anymore—I was now spending my days with my eyes glued to a camera lens—but I filled in behind the bar about once a week or so to bring in some much-needed cash.

"Hey," I said into the receiver. I put the magazine down on the couch. I considered bringing it with me on the subway but it'd probably wind up getting lost.

"Hey, is this Aaron Simmons?" The voice was male, fairly young, but unfamiliar to me. Immediately I thought bill collector. Damn, they had finally tracked me down at Nina's apartment. I thought it'd take them a bit longer. How'd they get the number anyway?

"Uh," I considered lying, "uh, yes, this is." I decided not to be a punk about it.

"Aaron, this is Phil Mahoney, from Manhattan Color Labs." He paused. I got the mental image of his face right away—stringy hair, scraggly beard, a torso covered with dark, angry-looking tattoos that were particularly unattractive on especially pale white skin.

"Oh, hey Phil. What's up?"

I heard him clear his throat. "I got a strange, uh, request today. A woman came in here with one of your contact sheets. A pretty black woman. Said she wanted us to figure out when the pictures were taken."

I quickly sat upright in my chair, as if my slouch had interfered with the processing of Phil's message. What was he talking about?

"A woman with one of *my* contact sheets? I don't get it."

Phil cleared his throat again. I got the feeling that he wasn't entirely comfortable making this phone call. "Well, she's interested in the pictures on the sheet. She wants to know when you took them."

Right away it clicked into place, like a bullet sliding into the chamber. Nina. She must have been doing her Inspector Gadget routine again and came across the pictures of Cocoa. Damn, I had fought with myself about whether I should keep that sheet with the rest of my stuff. On one hand I knew it'd be inviting trouble if Nina happened to stumble upon them—which in her case likely wouldn't be an accidental stumble. But on the other hand to hide them somewhere else or to dispose of them would be an admission that I didn't have the right to take sexy pictures of attractive women. I refused to put those limits on my craft, simply to shield myself from a jealous girlfriend. I was a photographer, working on my art, trying to hone my specialty, which was portraits. I should be able to take whatever kind of pictures I wanted to take of whoever I wanted to take them of, as long as I wasn't breaking any laws.

"Are the pictures kinda sexy shots of a black woman with long hair?" I asked Phil, already knowing the answer.

"Yeah, they are," he said. "Very nice stuff, I might add."

I grinned. Phil saw a lot of pictures during the course of the day, taken by some of the city's more gifted shooters. A compliment from him wasn't a trifle.

"Thanks," I said.

There was a momentary silence as my mind drifted. I was plotting my next move; for a second I had forgotten Phil was even there.

"Uh, so what do you want me to do?" Phil asked finally.

His voice startled me out of my thoughts. "Oh, I'm sorry. Uh, well, you don't have to do anything, Phil. I'll take care of it. If she should call you this afternoon, tell her you don't have anything yet."

"Okay, man. Will do."

"Oh, and Phil?"

"Yeah?"

"Thanks a lot for looking out," I said.

"Hey, no problem. I'm loyal to my shooters," he said.

The night at the comedy club dragged on; a succession of male comedians bored the crowd. The club wasn't a big enough name to get the top acts, so the manager was usually scraping pretty close to the bottom of the joke barrel for talent. He usually came up empty-handed. By my third week in the club, I was convinced that I was funnier than most of the comedians that played there. And I don't consider myself that funny. The fact that the comedians were awful only made my night more grinding—the patrons sucked down liquor with more intensity if the jokes on the stage weren't working. It was like they had a bottom line for their entertainment—if the guy on the stage couldn't get the job done, then they sought assistance from Mr. Jack Daniels or Mr. Johnnie Walker. On this Thursday night, the acts kept me busy with the drinks. The only relief I got from the monotony was a slightly buzzed white woman, a saucy brunette with big green eyes, who seemed intent on trying to pick me up.

"What do you do when you're not tending bar?" she said. She was sitting on one of the bar stools, ignoring the pointed stares of the women she had left back at her table—three other white women who weren't even in her league. Once I noticed the way they looked over at us, I decided I would play along with Miss Green Eyes just to fuck with her friends.

"Well, do you want me to start in the morning, maybe after I brush my teeth?" I said smartly, giving her a comely grin. She grinned back, clearly excited about my sudden interest.

"No, I want you to start before that, while you're still in bed," she said. I glanced at her with my eyebrows raised. Was she taking it there already? Wow, she didn't waste much time.

"And what do you want to know about my bed?" I asked, pausing from the operation of the blender.

She grinned again. "Well, for starters, how big is it?"

I refused to believe that she was being that plainly obvious about the sexual wordplay, so I ignored any other implications of her question besides the most literal.

"Uh, it's queen-size," I said. When I realized how easily mocked that statement was, I laughed.

She laughed, too. "Well, queen-size is certainly big enough," she said. "I've always felt like queen-size was a good fit for me."

Now this was getting fun. I leaned my elbows on the bar. I had missed the flirtatious games that had accompanied my last bartending gig. For the most part the best I did at this spot was occasional prolonged stares from the cute little blondes and brunettes who flowed through the doors every night. Apparently blacks and Latinos in New York weren't much into the comedy scene because they rarely made an appearance.

I pretended to let my eyes sweep down her body, though I could only see it from the midsection up. "You're sure that's not too big for you?" I said. "You look like you might be a little small for queen-size."

Abruptly she stepped back from the bar and, with a giggle, twirled around once to show me the rest of her body. I could see her friends in the background—their scowls spread across the table.

"Too small?" said Miss Green Eyes, after she completed her twirl. "You're kidding me, right? Does this look too small to you?"

I had to admit that the girl was packing some heat in her hips and thighs. They weren't as thick as I might find on a black woman, but they were pretty damn close. The short little Japanese-style kimono dress she wore fit snugly over her thighs and stretched across her ass, not leaving much to the imagination.

I grinned again. "Okay, you're right. I take that back—you look like a perfect fit for queen-size."

She was happy now. She plopped her plump behind back on the bar stool. "Well, my next question about your bed was whether there was anybody else in it." I kept the grin frozen on my face, not letting her question startle me. Once you entered a committed relationship, you were regularly confronted with such moments, the heart check. A lie could only take you so far, especially if you were cohabitating as I now was. But it still might be far enough to get a few pieces of ass broken off, a nice little juicy affair before you had to flee. I had discovered in the past, however, that I didn't really have the right makeup for all that stress and duplicity. I had known men over the years who could expend a large percentage of their energies trying to keep up the games, but it always seemed to me that they never had the time or stamina to do anything else. Even sharing a house with Inspector Gadget and harboring a great deal of rage at that moment, I still couldn't take that step.

"Yes, I'm afraid that there is usually somebody else in it," I said. Her smile flattened out a bit—but she was trying not to let her disappointment appear too obvious. She shrugged.

"Well, that's too bad, Mr. Cute Bartender. I would have been real interested in checking out the fit of that bed of yours," she said. She reached out and grabbed a cocktail napkin and pulled it toward her. She glanced up at me with a smile as she pulled a pen out of her tiny pocketbook. I saw her write down her name and number. She slid the napkin toward me.

"Well, hold on to that," she said. "If ever that bed empties out, give me a call."

Her handwriting was a bit hard to fathom. Her name looked like Susan or Swinn.

"Is it Susan?"

She nodded. "And yours?"

I extended my hand. "Susan, I'm Aaron. It's been a pleasure."

By the time I got back downtown later that night, the thrill of the little dance with Susan had worn off. I was back in the full bloom of my outrage. I wasn't sure how to confront my lady and her distrustful ways, but I knew something had to be done. If I didn't nip it now, it would only grow in ferocity over the years and eventually threaten to gobble both of us up. The confrontation probably wasn't going to be pretty, but it was necessary. I stormed up the steps, taking two at a time, convinced that Nina had to be put in her place if I had any chance of surviving a relationship with her. She was one of those black women who didn't respect you until you matched her strength with your own. If you let Nina punk you too many times, she'd eventually conclude that you were a punk. I opened the apartment door and stepped inside, wondering whether I'd step to her immediately if she were on the couch waiting up. But there was nothing in the small living room except the faint whirring sound of her fish tank filter. I glanced over at the fish to make sure there were no floating bodies at the top. Nina loved her fish—the fancier and more exotic the better. But the only problem with her highfalutin fish was that they seemed to have a life span barely longer than the trip from the pet store to your home tank. She got depressed when one of them died and she'd always make me dispose of it—even when I lived on the other side of town and we were friends and not lovers. I saw the red-black-and-green colored fish that she called Willy—she said the colors of the African-American flag immediately made her think of her father—darting energetically around the tank, looking for something to nibble on. Unfortunately, they often chose to nibble on each other—which certainly didn't help their already abbreviated life spans.

I stepped into the bedroom and heard Nina's roar before I saw her. I say roar because her snore sometimes reminded me of the mating call of some scary, mammoth beast in the bush—that's how loud it could get. At first it was amusing, providing us with many hours of good-natured mocking, but that wore off quick. Now I had taken to stuffing cotton plugs in my ears to fight off the noise. When Nina was roaring, there was no waking her—I had tried on quite a few occasions, usually hoping that I could rouse her from her deep slumber for some dead-of-the-night sexing. I knew from those experiences that the most I could expect of her was maybe a grunt of acknowledgment. I had never been able to elicit even a little kiss. A deal-breaking conversation was surely out of the question. I'd have to wait until the next day.

I didn't get the chance to tangle with her until the next evening, after she got home from work. She walked through the door with a pronounced slump to her shoulders, as if the day had been lengthy and uncompromising. This wasn't a bad time to hit her with my accusations—experience told me she might even be too tired to fight back with any zeal. I might get a quick technical knockout. That would please me just fine—though I was still trying to hold onto as much of my anger as I could manage, as a sort of amphetamine to get me through this fight, in the end what I wanted more than anything was to move immediately past conflict and get to the peace.

I waited for her to go to the bedroom and change her clothes. She walked into the kitchen, and I saw her glance at the stove and note its emptiness. I could guess what she was thinking—that I had once again failed to prepare dinner—but I wasn't exactly in the cooking mood on this night. Still, I couldn't help feeling a twinge of guilt as she opened up the freezer and pulled out a bag of something. From my seat in the living room, I couldn't tell what it was, but I guessed some type of frozen vegetable. The freezer was stuffed with big packets of frozen veggies that, when cooked, needed half a shaker of salt to be remotely edible, in my estimation. But I hadn't yet worked up the nerve to complain about it—Nina had placed any food complaints thoroughly out of bounds, off the discussion table. I took several deep breaths and headed for the kitchen.

"Listen, Nina, I need to talk to you," I said. She looked up at me with eyebrows raised. Nina knew I was rarely the serious conversation starter, so my lead-in had her immediately intrigued. "I got an interesting phone call today from the lab where I get most of my printing done. The guy said you had brought one of my contact sheets in there with some questions."

I crossed my arms and eyed her closely, waiting to see if she were going to defend her actions. But she didn't react. She just stared. I could see the chill behind her unblinking eyes, could sense the fury that simmered just beneath her surface cool.

"You care to explain yourself?" I said, after it became clear she wasn't going to offer anything.

Her lips pursed—a sure sign of her anger—and she scowled.

"I found that hooker's pictures, *man*," she said, putting a peculiar extra emphasis on the last word. Surprisingly she wasn't yelling. Her voice was stable and steady, maybe even calm.

"So what!" I shot back. "I'm a photographer. I specialize in portraits. It's what I do. Are you trying to take that away from me?" My voice acquired a pleading tone that I didn't expect—or welcome.

"I wish I could believe that's all you did, Mr. Photographer. I wish I could. I saw those pictures, Aaron. I'm not *stupid*."

I was blown away by the implications of her accusations. I wasn't supposed to be shooting any attractive women, was that it? She had such little faith and trust in me that I was supposed to limit my subjects to the ugly and unsexy? I was so exasperated, so speechless, that I turned on my heels and stomped back toward the living room. But I realized I wasn't done.

"Why can't you just trust me, Nina?" I asked. I heard my voice crack in desperation and I felt my face reddening from the embarrassment. I was glad she could no longer see me. "Why, all of a sudden, are you trippin' over the dumbest little things?" I paused to take a breath—then I thought of one more thing, something I knew would feel to her like a stab from a sharp blade.

"No wonder you couldn't ever keep a damn man!" I said loudly.

I heard Nina's footsteps approaching. A big nasty scowl blanketed her face and I could see the strain of her anger on her neck—gosh, her veins were even bulging. I hadn't seen that in years—not since high school. I noticed that the pot she was holding was trembling.

"Well, it turns out that every man I've ever known has been a lying, no-good snake," she said. Her voice was low, but the words cut into me. I felt a hot flash run down my spine. This was very bad. I needed to get away from this woman, my former friend who was now equating me with sleazy reptiles. I headed for the door, not knowing what I would do or where I would go. Before I finished my grand exit, I looked back at her face and saw the damning glare of what looked to be hatred. I shuddered and closed the door behind me. The big chill was on.

her

So the guy at the photo shop dimed me, and then had the nerve to refuse to give me the information I'd asked for: the date the pictures were taken. I'd found his message on my voice mail at work. "Ma'am, this is the Manhattan Photo Labs. I'm calling to tell you that these pictures don't belong to you—the name on the back says Aaron Simmons, and Mr. Simmons asked me to express to you that they are his private property. Now, I'm not going to involve the authorities, but I do ask that you stay away from the shop." I spent a few weeks consumed with outrage over that; how dare he take my private request to the streets and broadcast to the world—specifically, my world, Aaron—that I'd been snooping, prying, and doubting? Wasn't that a violation of *my* privacy? And did that white boy threaten to call the police on my ass? I had a mind to go over there and give him a good tongue thrashing—by the looks of him and the store, he'd probably never been privy to a good and righteous cussing-out by an angry black woman. A few times, I even marched my mad behind over to his shop to let him know to stay out of grown folks' business. The first time I went, some scrappy white chick with a thatch of blonde dreadlocks was behind the counter, and ol' boy was nowhere to be found. The second time I went, the shop was closed for some reason, even though I made it there well before it was supposed to be. The third time, about a week and a half after his revelations to my boyfriend tore our relationship apart, I went back to the shop during my lunch break, 'round the same time I'd dropped the pictures off, hoping that this time I'd catch him. But when I rounded the corner, what I saw stopped me dead in my tracks: Aaron was leaning over the counter, alternately pointing at and talking about what appeared to be a black binder full of prints. The white boy was leaned over, too, staring intently at the photos and nodding his head in agreement with whatever Aaron was saying. I just stood there, mouth agape. Heart broken. For it was then, as I laid eyes on my best friend for the first time since our knock-down, drag-out fight, that I realized that it wasn't anger that was fueling my contempt for the white boy. It was loneliness.

I missed my Aaron.

"Of course you do, jackass," Kenya said matter-of-factly, as we sat sipping tea at my desk in the office. It was a quiet Friday, the last of the summer, and quite a few of my coworkers had accepted an invitation to party at the Bridgehampton estate of one of the young senior managers, who seemed to work solely to pay for, party at, and brag about his place in the Hamptons. I declined the invitation: I couldn't think of a hell more worse than having to sit around and pretend to be having fun with a bunch of my coworkers, hopped-up on warm Budweiser and bad barbeque, for an entire weekend. The only ones left in my office were me and the other sistah who worked there, Florine. She was cool and all, but our relationship was strictly a work thing; outside of that, Florine and I didn't really talk. She was a little, well, a nice way to put it: country and corny—fresh out of B-school, and in the big city for the first time. Wide-eyed and wet behind the ears, is what my mother used to call folks like her. I didn't tend to pay the girl much mind, even though we were the only two black folks on the job. We'd tipped out for lunch a few times, but that was about it.

And so I invited Kenya over to lend me her ear, cheer me up, and tell me I did the right thing by confronting Aaron, despite that it'd gone down all wrong. Unfortunately, Kenya wasn't playing along with my program. "You just kicked a perfectly good man to the curb over some pictures," she said.

"They were pictures of a stripper. That he dated. Half-naked. You mean to tell me you wouldn't have had questions if you found those in your man's dresser drawer?"

"Well, your man is a photographer, and you didn't find those pictures in his dresser drawer; you found them in his portfolio of pictures, along with the rest of the pictures he's taken to perfect his craft, fool," Kenya said plainly. "You're acting like you found them between his mattress or something."

"I hardly think nearly naked pictures of a bitch he was boning counts as perfecting his craft—at least not the one he uses his camera for," I shot back.

"Whatever, Nina," Kenya said, trying to look as nonchalant as she was sounding. "You was dead wrong."

The room was quiet, save for the copy machine, which was stapling some papers Florine had been running off the printer. I could tell that she'd been listening, but, until then, she was careful not to put her two cents in. "Nina, not to get all in your business or anything, but I was wondering, since you and your man are, um—well, to cheer you up, I was wondering if you'd like to hang out tomorrow night. There's a new Red Lobster in Times Square I've been dying to try out, and I got an extra ticket to a jazz concert at Club Savoy if you're interested," Florine said.

I shot a look at Kenya, one that clearly read, "Save me." This girl thought good eating in New York was Red Lobster! And while I was into jazz, I was pretty sure I didn't want to have to sit up in any smoky bar with this chick. My eyes were searching Kenya's for the right words to decline the invitation without hurting poor Florine's feelings. But my best friend, my ace boon coon, left me hanging. "Hey girl—all-you-can-eat shrimp! I saw the commercial the other day— nine ninety-nine," Kenya said, before taking a sip of her tea. She coughed—I wasn't sure if it was from the liquid going down the wrong pipe, or if she was laughing at her own stupid joke. I rolled my eyes at Kenya, and gave her an "I'm gonna get you later, heiffa" look, and then I smiled at Florine.

"That's quite sweet of you, and Red Lobster sounds like, um, quite the treat," I said sweetly. "But I'm in no mood to go out really."

Florine wasted no time with her pitch. "Come on—you said yourself you don't have anything to do this weekend, and I've got this extra ticket. It'll be fun!"

I looked over at Kenya again, but she was too busy hiding her giggles in her tea to help a sistah out. So I looked back at Florine, and reluctantly accepted her offer. I did, after all, have to work with this girl. I didn't want her to think I was a total ogre. And she was right: I didn't have a thing to do over the weekend, now that my Aaron was gone. "Okay—you're on. Here, take my home number and call me later with all the details, okay?"

"Great," Florine said enthusiastically. She gathered up her copies, laid them on her desk, and practically skipped out of the office. I was shaking my head. Kenya was hysterical. "Girl, bring me back a plate of them shrimp," she said between giggles. "I loves me some Red Lobster!"

I hadn't put much thought into getting ready for my hot date with Florine. I mean, what does one wear to Red Lobster, in the middle of tourist central—Times Square? I'd answer that question for you, but I didn't quite know, because I—and any other true New Yorker I know—usually did nothing more on that side of town but ride the subway through it. The lights, the flash, the story-high billboards, the cheap T-shirts and overpriced New York, New York snow globes, the franchise restaurants—they were all an insult to a true New Yorker, who remembered what Times Square was like before Mayor Rudolph Giuliani and Disney got a hold of it. Not that I liked the hookers and card sharks and trash and filth that had overrun the district, but it represented New York—tough, seedy, grimy. We had a reputation to uphold, and the Times Square of old represented to the hilt.

Besides, there was so much more to New York than that six-block radius, if you were adventurous enough to check it out. There was magnificent shopping and sites in SoHo, and a funky, eclectic crowd of restaurants and hospitality in Park Slope, Brooklyn; Ft. Greene, despite gentrification, was still a really cool place to go for a good plate of Nigerian stew, or some fine, custom-made gear sewn by some of the finest African-American designers of our time; and just past that neighborhood, in Bed-Stuy, was the Akwaaba House, one of the finest bed-and-breakfasts in the country. Then there were the ethnic shops and delis lining Delancey Street, where, for the price of a few of those stupid snow globes, you could find the tastiest pickles in the free world or bags of mind-blowingly sumptuous pastries, and, of course, Harlem, full of history and color and new day spas and shopping.

Times Square? For corn-fed middle Americans and the birds. That's what I was thinking as I pulled on my wrap jean skirt and a white wife-beater. Actually, I hadn't planned to dress that far down, but for some reason, my stomach was bloated beyond recognition and, despite my best efforts, I couldn't squeeze into my black mini, my Seven jeans, or my fitted floral Courtney Washington tank dress. I was due for my period any day now, and usually, when it was time for the flow, I had to make clothing adjustments, but this was ridiculous; even my period standbys were struggling against my bulging tummy. "No matter," I said to myself aloud. "It's Red Lobster." I threw on some jewelry to dress up the wrap skirt, put on a cute pair of mules, pulled my hair into a big Afro puff, checked my makeup in the mirror, and then opened the cabinet to grab a few tampons—you know, to avert any accidents. The first thing my hand touched, though, was Aaron's electric razor, which had been holding court among my toiletries and assorted beauty products months before he moved in. I guess he'd left it there because he found himself waking up in my bed so often, that it was just easier for him to shower and shave at my place, and, despite that he'd ended up moving in, I never actually made a place among my myriad of soaps, scrubs, lipsticks, foundations, shampoos, conditioners, and the like to put his things.

Not that he needed a lot of space; he kept his face trimmed, and went to the barbershop every other week. That was the extent of his beauty regimen.

Still, he was beautiful.

I missed him so.

I started to tear, thinking about him—how much I missed his company. Not just his touch, you know? But our camaraderie—the time we spent over the years laughing and sharing and embracing one another, sometimes without even touching. Aaron would have gotten a kick out of going to Red Lobster, just so that we could make fun of people like Florine—and I wished that he were coming with me. I wondered what he was doing at that very moment—could he be longing for me like I'd been longing for him? Or was he still mad enough to not want to be bothered with such thoughts? The thought of that made me sick to my stomach—literally nauseous. I closed my eyes and held my breath, willing the feeling away. And then I considered calling Florine to cancel. But it was only a half hour before we were supposed to be meeting in the Red Lobster lounge, and I stupidly forgot to get her cell phone number, so I couldn't call her and tell her I wasn't coming. Reluctantly, I headed for the front door.

It took a half hour for me to make it to Times Square, and the whole time, I was forcing myself to fix my face so that Florine would think inviting me to Red Lobster wasn't a bad idea. I mean, she couldn't help it if she was a cornball, and, truthfully, for all my trash-talking, I wasn't mad at the fried shrimp there, either. As I walked up to the glass revolving door, I pushed a smile onto my face. The place was packed; Florine was standing in the far right corner, looking much more glamorous than she'd ever looked making copies at the office.

"Hey Nina!" she said, a little louder than she needed to say my name in a crowded restaurant. "I'm glad you made it!" She reached for my arm, and turned toward two men who were smiling awkwardly at me. "I want to introduce you to my boyfriend, Lonnie. Lonnie? Nina."

No, this heiffa did not . . .

"And this is Maurice Atkins, a dear friend of ours from Dallas," she said, practically pulling me into the boy's arms. He was short—no more than about three inches taller than me in my stockinged feet—and, though his face looked relatively young, his balding pate added a good ten years to what was probably his thirty or so years.

"Hello, Nina!" he boomed, as he extended his hand toward mine and then squeezed. "I've heard a lot about you!"

"Oh, you have, huh?" I said, trying to force a smile onto my face and shooting a dirty look in Florine's direction. "Funny, Florine hadn't mentioned anything about you."

For some reason, Florine, Maurice, and Lonnie got a kick out of that—even though I thought it was quite clear that I wasn't joking. I couldn't believe it—ambushed by Florine and her cornball brigade. What nerve did this girl have to sock me with a blind date? I was in no mood for this—doing the awkward dance of trying to hold conversation with a tableful of strangers I wasn't really interested in getting to know, the uneasy feeling that came with the silences as everyone struggles to find something else to say. Who knew what she'd told this man about me—perhaps that I was desperate? I started going over in my mind what Florine had overhead me saying to Kenya in the office just yesterday—was ol' baldy over there privy to that information? My stomach started to boil at the thought—literally.

"Oh look! The beeper just went off," Lonnie said, pointing to the behemoth contraption the receptionist had given our party to alert us when our table was ready. He scampered over to the receptionist to show her the glowing machine, and, after shuffling some menus and papers on the counter, she came forward. "Right this way," she said, pointing toward the dining room.

My steps were uneasy already, and they became even more unsure as Maurice put his clammy hands around my waist—as if we'd been together for years. I'd considered pushing his hand off me, but with each step, I was growing more and more nauseous. My mouth was watering, as if priming itself for the rush of bile that was winding through my stomach and making its way up into my esophagus; I was starting to breath heavy, hoping that each bit of air I took in would force the vomit back down. Just as I took another breath, a waiter walked by with the biggest plate of fried food I've ever seen in my life—fried fish, fried shrimp, fried calamari, fried clams, french fries. The accompanying scent that wafted as he passed—something that distinctly smelled like a mixture of old grease and old fish—went straight into my nose and beckoned the vomit I'd been fighting to stay in my stomach to come into my throat. "Oh my God, excuse me—I have to go to the bathroom!" I shouted, louder than I should have. I twirled around, my eyes darting, searching for someone who could tell me where the nearest bathroom was. My hand instinctively moved to my mouth. The look on Florine's face told me that my face must have lost some color or something, because her face said it all: What's about to happen is not going to be a good thing.

"Nina! Over there," she said, pointing. "The bathroom."

My eyes followed the point of her finger to a door that had the universal stick-figure bathroom sign, and the moment my mind confirmed what my eyes were looking at, I took off running. I'd barely made it into the doors when the hot, chunky liquid spewed out of my mouth. I fell into the first stall I saw, bent over, emptying my stomach until there was nothing left, and then some. After a few minutes, I pulled myself away from the porcelain and stumbled over to the sink, grabbing some paper towels on the way. I ran them under cold water and placed the compress against my mouth and then my forehead and cheeks, then rinsed my mouth out as best I could. Florine rushed in moments later, practically sliding in on the vomit that had escaped my mouth by the entrance. I was mad she didn't fall in it; if it weren't for her, I'd have been home, warm, in my bed, curled up with some ice cream in front of the television, figuring out a way to get my Aaron back.

"Are you okay?" she asked.

"Does it look like I'm okay?" I shot back. I saw the hurt look in her eyes and decided such nastiness wasn't necessary. Yeah, she had screwed up—but the girl meant well. I wiped my mouth one more time, and did a check in the mirror to make sure my face was clean. "I'm sorry, Florine, but I gotta get outta here." I looked at her reflection. "The surprise blind date was not cool at all. Tell Mr. Maurice—hell, I don't care, tell him whatever you want."

And with that, I turned on my heels, pushed past my coworker, and out the door, without so much as a glance at the rest of our party.

The subway ride from "Tourist Square" was the longest I've ever taken—at least that's what it seemed.

Nina and Aaron,

Part VII

Nina placed the plastic stick on the edge of the sink, setting it down as gently as if she were handling a porcelain doll. Her pants pulled back up, Nina was perched on the edge of the toilet, her knees too weak to stand anyway; Aaron stood in front of the sink, his arms folded because he didn't know what else to do with his hands—and he didn't want Nina to see how tightly his fists were clenched. They exchanged no words, no glances, no touches—yet they were acutely aware of each other's presence. It would take three more minutes for the arc of their lives to be determined, as if they were awaiting their turn at the pearly gates for the brief audience with St. Peter. Nina could hear the heaviness of her breaths; she could feel the tension in her shoulders. It was a surreal scene, like something a scriptwriter had invented for a family-planning commercial. The frightened father, the mortified mother, the moment of truth.

Inside the gauzelike indicator at the end of the wand, the carefully packed combination of monoclonal and polyclonal antibodies were poised, ready to wade through the gushing sluice of Nina's urine in search of human chorionic gonadotropin. The urine soaked down into the gauze, mixing with the antibodies, flipping the switches that had been painstakingly checked and rechecked by well-paid lab technicians. All it took were twenty thousandths of an International Unit per milliliter of the human chorionic gonadotropin for the antibodies to pass the baton to the pink dye.

One hundred and fifty seconds into their trial, enough time for each of them to separately ponder—and doubt—their fitness for the awesome responsibility that was possibly about to be dropped on their heads, the circle started exhibiting vague signs of some change occurring. A faint discoloration was forming—not enough to be called a line, but certainly different than the bland whiteness that was there before. After 173 seconds, that discoloration began to lengthen and sharpen. By the 200th second, it was no longer just a discoloration—it was a heavy, distinct, solid pink line. The test was positive. Nina was pregnant.

him

Oh God. A baby. How did we get here? When did we get here? I can't remember not remembering the condom. And it never broke. Not to my knowledge, anyway. And I was always the one who had to assume condom disposal responsibilities, so I would know. I'm so dizzy and confused and scared right now, I feel like my body is about to liquefy. What am I going to do? A baby? Just when we were trying to figure out how to make *us* work, now I have to worry about a *we*. We're going to become another cliché, another black couple making babies irresponsibly, with no plans for a future life together? Nina looks scared too. She is staring at me so hard that I feel like she can read my thoughts. We hadn't gotten *that* close, had we? But now I'm remembering that time when she told me we didn't need to use the condom, a couple of months ago. She assured me that she was just about to start her period so pregnancy was damn near impossible. I had believed her—why shouldn't I? She said she was extra horny and wanted to see what it felt like without the layer between us. "For once, I want to really feel *you* inside of me," she had said. How many men are strong enough to turn their back to a come-on like that? Of course I had tossed the condom across the room. Of course I had dived into it with gusto, giddy at the idea of getting some raw. Having come of sexual age after the advent of AIDS, I had always taken extra precautions to protect myself. I wasn't taking no crazy chances. Up at UConn, I had even told one fine-ass girl that we would have to wait until we could get a condom. She was naked in my bed at the time. I remember being so damn proud of myself, proud of my dick control. Of course the girl proceeded to pleasure me orally, so it wasn't like any kind of Gandhi-like sacrifice we're talking about. Is that a tear I see in Nina's eye? Is she that broken up by the idea of having my baby that she's going to cry about it? Oh, but now she's smiling at me, so I guess it wasn't a tear. The fuckin' rhythm method, that's what that was. I remember reading about the rhythm method being terribly unreliable. How can you trust something white people call the *rhythm method* when they ain't got no rhythm? Why had I let her talk me into throwing the condom away? That was *so* stupid! And it wasn't even worth it. Actually, I'd never ever tell her this, but it was kinda gross. *Waaay* too juicy and messy for me. When I pulled out and looked down, I thought I was going to faint—apparently her period had arrived during the act. Made me think about that crazy night with Cocoa. She said sometimes that happened—that sex accelerated its onset. I wanted to ask her why, knowing that, she let me go ahead and—you know what? I'm not even going to go any further. Surely I've told you enough about *that*. What should I say to her right now? I don't know if I can be reassuring, pretend to be certain of the future, not when my gut feels like a washing machine on spin cycle. And anyway, the whole thing was over in, like, forty-five seconds, I'm embarrassed to say. My God, who knew removing the condom could be like that? I surely didn't expect it to feel like a thousand tiny masseuses had descended on my penis at once, working over every nerve ending from stem to stern until I was helpless in holding back the rushing tide. I got a quick picture of Nina's face that night, the surprise I saw there when I let go so fast—the shame that flowed through me when I saw her surprise. I had disappointed her. She tried to say it was no big deal, but she couldn't paper over that first stunned reaction, a look that said clearly, "What the hell was that?" But why does this occasion have to be so sad? Why am I trippin'? There's nothing more inspiring, motivating, to a man than having a baby, right? And having a baby with the person in the world I know better than anyone, the partner I love more than I love myself—what could be bad about that? She was my most trusted friend on the planet—despite our recent troubles. This was all good. Yeah, her family is about as stable as a mental ward and she can be controlling and even domineering, but she wasn't afraid to open her heart up to me. That was a place that most of us aren't willing to go, to give ourselves over to another person so completely that even the most perfect pleasures are mixed with the pain that things can only get worse because there was nowhere else to go. Shoot, my family was the Brady Bunch in blackface and we still got more than our share of destructive baggage. My brother Carney had never even held a real job for longer than six months. The boy claimed that a woman was stalking him and he was afraid to stay in the same place for too long. Go figure. I didn't even like to talk to him on the phone anymore—his bizarre declarations made me too mad. So if Josefina and Ray Simmons, in all their idyllic domesticity, could produce a loon like Carney, any spawn of Willy and Angelique Andrews had at least a fighting chance of not screwing up a child too much. But speaking of Carney and employment, I had to go get a regular gig now. No more pursuing my art—that shit was over. Time to get paid. For my family. Ha—imagine that!

her

Oh God. It's not turning pink. *Tell me the lines are not turning pink.* Pink means pregnant, right? Oh God. There's a baby in there. There's a baby in me. A new life, growing inside my stomach. What the hell are we going to do? No, what the hell am *I* going to do? Aaron can't do anything for me—for us, can he? He's got no real career ambitions. No real job. As far as I know, he doesn't even have a place to lay his head—much less one for a crib. Unless he's sleeping on that nasty couch at his old place. No room for babies there. Hell, I wouldn't even put a mangy stray dog in that mess. What could he do for me *and* a baby? Go back to making tips at the Honey Pot? Rush back into Cocoa's arms when the baby cried too much and our life got hectic? Cocoa. I wonder if he was with her when he rushed over here to answer my SOS. I hope she was half-naked and hot when he hightailed it to me. I always had the power to make that boy break into a full trot—all I had to do was call his name and he'd come running, no matter what it was that I ultimately wanted. That's what kind of friend Aaron is—my best friend. And a good boyfriend. But a father? Was he ready for it? Was I ready for it? Was I ready for parenthood with him? What was I thinking when I asked him to have sex with me sans condom? Since when was unprotected sex okay? I'd done that only one other time—with my first college boyfriend, and that was only because I was a punk-ass freshman too stupid to recognize that when the boy said he loved me and we would be married and so I shouldn't worry about protection because it was going to be me and him forever, that he was just trying to get some buck-raw ass. I'd conveniently forgotten about how after I found out he was sleeping with practically half the girls in the freshman *and* sophomore classes that I went to the campus clinic for counseling and an AIDS test. It was negative, of course, but that didn't stop the nurse from lecturing me on the importance of safe sex, and I sure as hell made a point of remembering every horrible thing she said about venereal diseases and the slow death that came to HIV-positive people too stupid to have protected sex. How many times did I demand the trifling Negroes I laid with over the years wrap their dicks up tight? Why the hell did I make the exception for Aaron? I don't know what that boy's got. And at the very least, I should have thought through the fact that I could get knocked up. By a no-job/no-home/no-ambition man. Just what I needed, huh? To end up like my sister, Nikki, sitting up in a studio apartment with a two-year-old and a pile of bills and no daddy to speak of to help her feed him or diaper his butt or comfort him when he's sick or just, like, be there for him. Nikki's a mess. I don't want to end up like that. Maybe I should reconsider my opposition to abortion. Maybe that's what Aaron will tell me to do, to get rid of this life growing inside me. Or maybe he'll tell me he doesn't want to have anything to do with us. I don't know what he'll want to do. I wish he would say something. Whatever comes out of his mouth, I'm prepared to tell him this: He shouldn't feel any obligation to me or this child, because clearly this relationship is over.

him

A warmth flows through me, as if a kindly spirit has stepped into my body. I smile broadly, happily. It is the first manifestation of a reaction by either one of us to the two solid pink lines on the wand: a broad smile. I open my arms and step forward, folding Nina inside a tight bear hug. I can feel her body start to wrack and I am momentarily confused. I pull back and see that she is sobbing. Heavily. Her face is scrunched up into a crying, disfiguring mess. What does that mean?

"What are you thinking about right now?" I ask, using a query that I had once prohibited her from ever mouthing to me. That was during the friendship, when I could make all sorts of demands and not be taken to task for them.

She shakes her head, telling me that she will be unable to verbalize it for a few seconds. I wait, watching the tears continue to pool on her face, fighting against my own quickly escalating emotions.

"I was _so_ scared!" she says, pulling me to her once again. "I really didn't know _what_ you were going to say!"

"Really?" I say, a little surprised. "Like you thought I would be pissed? But you know how much I like kids."

I can feel her shaking her head. "Yes, I know you like other people's kids," she says, speaking into my chest. "But that's *waaay* different than having one of your own."

I look up, around me, at the shelf above the toilet, which contained about a dozen of her beauty products—she is an admitted beauty-product junkie. Actually, she described it as a "beauty whore." I chuckle to myself, years after first hearing her use the line. God, we have so much vibrant history together, so many overwhelming memories. I could keep myself entertained for hours just recalling funny moments, replaying some of her best lines. I glance down again and see the solid pink lines on the wand. Wow, a baby. I'm staggered all over again.

"I'm not going to tell you I'm not scared to death," I say. "The thought of all that responsibility is enough to make me piss in my pants." I can feel Nina's laugh vibrate against my chest. "But I'm thirty-one years old. I got friends from college whose kids are damn near in high school already. I can't afford to do the starving young artist thing anymore. For one thing, I'm not all that young anymore. And I am starting to see that I like having some of the finer things. That realization has hit me hard over the past three weeks, sleeping on Andy's couch in that nasty-ass apartment and trying to pretend that I wasn't miserable as hell. I had started to get used to a clean, sweet-smelling bathroom with all kinds of little frilly decorations. To clean sheets on the bed that were not purchased during the Reagan administration. To having more than one pot in the kitchen cabinets. Me and Andy were living like college students. Fuckin' slobs. That shit's not cute anymore. So right here and now, let me make some promises to you—the mother of my child."

Nina pulls back and stares up at me. The tears are still streaming down her face, but now they are accompanied by a wide smile. She waits, her eyebrows rising in expectation.

"I promise to you that I will go out and get a real job. I know that you said before that I needed to pursue my art, the photography thing, but things are different now. I have a family to support. That's what a real man does. I wasn't exactly thrilled by my parents' ways when I was growing up, but the one thing that I can say about my dad is that he took care of his family. I'm sure he had dreams of his own and that his grand plan wasn't exactly to be a doorman, but that's what he did. What he still does. He puts on that goofy-ass little burgundy uniform and he takes a six thirty A.M. train into Manhattan so that he can open doors for a building full of white people and smile up in their face. He once told me that he had been a pretty good artist when he was younger, that he used to paint and draw in high school, and he really wanted to go to art school and try to make a career from his artistic talents. But when he married my mom right after high school, he had to go get a job. He couldn't afford to indulge his art. I've been thinking about that a lot lately. At first when you told me that you wanted me to pursue my photography, I thought it would give me a sense of freedom. But actually the opposite happened—I felt even more trapped than before, but this time I was trapped by my guilt. I'd see you get up and go to work every day and I knew that I wasn't doing right by you. I can still take all the pictures I want, but right now I gotta help put food on the table. It's what my father did all these years and it's what I'm gonna do now. And I promise to you that I will work hard as hell to get our relationship back to what it was before, when we were friends and not lovers. I've been thinking about that a lot too, going back over the incidents of our childhoods together, remembering how incredibly close we were, how much we cared about each other and protected each other. It was unlike any other relationship I have ever seen two people have. And isn't it amazing how quickly we fucked it all up when we became lovers?"

I look down at her and Nina nods her hearty assent.

"Why is that? I've been trying to answer that question for months, even before we had our big fight. All of a sudden, things that I used to love about you became annoying to me. I started taking you for granted, I think, which is something I never did when we were friends. It's almost like we come to our friends without any pretensions, without any walls around us, and that gives us the chance for true honesty and sensitivity in the relationship. I've opened myself up to you, you've opened yourself up to me, so neither one of us has anything to be afraid of because it's all hanging out there. Then we become lovers and start accumulating secrets and jealousies and suspicions and suddenly there's no trust and no honesty. I never thought we would get there, but it happened. Even to us. It's some complicated shit."

The tears are gone now. Nina, nodding, stares at me lovingly. I feel a tremor of delight slip down my spine.

her

God, Aaron's so sexy. Those lips, those eyes—so earnest, so raw with emotion. His head is perfectly round—I always made fun of his little perfectly round head. Always loved falling into those lips of his. Makes me want to fall into them even more now that I know he loves me and this baby. A family. We're going to be a family. How cute will we be strolling to the park, baby in tow? I wonder if it'll be a boy? If he'll look like his daddy? Aaron—a daddy! Me, a mommy! Maybe a girl? Wouldn't be a bad-looking kid if she looked like her dad. I think I'll call her Skyy.

"That's my girl," Aaron says, as a smile spreads across my face. "That's my Nina. We're going to be all right—trust me. We're going to be all right."

"Oh my God, Aaron. There's a baby in my stomach! We're going to be parents!" Excitement is washing over me—I search his eyes to make sure that he really does feel the same way, too. I haven't, after all, given him any good reasons of late to want to be with me. I take his hands into mine and put them on my stomach, then raise them to my lips and kiss them ever so gently. There are a few moments of silence. "Aaron, I need to tell you something."

"Shoot," he says, without hesitating.

"These past few months have been absolutely atrocious, and I'm sure that my behavior had a lot to do with why we haven't been as close as we've always been. Hell, I didn't expect you to come over here when I called, and I certainly didn't expect you to say you were going to be here for me and this baby—not after all the heartache and drama I've caused. But I need you to know that I did it because I love you and even the thought of not having you in my life, or someone else having you, makes me absolutely crazy. And I didn't realize it until I thought I was going to lose you to someone else."

"Who?" he asks quickly. "Who could I possibly love more than Nina Andrews?"

I can hear a little annoyance in his voice, but I continue on. I have to let him know that I'm not always going to be as crazy as a bedbug. Not every day, at least. "I love me some Aaron, and I just want you all to myself." I take a step back and sit on the edge of the tub. "I didn't go snooping through your things because I don't trust you. I was looking through your pictures because my job was looking for a photographer to shoot publicity portraits for a few of the bigwigs, and I wanted them to consider you. And so I went through your things. I know I should have asked before I did it, but I was in a rush, and when I saw Cocoa's pictures, I didn't know what to think.

"Now, the old Nina just assumed that y'all were doing some kinky stuff and that they were evidence that you were tipping out on me," I continue. "But the new Nina? Well, she's not going to make any assumptions or jump to any conclusions. She's not going to take her man for granted, or piss him off over stupid stuff, or forget that he's the best thing that ever happened to her."

Aaron takes my hands into his and guides my body up toward his. He kisses me gently on my cheek, looks into my eyes, and then runs his hands across my belly. "You're my baby daddy," I whisper. A smile spreads across both of our faces, and then we fall out in laughter.

I want to kiss him.

I think I will.

"We're going to make it," he says. "We're going to make it."

Nina and Aaron
—and Skyler

The waiting has been hard on both of them, but only Nina's is interrupted every two minutes by pains so wrenching that she is becoming increasingly fearful that she will not be able to go through with this. She can just picture it: an astounding medical first—FEARFUL PREGNANT WOMAN REFUSES TO GIVE BIRTH. Splashed across the front page of the *New York Post*. On the other side of the pain will come unparalleled joy— she's fully aware of this and has not been appreciative of Aaron's need to remind her five times over the past twelve hours. That doesn't make it hurt any less. Different women have profoundly different reactions to mind-blowing pain; Nina was a Manic Laborer. Each excruciating contraction of her torso was greeted by her as a catastrophic event that needed to be felt by everyone around her. So as the unending parade of doctors and nurses and anesthesiologists and food servers came strolling into their small room at Columbia Presbyterian Hospital, Nina's mood turned increasingly sour and abrasive. Of course the hospital staff saw this many times over every day and had no appreciable reaction to her behavior—other than a mental reminder to avoid her room when at all possible. But as for Aaron—who didn't have the option of avoiding her room? He sat quietly in the cheap uncomfortable wooden-and-cloth chair and prayed that he could disappear into the wallpaper like an apparition. He kept telling himself that this wasn't the real Nina in the room with him—not his Nina. This was a Nina possessed by an all-consuming fear that he could never understand. On the occasion of a childbirth, perhaps more than any other time, the man felt acutely his status as the nonessential other. Conception itself was impossible without his sperm—though science had turned even that into a tenuous fact—and he could transform himself into the errand boy during the pregnancy, fetching and retrieving without complaint. But even when he had pushed himself to make the weekly trek to the two-hour birthing classes at the hospital and had faithfully memorized every word uttered by the class instructor, once labor commenced he became irrelevant with each passing contraction. The breathing exercises become nothing more than an annoyance to his woman and, short of eliminating her pain, there was very little he could actually do to make himself useful.

Nina's mood was profoundly affected by three facts, none of them related to each other but all swirling together to tug her into a deep funk. First, her doctor had chosen this week to go on a weeklong vacation. Nina hadn't discovered this until three weeks before her due date, when a casual call to Dr. Henrietta Hankerson's office revealed that her vacation was due to start two weeks hence. Nina hung up the phone thinking that it would be just her tough luck to go into labor a week early, before Dr. Hankerson had returned. And that's exactly what happened, almost as if Nina had willed it by giving it so much energy. As Aaron helped her down the stairs of their Lower East Side walk-up, Nina had silently cursed her doctor's absence. She was mortified about what awaited her uptown at Columbia Presbyterian, even when she thought the doctor was going to be at her side. Now she was practically apoplectic. Aaron had no idea of the troubles that weighed on his woman's mind—all he knew was that he had lost the ability to turn Nina's frowns into smiles, something he had always been able to pull off with ease.

Second to the doctor's absence was her worry about what might be transpiring in the maternity ward's waiting room. After the drama of her father's arrest and eventual release, her parents had lobbed increasingly hostile missives at each other, back and forth, week after week, usually using Nina as the courier. Even after Nina refused to carry their messages anymore, the nastiness didn't let up. In fact, it intensified because neither one of them was tempered by the possibility that their statements would actually be delivered to the other person. So Nina was treated to brutal phone conversations during which her mother would march through the last three decades, noting every slap, push, threat, and unkind word that she had received from Willy Andrews. At first the conversations, as unpleasant as they were, proved to be fascinating for Nina, who had never really understood her parents' relationship—the hostility and the strangely powerful magnetic pull each seemed to have for the other. But after a while she started to feel like the poison her mother threw at her was starting to seep into her pores and taint the way she viewed her own relationship—and, more specifically, her willingness to support Aaron while he pursued his photography passion. And her father wouldn't even bother with stories—he'd just fill Nina's ears with ten or fifteen minutes of pain-laced profanity directed at his wife for turning him in. So now the two of them were in the same hospital, conceivably breathing the same air in the waiting room. She couldn't imagine how stiff and unpleasant the air around them must feel. She sent Aaron out to the waiting room at least once every half hour to make sure they hadn't thrown down on each other, dropping their gloves to the floor (yes, it was June, but the image didn't work without the gloves) and squaring off like the hockey players she had seen in her one visit to a Rangers game at Madison Square Garden. Aaron would scurry back into the room and dutifully report whether he had seen or heard a word or even a glance pass between them. Usually there was nothing to report because they were intently pretending to ignore each other, instead pulling Aaron's parents Ray and Josefina into awkward and unnatural conversations about nothing at all.

The last thing that weighed on Nina—and its placement at the end probably shouldn't be taken as an indicator that it was least important—was her and Aaron's treatment by the hospital staff. Early on Dr. Hankerson had told Nina with what sounded like pride that she was affiliated with Presbyterian Hospital, which was connected to both Columbia and Cornell Universities and one of the top hospitals not just in New York but anywhere in the world. Dr. Hankerson, a warm, generous black woman with a gentle demeanor, had such a hold over Nina that she would have traveled to Wisconsin to have her baby if the good doctor insisted. But the fact that the doctor was so proud of her hospital clinched their decision to have the baby uptown, even if it meant a potentially harrowing cab ride over more than 150 Manhattan blocks. The cab ride turned out to be pleasant compared to what awaited them at the hospital. Early on during their stay, even before the staff had assessed that Nina was only three centimeters dilated and thus still could be more than a day away from giving birth, they had realized the impact of traveling to a hospital that was essentially in the middle of the 'hood. When Aaron accompanied Nina upstairs and helped her hobble into the pre-labor room—which was basically a holding cell for the laborers who weren't even close yet—his presence got more than a few double takes from the hospital staff. At first neither he nor Nina knew what they meant—until a slip up from a nurse with a looser tongue than most.

"Are you the father?" she asked, the surprise evident on her face as she looked up from the paperwork she was filling out. When he nodded, she smiled. "You came here to help her get through it, huh?" she said, chuckling softly. "That's nice." Then the nurse pivoted and was gone—leaving two stunned future parents in the room.

"Wait, hold up," Nina said, struggling to sit herself up in the bed. "Did that just happen? Or am I fuckin' dreaming?"

Aaron was shaking his head in disbelief. "She acted like she had never seen a father in the delivery room," Aaron said. "Like I was some kind of foreign creature."

Nina felt a wave of rage threaten to wash over her. She knew this was not the time to indulge nonproductive emotions like outrage, but she couldn't help it. It brought up something that had been poking at her for months but she hadn't verbalized—their impending single parenthood status. She wasn't so old-fashioned that she would be embarrassed by the idea of having a baby by a man she wasn't married to, but she did at times wonder if they were doing the right thing by adding to the woeful statistics in the black community. If Aaron was going to ask her to marry him, what was he waiting for? And how ugly it was that his failure to step forward and do it had opened them up to the sad assumptions of some ghetto nurse up in this ghetto hospital?

After the nurse's comment, they both started looking more closely at their surroundings and noticing other signs of the hospital's unglamorous location—the scruffy furniture and linens, the scuffed-up walls, the subtle disrespect shown by most of the staff, which apparently was used to dealing with a long line of ghetto mothers who they didn't feel were worthy of any special attentions.

After a check by yet another unidentified hospital resident revealed that Nina had enlarged to five-centimeters dilation, they announced that she was almost ready for the actual birthing room. They were both relieved at this sign of progress—at one point they even exchanged smiles. But then Aaron suddenly felt overwhelmed by a bad case of nerves. He was conflicted now about whether an important decision he had made was the correct one.

The ring had been burning a hole in his pocket for weeks. When to propose? He knew it was the right thing to do, had decided that it was time to make him and Nina officially recognized by the State of New York as an entity of one. And though the preponderance of unmarried mothers in society at large and the African-American community in particular had rendered the term *bastard* a near-anachronism, Aaron still held the quaint notion that his child should have married parents. It wasn't something he and Nina had given more than five minutes of discussion, but he could sense that a proposal would be important to her. But when to do it? Initially he was going to drop the bomb well in advance of her labor and delivery. He had cobbled together $3,000 over the last several months, primarily by tending bar at the comedy club after he left his new job at the magazine. With a new baby on the horizon, Aaron had begun a real job search in earnest, sending out feelers and making the kind of contacts that you need to make to get a job. The want ads were virtually useless in this process. It was all about your friends and acquaintances. One of Aaron's photography buddies called him up one day and told him that a well-respected, hip downtown magazine called *Sway* was looking for a new assistant photo editor—someone to stay in contact with the shooters, give them the guidance and support they needed to produce the slick, edgy photos that *Sway* was known for. Aaron rolled up to their offices in the Village with his portfolio and secured the job by the time the photo editor had eye-

balled the fourth picture. He said that he could see in Aaron's work a
real shooter's eye and a respect for the profession. Aaron started work
the next day—making Nina practically giddy with delight.

So the ring, an elegant round-cut three-quarter-carat diamond with
an eighteen-karat white gold band, sits in a black box in his pocket,
drawing his anxious hand at least once every ten minutes to make sure
it was still there. Aaron's plan to present the ring in the weeks leading
up to the big moment had been spoiled by his mother when she informed him that the father of the baby was tradition-bound to give the
mother a gift upon the birth of the new baby.

"Wait," Aaron had said to her. "The new baby isn't gift enough? You
know, the miracle of birth, new life, all that?"

His mother had just shaken her head, indicating that the matter was
nonnegotiable.

So his latest plan was to wait until she held the new baby in her
arms. But she's in such a foul mood that Aaron is tempted to alter his
plans, to do it now just to bring a smile to Nina's face. His deliberations
are interrupted by some surprising news.

"You're almost there—time to move it into the delivery room," says
the latest resident, a cocky, good-looking young white guy with the
bedside manner of an IRS auditor. With Aaron in tow, Nina is transported by wheelchair into the next chamber.

Twenty minutes breeze by. Aaron and Nina are quiet, their eyes
trained on the monitor that's strapped to Nina's belly, indicating the
onset of each contraction. Nina's lower regions have been deadened by
the epidural so she can't feel them anymore. Finally she's been released
from the cycle of pain. Just one more big job to be done.

A nurse scampers into the room and positions herself in front of
Nina to check dilation. Whatever she finds catches her by surprise—her
eyes widen.

"What is it?" Nina asks, concerned.

"I think you might be fully dilated," she says. "Let me go get a doctor."

Nina squirms on the bed, her face a mask of worry and excitement.
Aaron walks over and strokes her head. She looks up and forces a
smile. She is trying to convince herself that she's not frightened out of
her mind. The end is right in front of her. She is about to get this done.

Aaron fingers the black box. Is it time now—or should he wait?

A large, regal figure strolls into the room, clad in the blue hospital scrubs. Aaron hears Nina's gasp and jerks his head to the left.

"Dr. Hankerson!" Nina shouts. "What are you doing here—I thought you were on vacation?!"

The doctor is wearing a big grin on her smooth brown face.

"What—and miss this big moment?" the doctor says. "You ready to have this baby?"

Nina shows a big grin to match the doctor's. Aaron is grinning too. The tension flows out of Nina's body, leaving her in the most relaxed state she's felt in weeks. Her doctor has arrived on the scene, like the cavalry riding to the rescue of a damsel in distress.

In a matter of seconds, Nina is prepped for delivery, her legs positioned, the cloths draped and laid around her, the doctor and the nurse scurrying about preparing the instruments for the baby's arrival. Aaron moves to the side, out of the way, his heart firmly positioned somewhere in his esophagus. Nina looks anxious but no longer afraid.

It takes only six pushes for a slimy, squirming baby to slide into the world. She gags until the nurse grabs the suction and pulls the mucusy liquid from her throat and lungs. The baby responds by belting a huge, lusty note that would make Aretha jealous.

Out in the waiting area, Angelique Andrews discerns the meaning of the loud cry before anyone else. "There she goes—that has to be Nina's baby," she says, looking around, laughing. "Her mother screamed just like that when she was born—and she been screaming ever since."

The baby, swathed and warm, is placed on Nina's chest. "Hello, Skyler," Nina says softly, cooing.

"Skyler?!" Aaron says loudly, angrily.

Nina cuts him a look. "Aaron! We already agreed on it!"

Aaron breaks out into a grin. "I'm just playing," he says, chuckling. "Skyler it is."

Aaron finally reaches down into his pocket and produces the black box. His hands are shaky as he tries to open it.

"What's that?" Nina asks.

Nina gasps when the diamond catches the fluorescent light and sends a flashing sparkle around the room that renders the doctor and nurse motionless.

"I guess I've been preparing for this moment for the last twenty-six years," Aaron says, his voice a little shaky. "Nina Andrews, will you—"

"Yes, yes, I will, I will!" Nina says excitedly. She reaches up with her right hand and pulls Aaron's face toward her own. Aaron kisses her softly.

"You didn't even let me finish," he says.

They both hear the clapping at the same time. Dr. Hankerson is smiling as she claps, as is the nurse. Aaron looks down at his new baby, her round perfect face a little yellow version of her mother's. It may have been an illusion, or maybe the early onset of gas pains, but he swears that Skyler is smiling too.

Denene Millner, author of *The Sistahs' Rules,* has written for the Associated Press and the *New York Daily News,* and is an articles editor at *Parenting* magazine. **Nick Chiles,** an award-winning journalist and editor in chief of the multicultural travel magazine *Odyssey Couleur,* has written for *Essence, The Dallas Morning News, The New York Times, Newsday,* and other publications. Together they are the *Blackboard* bestselling authors of the *What Brothers Think, What Sistahs Know* series and the *Essence* bestseller *Love Don't Live Here Anymore,* and *In Love and War.* They live in South Orange, New Jersey.